Your name is Bryan Alexander.

Once you were a college professor in Twentieth-century America . . .

. . . until you inherited the fortune that give you your freedom . . .

. . . until you stumbled upon the manuscript of an ancestor who had moved from one world to another on a mysterious pathway through time and space . . .

. . . until you inherited the fortune that gave you your find yourself face to face with a man who turned out to be fact not fiction . . .

. . . the man who called himself Captain Nemo, and who made you both his guest and his prisoner aboard the vessel that his genius created and commanded— **The Nautilus. . . .**

D1530305

Also by Thomas F. Monteleone
and available from Popular Library:

THE TIME CONNECTION
00417-7 $1.25

THE TIME-SWEPT CITY
04081-5 $1.50

UNABLE TO FIND FAWCETT PAPERBACKS AT
YOUR LOCAL BOOKSTORE OR NEWSSTAND?

If you are unable to locate a book published by Fawcett, or, if you wish to see a
list of all available Fawcett Crest, Gold Medal and Popular Library titles, write
for our FREE Order Form. Just send us your name and address and 35¢ to help
defray postage and handling costs. Mail to:

FAWCETT BOOKS GROUP
P.O. Box C730
524 Myrtle Ave.
Pratt Station, Brooklyn, N.Y. 11205

(Orders for less than 5 books must include 75¢ for the first book and 25¢ for
each additional book to cover postage and handling.)

THE
Secret Sea

by
Thomas F. Monteleone

POPULAR LIBRARY • NEW YORK

*This is for
Damon,
my son.*

THE SECRET SEA

Published by Popular Library, a unit of CBS Publications, the
Consumer Publishing Division of CBS Inc.

Copyright © 1979 by Thomas F. Monteleone

All Rights Reserved

ISBN: 0-445-04404-7

Printed in the United States of America

10   9   8   7   6   5   4   3   2   1

ONE

THE LETTER was from a lawyer in Brattleboro, Vermont.

Now just about at that time, I was particularly leery of letters from lawyers—a natural, inevitable conditioning which stemmed from Judy's divorce proceedings (but that's another story)—and I was not excited about reading more legal obfuscation. So I threw it on the desk and worked through the remainder of that morning's mail before considering it.

I like to get mail, however, because it has always seemed to me to be a more civilized way of communicating with your fellows. And it is fast becoming a vanishing art, letter writing, mainly because of the proliferation of the telephone—that squat, toadlike thing which lurks in the corners of our homes, which invades our thoughts, and interrupts our sleep with its senseless bleatings. I hate telephones. They have made us less human, robbed us of our chance for intimacy or posterity or sincerity.

Fortunately, a few of my friends—my real friends—share my views on this, and we enjoy lively, revealing, soul-searched correspondence. As I sat at the breakfast table of my now-solitudinous split-level, I read a letter from Jay. Before a single "I" appeared in his letter, he had spent a page and one half describing the change of seasons on his farm, the peacefulness of the early-autumn days, the starry brilliance of crisp October nights. Beautiful. We need more Jays in this gadget culture of ours.

Checking my watch after two more letters and one more cup of coffee, I discovered that time had ambushed me yet again. I slipped the unopened lawyer's letter into my attaché case, wolfed the rest of the coffee, and ran out the door. It was Tuesday, and I had posted office hours

5

from 10:00 until 12:00 that day each week. Since I was late, I knew there would be a small knot of students waiting at my door, their seminar papers dangling from angry hands.

I ended up being only fifteen minutes late, and to my surprise, there was no one waiting for me. Unlocking the door, picking up some interdepartmental memos slipped under the sill, I collapsed behind the cocoon of my desk and bookshelves. The office was small, no larger than eight feet on a side, and it was crammed with bookcases, the desk, a guest chair, and a few posters and pictures. All the offices in the building were like mine, but that did not deter a colleague of mine from bringing in a bedroll and a hot plate, and setting up his home in its torturous confines. Seems as if his wife had left him so financially bereft that he simply could not affort a residence of his own—especially on the salary of a college professor. He continued to live like a beaver in his lodge for almost a year before being discovered by Doctor Luzinski, the department chairman. Luzinski fired the colleague, but the rest of us threatened to go on strike unless he was reinstated. I think it was the first instance of collective bargaining among English literature professors at the university, and I was shocked to see that it was successful. The colleague was reinstated but was forced to find housing off campus.

But I digress.

The issue at hand was the letter from the Vermont lawyer, and I was now forced to attend to it, what with no students clamoring for a change of grade. Opening it, I found a short, personal note which read as follows:

James Fairly
Attorney-at-Law
Warren's Grove Road
Brattleboro VT 05301

Bryan D. Alexander, Ph.D
1804 Brennan Terrace
College Park MD 20740

Dear Doctor Alexander:

Please contact me at your earliest possible convenience during normal business hours. As executor for the late Mrs. Agatha Rochemont, I have been instructed to inform you of your status as the sole heir to Mrs. Rochemont's estate.

My phone number (802)-874-1010. Thank you very much.

Sincerely,
James Fairly

Although the letter implied the death of my mother's great aunt Agatha—a woman whom I had not seen since I was ten years of age—I could not suppress the smile that crept upon my face like a sly cat. I found it somehow comical to be in that most mythical of American situations: to be the sole heir of a (presumably) rich, (probably) eccentric, and (assuredly) distant relative.

Now I did not want any intrusions, so I Magic-Markered a hasty note: WILL RETURN IN 15 MINUTES, pulled off a slab of Scotch tape, and stuck it to the front of my door before closing it, sealing me in. Picking up the phone, I dialed a 9, which patched me into one of the cold, gray fish who pose as campus telephone operators.

"Can I help you?" intoned a flat, slightly sinusited voice.

"Yes, operator. This is Doctor Alexander, extension 6544. . . . I'd like to make a long distance call please."

"Is this university business, Doctor?" They always asked that.

"Certainly," I said.

"Where do you want to call?"

"Brattleboro, Vermont. The Peraclean Textbook Company." English professors are notorious callers of textbook publishers.

"All right, Doctor, you have an outside line now."

There was a click and a familiar drone in the receiver before I could mutter a thank-you.

I dialed Fairly's number and heard it answered on the first ring.

"James Fairly," said a young voice.

"Mr. Fairly, this is Bryan Alexander. . . . I received your letter this morning."

"Good morning, Doctor Alexander. Before I go on, let me express my sincerest condolences . . ."

"Oh that's all right, I didn't even know that Agatha was dead till I got your letter," I said quickly. "And please, don't call me 'Doctor,' makes me feel like an old fart, if you know what I mean. Bryan's fine."

There was a pause. Fairly cleared his throat. I reached into my pocket and pulled out my Carltons, lit one, waited.

"Oh, I see. I'm sorry that I was the one to convey the bad news. I must admit that I was curious as to your absence at the funeral."

"I'm surprised that Agatha had one. She always said she loathed them. I don't care for them either. Too ritualistic for me. I probably wouldn't have gone even if I *had* known about hers." I exhaled slowly.

"Oh, I see . . ." Mr. Fairly let his voice tail off, obviously thinking.

"Well, anyway," I said. "You wanted to talk to me about her estate, right?"

"Oh yes, of course." There was sound of papers rattling near the phone.

"I hope you don't think I'm just a coldhearted bastard who's merely interested in my aunt's money, but you've never taught college, have you?"

"Why no, I haven't, but I think I understand what you're getting at."

I laughed but said nothing, drew on the cigarette.

"Well, basically, it's like this, Doct—ah, Bryan: Agatha Rochemont left an airtight, perfectly legal will and testament with my former partner, the late Elihu Webberton. The document leaves all her worldly possessions, her real estate, her bank accounts—everything—to you."

8

"What about her debts?" I asked, feeling my pulse jump.

"She didn't have a one."

"Any chance of probate? Contestation?"

"Not a chance that I see."

"Now the important question," I said, smiling. I liked this young guy, Fairly. "How much?"

"Well, I'm not sure we should discuss things like that over the phone, Bryan. I was going to ask you to come up to Brattleboro at your earliest convenience so that we could clarify those types of things."

"Well, let me tell you something, Mr. Fairly. I'm not much for that kind of propriety. Now as you know, I'm trapped in this teaching job. I have a department chairman who thinks he's a Prussian army commandant, and a schedule that's tighter than a rat's—"

"I think I understand your position," he cut in sharply.

"Wait, let me finish, it's quite simple really. If my aunt left me enough, then I can simply tell this place where to go. *Then* I can come visit you at my 'earliest convenience.' Otherwise, I'll be expected to crawl around on the chairman's rug for an hour or so. Do you get the picture?"

"Perfectly."

"Well?"

"If I told you it was substantial, would that be enough?"

"Listen, Mr. Fairly. I don't want to play games. Is it enough for me to go out of this office and never come back? How much the hell is it?" Now I was no longer sure I liked this guy.

Fairly let out a long, labored breath that was tempted to become a sigh. "All right, let me see . . . counting up everything, including the house but not the value of the furniture inside—lot's of antiques, you know—I'd say it's in the neighborhood of $600,000."

I paused for a moment, fighting the pure biological responses to the figure. If you have never been told that you are suddenly rich, you will probably never understand what it actually *feels* like. Let me only say that I thought

I was going to (a) suffer a coronary (b) experience an aneurysm (c) become hysterical (d) undergo locomotor ataxia (e) all of the above.

Instead, I found myself saying, quite inanely: "Gee, that's a lot of money."

Mr. Fairly laughed, establishing his humanity once again, and I joined him in a burst of pure joy. The laughter pealed out of me like cathedral bells, and it was the most wonderful sound I had ever heard.

After I had calmed down somewhat, I received specific instructions and directions from Mr. Fairly. I could catch a Dulles flight into Springfield, Massachusetts, then take a limousine to Brattleboro. I could easily be in Fairly's office by 1:00 in the afternoon if I left early the next morning. We agreed on that and said our goodbyes.

Hanging up the phone, I realized that I was still giddy, flying high on the potent mixture of adrenalin and *argentum*. God, I felt *good!* I fired up another Carlton, being careful to cover up those little "airstream filter" holes so that I could taste the smoke. I was so excited that I didn't know what to do first. My mind flickered like old movies with images of myself and my new life: sweeping homes of *nouveau* architecture, European automobiles, double-knit suits, cocktail parties at the Windows On The World, breakfasts on the Left Bank, a kidney-shaped swimming pool filled with naked women . . .

And suddenly I was going down like an old Spad with a smoking engine.

What was happening to me? What the hell was I thinking about? I didn't want any of that bullshit. Not *really* want it. At least that's what I had always told myself when I was sitting in my library at home. I looked about the office, feeling the warmth that radiated from the crammed bookcases, the solace of the worn, battered furniture, the *rightness* of it all. Perhaps B. Traven was right. Gold was the catalyst that turned simple men into calloused trolls.

What *would* I do with all that money?

I did not, at that moment, honestly know. It required several minutes and another Carlton (they burn very quickly) to adjust to that self-realization; then I began thinking rationally once again. The first thing that had to be done was to deal with Doctor Luzinski.

I left the office and entered the corridor just as the 10:00 classes were letting out. The main corridor at the end of the hall was filled with blue-jeaned bodies and the gentle murmur of conversation. Maneuvering through the young crowds, I entered the English department offices—an area which closely resembled the expediting section of a large warehouse. It was a series of cubicles set off by flimsy pastel panels, flanked by two secretaries' desks, a wall of pigeonholes for all the instructors, and *everything* painted a sickening turquoise. Well, not everything; but, it *was* tasteless to the point of being dull, which seemed to be appropriate for a department such as it was.

Mrs. Wynegar, the chairman's secretary, studied me with the bland mask that was forever the cast of her middle-aged Visigothic features. "Can I help you?"

"I'd like to see Doctor Luzinski," I said, putting my hands in my pockets.

"Can I tell him who's calling?"

"Who's calling? For Chrissake, I'm a member of his department—Bryan Alexander!"

Unfazed by this, she announced me on the intercom with all the panache of a mortician at day's end.

"Tell him to make an appointment. I'm quite busy right now." Luzinski's voice, normally a not unpleasant alto, sounded tinny and cheap.

As the intercom clicked off and Mrs. Wynegar looked up to repeat my master's words, I started moving past her desk toward Luzinski's closed door.

"You can't go in there," said the secretary, her voice rising above its dull drone for the first time in memory.

I could only smile at this. "Oh yes I can," I said and strode forcefully up to Luzinski's door, grabbing the knob and twisting it open in one fluid motion.

Before Mrs. Wynegar could disengage herself from her desk, I was already inside the door and closing it swiftly behind me. As he turned around, I saw Luzinski stuff a

11

slick-covered men's magazine into his right-hand desk drawer.

"You *look* very busy, Doctor Luzinski," I said, smiling as I approached his desk and sat down in the interviewee's chair which was prosaically termed the "hot seat" by the less imaginative members of the department.

"What's going on, Alexander?" said Luzinski. He struggled to assume control of the situation and was not doing badly.

"I have to talk to you and I don't have time to make an appointment," I said, reaching for my cigarettes.

"Your conduct is highly irregular. You could receive a severe reprimand for this sort of thing. A note in your file wouldn't look good if you ever had to seek work at another institution, you know." He sounded as if he were in complete command of things now. He was as stuffy as I'd ever seen him.

"Listen to me, I've just received word that a close relative has died, and I'm going to have to leave immediately for the funeral. Does that change things any?"

His eyebrows arched for a moment, and he made a steeple with his hands across the barren desk-top. "Oh I see . . . Where do you have to go?"

"New England. Vermont, actually."

"How long will you be gone?"

"Indefinitely," I said.

"What?!"

"You heard me. I'll be gone for an indeterminate amount of time . . . like forever." I smiled and blew smoke at him.

"You mean you're resigning?"

"That's right. I thought you'd like to know about it."

"But why?" Luzinski looked truly puzzled, as if he could not comprehend why anyone would wish to leave the groves of academe, once firmly entrenched.

"Why not? And what do you care? There are at least four or five hundred able and willing replacements that you can choose from. Ph.D.'s in English are working in lots of supermarkets all over the country."

He shook his head. "You puzzle me, Alexander, you

really do. You're young, bright, you have a whole future ahead of you. Your students like you, you've published in all the prestigious journals, you—"

"No I haven't," I said, cutting him off.

"What?"

"I said 'No, I haven't.' I haven't published anything. Anywhere."

"What are you talking about?"

"Those publishing credentials in my resumé are phony. The whole resumé's a phony." I drew on my Carlton and exhaled slowly. The expression on Luzinski's face was an ugly blend of emotions. His hands gripped each other in a white-knuckled embrace.

"Impossible!"

"Oh come on, Phil," I said, emphasizing his first name—because *no one* was ever supposed to address him thusly. "You know nobody ever checks resumés. Too much work."

"I don't believe you!" His features were slowly tightening, his complexion flushing nicely all around. A large vein started to bulge across his forehead. He was starting to look like a sketch in an anthropology text.

"Sorry, but it's true," I said. "In reality, I am Doctor Bryan D. Alexander, ex-physics professor from the University of California at Irvine."

"Bullshit!" he cried, shocking *me* with his decay into good old human vernacular. "*Bull*shit!"

"Not this time, Phil. About six years ago, I realized that physics was not what I wanted to do with my life, so I decided to try an experiment. I had always liked to read . . . figured I knew just about as much about the classics as any English major. So I applied for jobs in English."

"But . . . but . . . *physics*!?" He mouthed the word as if it were a true obscenity, as if it were a vileness unspeakable upon his tongue. It was beautiful, and I almost laughed in his face.

"Sadly, yes."

"But your references, the letters of recommendation? . . ."

"All phony. Wrote them myself. Used box numbers

13

and addresses of friends at some of the right universities, that's all."

"I don't believe it. I simply can*not* believe this, Alexander," he said in a final attempt to regain control of what must have been for him a terribly embarrassing situation.

"Well, you'll have plenty of time to check up on it if you want," I said, getting up, "but I'm leaving. Goodbye, Phil."

"But why? *Why*, Alexander?" He was pleading with me now.

I wanted to tell him that my experiment—all true, by the way—had served to prove what probably all academics secretly think as they lay in the darkness when sleep will not take them: that what they do is the biggest cultural sham in the history of the country. I wanted to tell him that people like English Ph.D.'s serve no other purpose than to create *other* English Ph.D.'s, and thus serve the centuries *ad infinitum*. I wanted to tell him that all the dead hours and reams of paper spent on the one hundred and thirty-two thousand six hundred and forty-second monograph on Shakespeare would serve the existential essence, the biological survival, of humanity not in the slightest. That the bulk of us were nothing more than the twentieth-century equivalents of the friars stooped and stooled at their illuminations. That we were not special in a specialized world; so much so that any one of us—with a little intelligence and a lot of nerve—could do the job of any other of us. And that no one would suspect a thing.

I wanted to tell him all these things. I wanted to raise my voice and prance dramatically about his office like Clarence Darrow.

But I was already tired of the game. In a flash of Zen-like recognition, I suddenly saw Luzinski for the creature which he was. A rumpled little man who could never admit to himself that his life was an endless maze of faculty teas, oral examinations, comprehensives, desiccated little bibliographies, dissertation committees, and freshman quizzes. A compendium of nothings.

And so, I turned to leave, pausing only to say: "I don't

really know, Doctor Luzinski, but it seemed like a good idea at the time."

I closed the door behind me, ignoring the stares of the two secretaries, and walked quickly into the corridor. I did not now feel the dizzying rush of confidence and sense of satisfaction that I had so glibly expected. Somehow there had been little joy in exacting my personal brand of revenge upon my department chairman.

As I reached my office and began to clean out my desk drawers by throwing oddments unceremoniously into my usually empty briefcase, I reflected upon things. It is unpleasant for any of us to discover chinks in armor, especially when they are of our own devise.

TWO

WHEN I was growing up, battling the years of adolescence, my father had always stressed the fact that one day he wanted me to "be somebody." To Be Somebody. He had toiled all of his life as a construction worker, and he nightly came home to the rest of us, lunch pail in one grimy hand, the evening news tabloid in the other, to tell me that he did not want me to turn out like him. He wanted me to have a job where I could wear a *white* shirt to work. And a tie. *And* a suit.

Sometimes I feel guilty when I realize that I grew to loathe white shirts and ties. *And* suits.

But in those early years, there was a burning desire to please my father. I wanted to please him because I *knew* how hard he had worked all through the years, and because I loved him and wanted to make him happy. It's simple enough: when you love someone, your real joy comes from giving them joy. I don't think anyone would quarrel with that. And so I found myself wanting to be an astronomer, then a paleontologist, and finally, a dentist.

No matter that now the thought of myself in a trim, white smock, dutifully probing and drilling in all manner of mouths strikes me as ludicrous. Because at the time, it was a deadly serious ambition, and I strove toward that goal with all my worth. I escaped the possibility of becoming a modern McTeague only because I found organic chemistry to be far more inscrutable than Linear B. Oddly, as I struggled through the University of Pennsylvania's pre-dent program, I found that I possessed an uncanny understanding—a "knack," if you will—for physics. When the dental schools rejected me, I simply continued on in physics, playing the academic game until they called me

16

"Doctor." My father was pleased. The University of California at Irvine was pleased. Even I was pleased. For a while.

But what I really wanted, what I had thoroughly ached for through all those years, was a nebulous, nonpaycheck kind of vocation known loosely as a soldier of fortune.

Don't laugh. I am perfectly serious about this.

I had always been fascinated with geography and the lure of travel to foreign lands. I thought of places with names obscured by misty enigma: Cathay, Macao, Hollandia, Caledonia, Bambasi, Dar es Salaam. My Latin classes were endurable because of my daydreams: steaming jungles and oven-breath deserts penetrated by my four-wheel drive Jeep, a ring-mount twin-sixties machine gun in the rear seat. I spent years escaping ice floes in McMurdo Sound, hacking through willowgrass near Murchison Falls, discovering the ruins of Tiahuanaco in the green pit of the Amazon, roaming the lengendary elephant graveyard.

As I grew older, and presumably more rational, I began to question the romantic pursuits of such "soldiers;" not because of the possibility of actually doing it, but rather the feasability. I mean, it was not the kind of profession that normally overflowed the classified sections of the *Washington Post,* nor was it a readily accessible curriculum at many universities. And so the dream, like a million other adolescent fantasies of baroque construction, dissolved like morning mist.

Until now.

I was sitting in the smoking section of a 707 that was banking up and away from Dulles International when the old dreams touched me once again. I had been thinking of how my inheritance would bring me, more than money, *freedom.* Wealth is, when one considers it carefully, not actually material, but time. And if what Aunt Agatha's lawyer told was even half-correct, I would be, to coin an expression, filthy with *time.*

The stewardess, a petite, slender blonde with a wholesome, Nebraska-and-freckles kind of face, appeared at my right and asked me if I wanted a cocktail. I don't

17

normally care for liquor, although I find the occasional mixed drink a novelty. I think it stems from my adolescence when I wanted to act like a sophisticated adult so badly that I could almost taste it. Back in those simpler times, to sit in a bar in a strange city, fondling a Scotch and soda (which tasted like medicine), made me feel worldly and wise.

Not so any longer. And yet, I still get the urge to take a cocktail in situations which are out of the ordinary: a long train-ride, a first dinner date with a mysterious woman, a plane flight. The stewardess looked into my eyes with such a willing-to-please expression that I simply could not say no, but as usual, I could not think of one drink that I would really *like* to have.

"How about a White Swan," I said finally. It was something I had remembered seeing in a bartender's guide but had never sampled.

The stewardess puzzled over it for a moment, grinned knowingly, and said: "What's *that?* Something for girls named Leda?"

I laughed at her wit, smiled, and answered her. "No . . . it's for a guy named Bryan, actually."

She smiled yet again, and I was wondering what I was getting myself into.

"I'd be happy to make it for you . . . if you'd give me an idea of what's in it."

"Amaretto and cream over ice. You have any Amaretto?"

"I think so. I'll see what I can do, okay?"

I nodded and she glided down the aisle. I watched her, thinking back to a story a friend of mine once related to me. In fact, I think about it every time I take a flight somewhere. My friend is a writer, and he logs hundreds of thousands of miles flying all over the country on the university lecture circuit, giving dramatic readings of his work and generally bombastic and highly personal assessments of the world at large. He is immensely popular and is a well-known appreciator of beautiful women. Once, while flying from Los Angeles to Chicago, just as he entered the restroom in the tail section of the plane, the

18

door was opened, and a young, dark-eyed stewardess slipped in with him and locked the door. "Whatever happens next is up to you," she said with complete seriousness.

Afterward, the stewardess informed him that he was now a member of the infamous "Mile-High Club."

I have often wondered what I would do in a similar situation, and I was thinking such thoughts when my stewardess returned with my White Swan. I accepted the drink with my most sincere smile, but she merely deposited it on the fold-down tray and continued down the aisle.

Tasting the drink, I found it to be quite pleasant, a hint of almond in creamy coolness. The no-smoking lamp had been out for quite a few minutes, so I pulled out my cigarettes and lit one. I hadn't drawn more than two inhalations when I felt someone touch my sleeve. Looking to my left I stared into the sea green eyes of a strikingly attractive woman of perhaps twenty-five.

"Excuse me," she said, and my imagination sparked and flashed. To be sought after was an exhilarating feeling.

"Yes?" I said as casually as I could, even though I was stunned by her classic beauty: almond eyes; slightly parted, slightly pouted lips; long ash-blond hair. I quickly conjured up possible repartees to her obvious come-on.

"Your cigarette . . ." she said, the sensual mouth drawing tight, grim.

"My *cigarette?*" Some vital part of me started to lock up, stagger, and finally stop.

"Yes, I was wondering if you would mind not smoking?"

Now you must understand that this sort of boldness in people irritates me greatly. Compound this with the fact that I was expecting a sultry introduction which never materialized, and you will see why I became instantly hostile.

"But I'm sitting in the smoking section," I said, trying to keep my voice even, controlled.

"Well, I know that, but I'm sitting four seats up and your smoke . . . well, it's *bothering* me." She stared at

19

me with a reproachful expression that I would imagine was supposed to make me feel like a properly admonished little boy.

When I am in public places, I often see other individuals doing things—picking their noses, hocking up great gobbets of phlegm, jiggling their little fingers in their ears as if pumping water, blueing the air with blimplike cigars, using "you know?" at the end of every sentence they utter . . . the list is endless—that I find anywhere from mildly annoying to utterly contemptible. But *never* have I ever thought to approach that person and ask them to stop on my account. It is simply unthinkable to me. The reasons for this are numerous: one being that I subscribe to the fact that there are an infinitely greater number of psychos on our public streets than in our asylums, and you just never know when you might say the wrong thing to one of their number; another being my philosophy that the word "public" is self-explanatory, and that anyone who goes out into it does so with the understanding that on occasion they must suffer small affronts to their personal *Weltanschhauung*.

And so I sat in my seat, transfixed by this woman's stare, like a butterfly under a pin, my cigarette sputtering and snaking a thin stream upward, as I tried to decide upon my course of action.

"I *said* it *bothers* me," she said again, as if I had not reacted quickly enough for her.

Slowly, and with great panache, I drew the cigarette to my lips and inhaled. She, by her last, venom-soaked barb, had made my decision for me. Exhaling, I directed the tight stream of smoke squarely between her sea green eyes, wishing for an instant that it was a laser beam.

"*You* . . . bother *me*," I said slowly as I exhausted my supply of smoke.

Her lower lip trembled, and something like hate lurched behind her eyes, but she said nothing. The moment of confrontation hung between us like a slab of lead shielding, cold and impenetrable. I stared into her eyes until she finally gave up the contest, whirled, disappearing up the aisle.

20

I felt no joy in the small victory, and I even felt sympathy toward her as I saw her get the attention of a steward, whisper angrily, and point back in the direction of my seat. I did not smirk as the steward indicated the proper division of the smoking and nonsmoking sections, and that I was not violating any rules.

"Good for you, Jimmy," said an elderly woman who was sitting in the window seat next to me. Previously, she had been so silent and unobtrusive that I had not even noticed her there.

"What?"

"She deserved that," said the old woman, nodding her head in the direction of my assailant.

I nodded and took another sip of the White Swan. Actually, the woman did not deserve it. In fact, I would have probably offered to move to another seat in the smoking section of the plane . . . if she had not repeated her demand. But she had repeated it, with not a small amount of nastiness. And when people are nasty with me, some inner, totally automatic circuit clicks into play: I become equally nasty. I don't like it, but it happens nevertheless, with the result that I feel vaguely unsatisfied, even disappointed with myself.

But it is a survival tactic, I suppose, and we all seem to evolve our own subsets of tactics. The ones that we retain are obviously the ones that work most efficiently. Life is learning to live with one's self, I think.

Outside the cabin, the clouds seemed to drift by, despite our airspeed of close to 500 MPH, and through an occasional gap in the cover, I tried to distinguish a familiar landmark. Of course, I could not. The only thing I ever recognized from the air was the Grand Canyon when my flight crossed directly over it during a returning flight from a convention in Los Angeles. It was so goddamned big, even from 30,000 feet, that *no one* could mistake it for anything other than the Grand Canyon.

The plane approached the Massachusetts border as I found myself approaching the possibility of being *nouveau riche*. There would be a few bills to pay off first, but nothing outlandish, since I rarely used credit cards or

21

bought anything that I could not pay cash for—nothing except the house, which had a $35,000 mortgage. And since it might be to my tax advantage *not* to pay off the mortgage, I was not completely sure what I would do with the bulk of Aunt Agatha's estate.

As the 707 eased into its landing pattern above Springfield, I found myself designing an artists' colony on Agatha's property and in her large manor-house. I would invite promising young creators to dwell within its tranquility for months-long sojourns, free of charge, while I myself learned to play classical guitar. (It occurs to me sometimes that all mathematicians and physics types are frustrated musicians.)

My stewardess aroused me from the daydream, reminding me to fasten my seat belt. Whatever happened next was definitely *not* up to me. I did not breathe with regularity from that point on until the plane's landing gear touched down on Springfield's runway. Planes had always made me apprehensive, probably because I did not fly very frequently. But I think a large part of the reason lay in that I had no control of my own life when flying. If there was every any trouble, I would be virtually helpless, and I do not like that feeling.

But this time I was lucky. The pilot eased the big jet in so smoothly that I barely felt the scritch of its massive tires as they touched the asphalt. I disembarked quickly, not wishing to face the young woman whom I had bothered, not wishing to see the stewardess who had bothered me. I succeeded in these objectives and was soon alone in a rather small, functional, but uninspired, terminal. There were so few people in the building that I could almost hear the slap of my shoes on the featureless, tiled floor.

After a quick check on things, I found that I could charter a small Lear to a private airport outside of Brattleboro instead of taking a cab or special airport limo. The cost was not as prohibitive as I had imagined, and despite my fears of flying, I chartered a flight with a small outfit called New England Business Shuttles. Even though statistics stridently point out that the percentage of air accidents is higher with small, private planes than with the

22

big commercial transports, I *feel* safer in a plane like a Lear or a Hawker-Siddeley. I am told that small planes have an acceptable glide factor (whereas the 707's, without power, will drop like a stone), plus there is the possibility (slim though it may be) that I could grip the copilot's stick and save myself should the pilot suddenly slump over his controls under a coronary attack.

The flight was swift and uneventful. The pilot, efficient and taciturn. I arrived at the private field outside Brattleboro a few minutes after noon, called a cab, and was driven into one of Vermont's patented beautiful towns.

Brattleboro, Vermont: one main street, a brace of intersections clustered with clapboard and brick-front shops and offices. Lots of specialty businesses like cabinetmakers, metalsmiths, stationers, potters, chemists, glassblowers. The streets are like green caves, so thick and complete are the large trees that line their perimeters. The houses are full of gingerbread and filigree, turrets and cupolas, porches and bottleglass windows. If there ever was a true time-machine, it is the small towns and villages of Vermont.

The cab driver had never heard of my lawyer's name, but he did know the address of Elihu Webberton, the recently deceased *juris doctor*. He drove me straight to the establishment, a small townhouse office in goldenrod tongue-and-groove slatting, black shutters, and small brick stoop. I was a half hour early, and I was tempted to take a leisurely walk up to the main thoroughfare. But the thought struck me that there would be plenty of time for that sort of thing. Time was my servant now, instead of the usual arrangement. I decided to see Fairly, get things over with.

There was no receptionist in the front room, no plastic furniture, no Woolworth prints of famous masters on the walls, no *Times and Newsweeks* in those hideous clear-plastic binders on the end tables. The room looked like someone's study: warm, woodsy, lived in. Opposite the entrance was another door, whereupon I knocked.

"Just a moment," said a muffled voice.

The door swung open, and I stared at a young man with hair down to his shoulders, wire-framed glasses magnifying pale blue eyes, sallow cheeks, some freckles for color, a long nose, and thin lips.

He looked at me blankly for a moment. "Can I help you with something?"

"Yes, I'm Bryan Alexander. You Fairly?"

He brightened a bit and looked me over quickly, probably surprised at my casual attire of blue denim jeans and an old brown herringbone sports jacket that did nothing to accent my plain white shirt. "Oh yes, of course! Please come in."

His office was large and lined with the expected panoply of leather-bound law books, properly framed degrees, a bronzed statue of blind Justice with the scales (a gift from practically every ex-law student's relative), and a desk large enough to withstand a cavalry charge.

He directed me to a chair by his desk, arranged himself behind it, and cleared away the remains of a ham and cheese sandwich wrapped in tan butcher's paper. "Just finishing lunch. Hope you don't mind . . ."

I shrugged and reached for my cigarettes, lighting one up.

Fairly adjusted his glasses and reached for a stack of papers on the corner of the desk. "Here's just about everything, except for some policies and other personal documents that your aunt kept in a safe deposit box at the bank. We can examine those once you have signed some papers which will give you access to it. If you want to read through this stuff, be my guest . . ."

I waved my hand casually. "No thanks, it's not going to make much sense to me anyway. You look like an honest kind of guy. I'm afraid I'm just going to have to trust you."

Fairly smiled and he looked no older than sixteen when he did this. "Frankly, I don't blame you. The language bores me silly. When I read it, my mind kind of goes on automatic pilot, and I understand what I've read without really having to *read* it, if you know what I mean."

He shuffled through the papers, rearranging their order

24

slightly, then picked them up one by one and briefly explained the purpose and declaration. There were depositions, reassignments, powers-of-attorney, executorships, tax forms, inheritance riders, insurance binders, and a raft of other legal terms which I did not recognize. Most of them required my signature at least two or three times, not counting the copies, and I rushed through this task with all the enthusiasm of a small boy accepting a sales receipt for a much-awaited toy which he has just bought.

Afterward, Fairly took me up to the main branch of the Brattleboro People's Bank, introduced me to the president as Agatha's rightful heir, acquired possession of the safe deposit box keys, signed some more papers which gave me signature to her numerous accounts, and escorted me out of the solemn place.

"Would you like to go up to her house and look around?" he asked as we climbed into his Chevrolet at the curbside. "I have the keys with me."

"Why not," I said, still not accustomed to being a man of considerable means.

The drive took us through winding, hilly roads that must have been hell when the snow started to fall, but which were now lined with forty-foot oaks and smaller maples just beginning their spectral slide into oranges and reds. The houses were all meticulously painted and landscaped, and the driveways were lined with small evergreens and whitewashed boulders. American flags were in abundance on private flagpoles. And just beneath the surface of all this neat propriety was the rippling spirit of the New Englander—muscular, proud, industrious. It made me feel good just to be in its midst.

Fairly's Chevrolet slowed as we approached an entrance partially obscured by tall, expertly trimmed hedges which continued to form the walls of a green corridor curving slightly to the left. The hedges broke upon a tree-shaded garden, lush with late-blooming geraniums, coleuses, and begonias. The ground was covered with pachysandra, and the air smelled of pine cones. Beyond the garden was my Aunt Agatha's house, unchanged since my childhood visits to the place—a three-story, squarish-

25

looking affair, its lines broken only by the expansive front porch, the widow's-watch tower in the eastern corner, and an ornate cupola above the center peak of the roof.

We parked out front, and Fairly led me up a gravel walk to the front door. Keying the lock, we entered, and I was caught up in a rush of memories, triggered either by the unchanged positions of the furnishings, or by the warm, almost spicy, smell of the place. Smells had a way of cuing old memories in me, especially since cigarette smoking all but killed my sense of smell for current odors. Fairly walked me around the place, pointing out a particular piece of antique furniture or a singularly nice painting. As we passed through the rooms, I could almost hear the old conversations I had enjoyed with Agatha years ago in the same places.

"The place looks so clean and well kept," I said, and meaning it. The house did not have the silence and pallor of one recently deceased; it was bright and warm—alive.

"Yes," said Fairly. "There's a maid who lived with your aunt. She did a nice job it seems."

"A maid? Where's she now?"

"She's taken a room at a boarding house in town. What with your aunt's passing, her future is up in the air right now."

I nodded. "Is she young?"

Fairly shrugged. "Depends upon your definition of the word . . ."

"How old *is* she?" Lawyers' evasiveness always had bothered me.

"Forty . . . forty-five, I'd say." He smiled as he saw my dream of playing master-and-mistress fade rapidly away.

"Well, why don't you get in touch with her and tell her to come on back to the house. It will need her."

"Even if you won't?" said Fairly, smiling.

"Depends on your definition of the word," I said.

THREE

I HAD BEEN living in the house for almost a week before I found the manuscript.

Mrs. Carrington, my aunt's maid, returned to the house the day after I signed the papers at Fairly's. She was a slender woman of perhaps forty, although when the light was right, she appeared to be five years younger. She had long brown hair tied up in a loose ponytail. She had small brown eyes that looked tired, despite the long natural lashes which telegraphed her every blink and *coup d'oeil*. She had a tight but pleasant smile, and disposition to match. The first thing I told her was to get rid of that ugly black uniform with the lacy apron and funny hat.

Now that does not mean exactly how it sounds. What I suggested was that she replace her traditional maid-clothing for something more casual: jeans and jerseys, sweaters, and things like that.

Mrs. Carrington agreed, and with her change of apparel there came a more relaxed, casual atmosphere to the old house, which I greatly enjoyed. She had been showing me all the myriad aspects of the place, and I spent long days and nights exploring, sorting, collecting, and discarding. My aunt had lived a long, prosperous life, and she exhibited all the pack-rat tendencies that seem to be rife in my family.

It was an early-September Sunday morning when I finally worked my way up to the house's expansive attic. There in that roof-beamed mustiness I found a cache of old treasures—the kind that every young boy dreams about. I rummaged and rooted and pried, feeling as Flinders Petrie may have felt when he thrust his first torch into his first Egyptian burial chamber. I came to discover, both by deduction and then verification of my maid, that my aunt's husband, Valery Rochemont, had been a famous antiquarian before his private sailing vessel was lost at sea off the coast of Bar Harbor, Maine, many years ago. His collection of early books and manuscripts must have been worth an enormous fortune in itself, although I would have great shame in selling some of these carefully preserved treasures.

I found a small chest made of oak, with brass fittings and cracked leather straps. It was locked, and there was no key, which led me to take a hammer and cold chisel to it. The metal was well crafted, but it finally gave way to several of my ugly blows. Inside, carefully wrapped in stiff linen were three leather-bound volumes. The single word, *Journal*, graced the cover of each volume in flaking gold intaglio. I glanced through the topmost volume and saw that the pages were a thickish grade of vellum, and that every page was filled with a roughish handwriting that was not instantly legible, although it was written in English. I picked up the first volume and flipped to the first page where the following was scribed in the center of the page:

DURHAM KENT

13 RUE KERVEGAN
ILE DE FEYDEAU
NANTES

The name meant nothing to me, although it may have been someone very well known to book-and-manuscript aficionados. I glanced through some of the pages and saw that it was nothing more than a fairly well drawn diary of the fellow's life.

I was about to replace it in the locked chest, when I decided to check out the first few pages, just to see if there was any indication of Kent's identity, which might thereby give a hint as to the value of the manuscripts. After all, my uncle had thought highly enough of them to keep them under lock and key. . . .

April 14, 1860

I have decided to begin a journal of my activities. I do this in the event that I may one day return to my own world. A detailed record of my adventures may serve me well. It has been four years since shipwrecking upon the Normandy beaches. The first few years were those of a beggar and a vagrant. Worked odd jobs along the road to Paris, seduced a woman or two, lived from hand to mouth. To get another ship! God, I'd give anything to leave this land of effete Frenchmen! But finding the exact place where the fluxes are working would be difficult work. Still, it is a dream, a workable goal that gives me strength to carry on a largely miserable life.

April 30, 1860

Paris is a cosmopolitan place, but I do not take part in much of it. Early this year I obtained work with a shipwright whose dock on the Seine is highly respected. Business is high, and I am one of his best workers. Learning French has been a hardship, but I am managing. Man is ever-adaptable, I fear, no matter what time or place he finds himself in. The work is hard, the tools inadequate (despite my "inventions" from time to time), but it keeps my mind off my troubles and it gives me for the first time in this world some money and a place to hang my hat at day's end.

May 12, 1860

After work today, I ventured into my favorite tavern, a warm place called La Belle Donzelle. Means "the pretty wench," but there are few of them in this place. But the ale is good and so is the wine. The company's acceptable too, because it's not the usual wharf riffraff. Literary types come here to sample "real life" as they call it. They talk amongst themselves and also with the "real livers." Saw Dumas in here once. A real earthy sort, not what you would

29

think of a person who wrote stories of the court. Napoleon III not terribly popular in here, by the way. Me, I could care less.

May 18, 1860
Today, at La Belle Donzelle, I met a nice sort of chap. Says his name is Jules Verne and he's got quite a mind on him. He's the son of a prominent Parisian barrister, and he himself is an on-again off-again law student, although he claims to hate it. Wants to be a writer, he does. Comes to the Belle to rub shoulders with the literary lights, and maybe get some help from them. Can't blame him. Law bores me, too.

It took me almost a half hour to read that much of it. Kent's handwriting was close to indecipherable. But I could instantly understand why my uncle had been interested in the journals of old Durham Kent. This stuff was probably quite valuable, especially since there were no copies and it was the original manuscript. I decided that I would bring the chest downstairs to the library, clean it and its contents up, and cart them off with a few other questionable treasures to one of the larger book-dealers in the area.

After supper, in which Mrs. Carrington was proving herself to be a competent cook as well as a maid, I went to dusting and polishing the leather-bound journals. Over a cup of coffee and a Carlton, I fell to the temptation and began reading Mr. Kent's revelations once again. I found that as the hours passed the legibility of the manuscript increased, since I became more accustomed to the odd curlicues and slants that were Kent's distinctive symbols for the alphabet.

As I continued to read, I had the growing feeling that there was something odd about the journal. It was nothing that I could immediately single out, but there were recurring references by the writer which left me dangling, others that were so totally cryptic that I had no idea of what he may have meant. There were certain words—

"fluxes," "fluxgates," "the submersible," "fluxworlds,"—that puzzled me completely. In the beginning, I had the feeling that Mr. Kent was at best a low-grade psychotic given to occasional lapses of sanity and enjoying fanciful pieces of hallucination.

In a note from *September 2, 1860:*

. . . I almost told Jules about my origins last night. The ale had flowed freely, and I had made mention of the possibility of a submersible. His eyes grew round and bright, his curiosity and imagination obviously piqued. I wondered what he would have thought of the concept of fluxworlds? Perhaps someday he will trust me. . . .

And another from *September 17, 1860:*

Tonight, Jules visited me in my quarters down near Rampal's docksite. He brought with him two of his plays—*The Gunpowder Plot* and an absolutely dreadful thing called *A Regency Tragedy*. He forced me to read them in that pathetically enthusiastic manner of his. And I was forced to comment on them. The plays are bad, I can say that now in the privacy of my thoughts, but they did demonstrate his ability to string words together coherently—at least they *appeared* to be nicely done to someone who has come only recently to French. Later on we talked about sailing, and Jules told me that he wishes to have one day a fine ship, since he fairly loves the sea. How I wished to tell him what burns in my heart of hearts! My imagination danced with pictures of me upon Jules' boat, searching for one of the fluxgates, then finding it, slipping through to the sanity of my own world. Again tonight, I almost told him the whole story.

My knowledge of schizophrenics had been confined to only what I'd read in the survey textbooks and the articles you can find in places like *Psychology Today,* but it had been my layman's experience that true psychotics lived in a totally unreal world, and that their world was so rigidly and completely structured that there was eventually little real contact with the world of us normals.

That did not seem to be the case with Durham Kent. His journals described a perfectly ordinary, fairly well lettered Englishman in France, who had the happy accident to meet the young Jules Verne and be fascinated with the young writer's company. It was only on the odd occasion that he slipped into his singular nonsense about "fluxes" and such. Now I was not so obtuse that I did not make the supposition that Kent's submersible might be his own term for the modern submarine, and of course, the most obvious connection would be that he eventually provided Verne with the inspiration for *The Nautilus*. Kent had said that he worked as a shipwright, and I assumed that maybe he had worked out the plans for a workable submarine, much as had some other early pioneers like Fulton and MacInnes.

In the end-analysis, I knew that there was no way I could arbitrarily pass judgment on Kent's state of mind. He *seemed* quite rational. I decided that I would resist the temptation to read ahead, skipping around and the like, and merely take each entry as they came.

A week passed before I had completed the task.

But it was *some* kind of week, let me tell you.

Either Durham Kent was the most ingenious liar I had ever read, or I held in my hands one of the world's most fantastic discoveries since electricity.

I won't belabor the narrative by reproducing all of Kent's entries word for word, since there are many passages that have nothing to do with the situation at hand. There are some parts which follow which will aptly demonstrate my amazement.

It seems as if Durham Kent and Jules Verne became the best of friends. So close, in fact, that in 1862 Jules invited him to live at his country home in Chantenay, just outside of Paris, where the young Verne lived with his lovely wife, Honorine. In fact, Durham Kent became

Jules Verne's manservant—his gentleman's gentleman, his valet, confidant, advisor, and constant companion. Durham Kent does not indicate how Honorine reacted to this arrangement, but from the descriptions of Verne's personality, I don't think it would have made any difference. The Frenchman was an outspoken, headstrong type who didn't take any crap from anybody.

That Verne and Kent shared many likes and dislikes seemed obvious, but the incident that seemed to cement their friendship and their subsequent agreements probably occurred on the following occasion:

October 14, 1862

Tonight I told Jules everything. We were strolling through the gardens of the Chantenay estate, enjoying pipes of good Virginia tobaccos, when he asked me something about my childhood. I don't remember the exact reference—probably because he had referred to some incident which I had concocted out of whole cloth to cover my true identity and reason for being in this particular fluxworld.

When he asked me that question, whatever it was, I looked into his bright blue eyes and realized that I could no longer lie to him. If it had not been for Jules, I would have been forever a miserable wretch. And so, I asked him to have a seat on one of the many benches among the hedgerows . . . because I had a great confession to make, and that I prayed that he would believe me. Jules nodded his head slowly, assuring me that he would believe anything I swore to be true.

Thanking him for his faith I proceeded to tell him the entire story. It would have been difficult to explain the complex theory and structure of what Nemo had always called *The Continuum* and its infinite number of fluxworlds, so I decided to cover each specific point as I came to it in the course of my story. To begin, I merely told him that I had originally lived in a "universe"—time and place completely *different* from his own. To my surprise,

Jules only nodded at what I had thought would be a major revelation. I was constantly underestimating his boundless imagination and open-mindedness to things scientific. I then told him of the life in England, as a seaman in her navy, the years of apprenticeship before meeting Captain Nemo, before joining his handpicked crew aboard his craft, *The Nautilus*. I told him about the incident which had me court-martialed by Nemo's own tribunal and set adrift in an open boat in the North Atlantic of my fluxworld earth. A punishment that was common aboard *The Nautilus*. Discipline was usually high and not breeched lightly.

I had drifted for three days and three nights. The prevailing current carried my provisionless boat toward the east. Without instruments, it was difficult to keep track of my position, but I fashioned a crude astrolabe from pieces of wood and iron from the boat, and attempted to make readings. It passed the time and kept me from thinking of my death. Jules questioned me about this, being very curious as to whether or not the different fluxworlds shared the same geographical landmarks. I told him there were variations in all things, but many of the worlds that Nemo had taken us to were in fact very similar geomorphically.

To continue the story, I told him that just as I had sighted land (the coast of Normandy) and imagined that I would be saved, I saw shimmering for a moment in an apparent path the glowing hemisphere of a fluxgate. I explained to Jules that the fluxgates were nothing more than portals between the myriad worlds of the Continuum. Nemo had been the discoverer of the fluxgates and had moved to keep them a secret from the world of man, since he felt that humanity had mucked up one world badly enough without further meddling in the worlds of others who might be more successful. To my horror my boat drifted through the gate and was transported to the earth of my present life. I drifted onto the beach exhausted and began the adventures that have been partially outlined within these pages.

To my surprise, and my relief, Jules believed me.

After first reading that passage, I thought that perhaps Jules Verne was a more gullible man than I could ever be. The story reeked of foolishness and absurdity. Although, I knew that learned men had scoffed at ideas far more fantastic and had lived to regret their skepticism. The urge was to immediately call in supposed "experts" in such things. I knew several professors back at Maryland who would have been able to determine things like historical accuracy of Kent's journals, others who could analyze the handwriting and the style to see if it conformed with that of the period. Even I, with the aid of the right laboratory equipment, could have discovered the age and condition of the leather, the vellum, even the ink which old Durham Kent had used.

But something kept telling me that all that business was not necessary. If the journals were a hoax, why would whomever my uncle had gotten them from have kept them secret from the rest of the world? If the words of Kent were nothing but lies, why had he not tried to publicize and capitalize on his lies?

There were other considerations. Many of my colleagues in the world of *physica theoretica* had been stretching my consciousness with proposals, theories, and seemingly absurd ideas for years. The idea of the parallelism of worlds, of entire universes, was a common one among the think-tankers. They carried the whole thing quantum leaps farther, into boundless areas of shadow where assumption was tantamount to whimsy. Theoretically, given an infinite number of combinations of the electron positions about the various energy shells of each atom, you could have a practically infinite number of "dimensions" corresponding to each positional state of matter. At least that's what Fred Leshinsky used to say over ham and cheese in the University of California faculty cafeteria.

But there was one more reason why I did not want to

doubt the veracity of Kent's journals: I *wanted* to believe it.

Think of it. A closet-dentist-turned-physicist, who ended up playing games with The System (and his own sanity), who is actually a frustrated soldier-of-fortune in a world which no longer offers much fortune to soldier after. What more could such a person ask for than a totally new *world* in which to seek out his shadowed destiny. I realize that may sound a bit melodramatic, but you must realize that it was simply that. There is something, I think, in New England that does love a melodrama.

After mulling over the journals for a few days more, I decided that I would seek out one of Nemo's "fluxgates" and try my luck at locating his marvelous submarine. I decided that this might be possible, because old Kent had mentioned somewhere in his text that "time," within the confines of the various parallel worlds, "flows at different rates." Although Kent had no way of documenting or proving his suspicions, he stated that he felt that time in Verne's world flowed much "faster" (a relative term, in the instance) than in Nemo's. His reasons for feeling thusly stemmed from biological rhythms within his own body which he sensed had been disrupted in barely preceptible ways. If Kent was correct, it was possible, were I actually to find Nemo, that the captain would still be alive in his own world.

The way I figured it, I had a one-in-three chance of being correct: time either flowed faster, slower, or in conjunction with my own "fluxworld." I know that is simplifying things, but let's face it, I wanted to try it out.

I spent another week at the Brattleboro library, making great use of their interlibrary loan services, studying navigation, star charts, instrumentation, and related subjects. From various references in Kent's narrative, I was able to localize three different fluxgates that he stated either existed in my own world or in Nemo's. The trick was to come upon one when it actually happened to be "in flux," or *active*. Kent claimed that there was a cyclic nature to the operation of the fluxgates, based upon some esoteric physical law. Although Kent could never verify it, he also
36

felt that Nemo had somehow cracked the secrets of the fluxgates and was able to control them, using them at will for passage from one dimensional level to the next.

All of which added up to a mountain of speculation and very little hard data. There would be much "dead reckoning" involved in any search for the fluxgates, and not a small amount of luck. It could take a very long time. But time is what I now owned in great quantities. Money equaling freedom as it does.

And so I outlined the procedures that I would soon initiate, pausing for a short while to consider including my maid, Mrs. Carrington, along in my adventure. The longer I knew her, the more I supposed that she might have been willing to accompany me, but there was an obstinate aspect of her nature that held me back from asking her. She seemed to have a traditional Vermonter's rock-hard skepticism for anything not concrete, and I felt that my adventure was going to be somewhat like that of Wendy, or Alice, or Dorothy. I felt that in order to have even half a chance at success. I would have to *believe* everything with all my heart. Somehow, I don't think Mrs. Carrington would be capable of that.

And owing to the fact that there were no available girls (named Dorothy) with time and dreams on their hands in all of Brattleboro, I decided to go it alone.

FOUR

I FELT no qualms in leaving Mrs. Carrington in charge of the estate. Although she asked no questions about my planned departure, I was dying to produce Kent's journal and *tell* her where I was going. I *wanted* to tell somebody, and there was no one—absolutely no one.

I felt like a boy with what seemed to be a spectacular secret, a secret that was too important to share with anyone.

The trip I planned was to Annapolis, Maryland—a small city on Chesapeake Bay. I took a plane to Baltimore-Washington International Airport, carrying with me only a small suitcase into which I had stuffed some extra underwear, a change of shirt, and Kent's journals. From the airport, I chartered a private jet down to Annapolis, and a limousine to the marinas which were clustered about the old city's harbor like hands reaching out toward the bay.

Annapolis is a city of narrow streets and colonial townhouses, of seafood restaurants and old families with a long line of graduated sons of the United States Naval Academy. It is also a yachtsman's paradise. There is every type of fishing and sailing craft anchored somewhere in the city's miles of coastline and docksides. I needed a boat that would be a worthy opponent for the North Atlantic, and I knew that I would find one in Annapolis.

There was an old man, dressed in an immaculate uniform of white-duck pants, blue deck-shoes, and a matching blazer, who was seated on a bench at the edge of a long dock filled with boats in the forty-foot and up class. I approached him and he smiled a greeting.

"Any of these rigs for charter?" I asked casually.

"Some of them, but not many. How long you want to go out?" He pulled out a gnarled meerschaum, fumbled for a tobacco pouch, and slowly began to fill the pipe's deep bowl.

"Well, that's the catch, I guess. I plan to be out indefinitely."

"That'll cost you," said the old man. "What you looking for . . . buried treasure?"

"No, not exactly. All I know at this point is that I need a boat that can afford to be at sea for quite a long time, maybe."

The man smiled and puffed, then remembered to strike a match, lit the tobacco. "Well, you don't want this dock, then. These're mostly pleasure craft."

"What *do* I want?"

"Go down to South Harbor, where the fishing fleets lay in. You'll see Johns Hopkins' big catamaran down there . . . can't miss it. Just beyond their quay's a whole bunch of big ketches and schooners."

"Got anybody you could recommend?"

"Got a few . . ."

"I'm listening."

The old man rattled off three names of captains and their respective boats. I let the captain's names slide past, concentrating on the names of the boats, told him thanks, and ambled down the walkway toward the center of the harbor area.

My advisor's instructions were accurate, and I found the correct dock without any hitches. Since it was late in the afternoon, many of the big boats were back in their moorings, and I could stroll leisurely past their sterns and read their names. I was, as always, dismayed at the utter prosaic quality of most of them: *The Mary-Margaret, The Seaspray, The Weekend Warrior, The Jonathan Livingston* (argh!), *The Peggy Sue II.* One of the names the old man had given me was *The Metamorphosis,* and I was captivated by the kind of personality that would name his ship after a Kafka allegory. I decided to seek out that craft first.

Of course, it was the last ship in the long line, at the very end of the dock. Climbing on board, I called out, stood on the edge of the gangway, waited. A muffled male voice answered me from below deck, and I waited for its owner to scramble topside. Using the time to best advantage, I tried to take in the condition and seaworthiness of the boat. It was a two-masted schooner in design, wide of beam, around forty-five feet in length, and appeared to be meticulously maintained. The deck houses were large and freshly painted, every rope and line was neatly coiled and stored, the sails gleamed so white that they seemed to have never been used, although I was sure that they had. It was a beautiful ship.

Spotting movement in a hatch on the fo'c'sle, I regarded the man who rose from that place. He waved and stepped forward, smiling genuinely. He was broad-shouldered, wore a knit jersey and blue jeans. His face had a chiseled-out quality: lots of sharp angles and lines, blue eyes, hatchet-edged nose, lantern jaw, lots of teeth in his smile, long blond hair. His age could have been anywhere between thirty and forty-five.

"Hi there! What can I do for you?" he said, extending his hand. "Ruffin's the name. Derek Ruffin."

"Hi, I'm Bryan Alexander. . . . An old man up at the yacht marina sent me down here. I need a good boat."

"That must've been Sam," he said, nodding his head. "Where you want to go and for how long? This ship's a deep-draft, ocean-going type, you know."

"That's what I want. The North Atlantic, most likely."

Ruffin pretended to be cold. "Whew, it's starting to get a little nasty up there. How *far* north?"

"Well, I'm not sure really. Somewhere off the coast of France. In sight of Normandy."

"Huh?" Ruffin looked at me like I was not wrapped completely tight.

"Listen," I said, "it's kind of a long story. Can I buy you a beer or something?"

Ruffin smiled and pointed out a rather seedy-looking bar all the way down the dock and across the street. I could barely see it, but I nodded as if it were familiar.

40

Once inside, I explained my needs and my motivations in as fine a detail as I wished to divulge at that point. I interspersed my story with questions which were subtle enough, yet gave me some insight into the type of character with whom I would possibly be sharing a microcosm for several months. Ruffin proved himself to be educated (a Space Program engineer-casualty), cynical (his boat was the only haven from all the world's "crazies"), adventurous (his *Metamorphosis* had once hired out as a gunrunner for a South American industrialist supplying some right wing guerilla group in a coup d'etat), and an aficionado of the Almighty Dollar (no examples necessary).

I told him that I was an archeologist on sabbatical and that I was working from a newly discovered manuscript that described the remnants of a pre-Paleolithic island-culture in the North Atlantic. I told him that according to my sources, there was a geologically old chain of volcanic islands, similar to the Spanish Canary group, just below the surface of the Atlantic and off the coast of France. It was a patently ludicrous story, but Ruffin did not seem to mind. In fact, if the price was right, Ruffin would be agreeable to whatever I told him.

Which it was and so was he.

He said that he had a few affairs that he would like to take care of before putting out to sea, and that it would require a day or two. That was fine with me, since I had planned to spend approximately the same amount of time assembling the clothing, supplies, and any other gear that might be necessary. I left him in the bar, walked down the street, and checked into a small roominghouse which promised fresh linens and free breakfasts.

By nightfall I had collected most of what I would need. This list included: six pairs of denim jeans, ten shirts of various design and weight, three turtleneck sweaters, a flak vest, two pairs of jungle boots, three pairs of deck shoes, a month's supply of underwear and socks, an all-weather slicker, an alpaca-lined sealskin parka, thermal underwear, gloves, and a couple of knit caps. I also

41

thought to lay in an entire trunk of paperbacks, picked semijudiciously from a large bookstore near the Naval Academy campus. I of course bought copies of as many of Verne's works that were available, plus other titles which ranged from anthropology through oceanography and philosophy, history, and poetry. I selected some fiction—covering classic stuff that I had always *meant* to read but had somehow never found the time for, plus some contemporary thrillers and speculative fictions. There was also some consideration given to the oddments and vices: a survival kit, a flashlight, a tool kit, a gross of Carltons in cartons, and a case of Amaretto.

There were several other items that I felt might be necessary, but I was reluctant to purchase them. The only thing that finally convinced me was the realization that no true soldier of fortune could be called thusly without decent weaponry for those tight spots.

Finding the sporting goods store was not difficult, but I had no conception of what to ask for in the way of guns. The clerk was your usual sporting goods guns department stereotype: overweight, prickly beard, small, dark eyes, red plaid flannel shirt, ruddy complexion, nose with the standard gin-ruptured capillaries. I told him that I knew nothing about guns but that I would be traveling to the Brazilian Amazon River Basin and would need the finest weaponry available. He looked at me as if the Amazon Basin was in southern Minnesota for all he could care, said nothing, turned, and pulled a large rifle off the top rack above the counter.

"You'll want this, then," he said. "Weatherby .300 Magnum. I can mount a Leupold Scope with three to nine times, variable, on it. Accurate to five hundred yards. Dead on."

He hefted the gun into his hands, and I held it tenderly. It was a black hulk that seemed full of menace. The oil of its innards stung my nostrils, and I half expected it to writhe into evil life even as I held it. I could not even make a pretense of shouldering it, sighting with it. I was afraid of the weapon, quite simply. The one and only other time I had touched a gun was a long time ago—twelve years old in Boy Scout camp, a skeet rifle which had refused to reach a single clay pigeon.

"This will be fine," I said as nonchalantly as I could manage. "I'll take the scope, too."

Red flannel shirt nodded and began fitting the Weatherby into a stylish, waterproof bag. "How 'bout a side arm?" he asked.

"A what?"

"Handgun . . . need a handgun?"

"Oh, yes, of course," I said. "I'll take the best you've got."

"It'll cost you plenty, mister," he said as he bent down beneath the locked display counter, twisted the lock, and reached in for a compact, blue black pistol.

"That's okay," I said casually, as if I were selecting grapefruits at a roadside stand.

"This here's a Walther PPK." He cradled it in his thick hands lovingly and smiled to reveal uneven teeth. "Just like that guy James Bomb—9 millimeter, short, seven shot clip, good to thirty yards. When one of these slugs comes out of ya, leaves a hole big as a pie pan."

"That's nice," I said.

"The only one I got in the store. Most folks can't afford somethin' like this baby. Ya want it?"

I nodded my head. "Does it come with a holster?"

"Waist or shoulder harness?"

"Oh, the shoulder, I guess."

He looked at me for a long moment, tilting his head slightly. "You ever shot a gun before?"

"Who, me? Why do you ask?" I said, trying not to sound so goddamned defensive.

Red shirt just harrumphed and smiled. Turning toward the back of the store, he said, "Be a few minutes while I get that scope mounted. Make yerself comfortable."

Thirty minutes later, I left the store feeling like an Israeli commando. I had had no idea how heavy the boxes of cartridges were, much less the weight of the weapons

43

themselves. Back at my room, I packed the guns into the bottom of the steamer trunk of books. Better that Ruffin not get suspicious, or start imagining some wild, paranoid scenario. I planned to explain everything in due time, anyway. Just not right away.

When I prepared to sleep that night, I lay in the darkness of the small room, thinking about what was to follow. Everyone probably dreams about the one great adventure in their lives. For most of us that adventure never gets past the dream level, and we carry it with us till it withers into something even less than a dream. But I lay there knowing that my own dream, my dream of exploring unknown worlds, could very possibly be coming true. I felt an adolescent thrill beat through me, and I was insanely pleased with myself.

By mid-afternoon, I had all my gear secured aboard the adequate quarters of *The Metamorphosis*. Ruffin was on shore, clearing up some final arrangements—probably investing the outrageous sum he had charged me for the journey—and I waited comfortably belowdecks. The ship itself was larger than I would have expected two men could handle, but it employed a ketch rig. There were quarters for eight people, and there seemed to be enough lines and sheets and stays to keep an entire galleon occupied. There was also a fine array of hand-crafted electronics gear cobbled together from Ruffin's NASA days—sonar, transponder, radar, radio, and a few things I did not immediately recognize. I decided that before this cruise was at an end, I would learn a few things about the exquisite art of ocean sailing.

When Ruffin returned and announced that we would be shoving off, it was almost sunset, and I was getting hungry. Mentioning this to him, I was told that there would be plenty of time for eating once we cleared Chesapeake Bay. I was in no mood to argue about that fact; there was nothing left to do, other than follow his instructions.

As we crossed beneath the towering span of the Chesapeake Bay Bridge, the sun was casting long shadows across our port side. The bowsprit pointed toward the open sea, and the salt spray was thick in my face. For the first time in my life, I felt totally free. Totally alive.

FIVE

A SINGLE SHIP upon a green-glass sea. The hypnotic cradle-rocking of the boat, tended by the crests and swells; the limitless breath of sky which surrounds you. There were many times when I would sit out on the deck, "standing watch," as Ruffin referred to it, and think that a single ship like ours was actually a prison cell. And we upon its decks were some metaphysical offenders locked tightly within the walls of Nature's vault. The sea is a silent, lonely keeper; it is capricious, untrustworthy, coolly objective. Men either love it or loathe it.

Me, I had yet to make up my mind.

The Metamorphosis was a fine vessel, and it practically sailed itself. Ruffin had equipped the ship with a fine array of modern gear, and its design clearly demonstrated centuries-long experience with the sea. Within two weeks, I had mastered the tasks that my captain had assigned to me. They were few and hardly exhausting, although I could feel a difference in my arms and legs as they adapted from the sedentary life to one of even mild activity.

I did less reading that I had imagined I would; more drinking; and a lot of talking. When two men are continually in each other's presence, one of two things happen. They either begin to hate each other intensely, or they become fast friends. For Ruffin and me, it was fortunately the latter. He was taller than I, muscular, long on breath and stamina. He talked slowly, as if he were considering each word carefully before using it. In some people, a characteristic like that can make you think they are insipid, unaware, unlettered; but in Ruffin, you just knew that he was sharp and *very* aware of what was going on around him. His reflexes were finely honed, quick, smooth. His eyes moved with trained swiftness, in the same fashion as his mind. His whole body functioned in a controlled, *mastered* way that announced that Ruffin was a *survivor*. He was a man who knew the world for what it was, who knew what he would have to do to survive within it. I admired him for what must have taken years to develop, and I admired him more for not bragging about it, for not trying to impress me with how god-damned tough and smart he was. People like that are worse than obnoxious; they are repulsive.

Ruffin *was* his real name. One night, over some White Swans, I asked him if it was, because it *did* sound phony, albeit appropriate to his personality. We both had a laugh over my observation, and then he swore that it was his true surname.

As time passed during the first few weeks, I had just about covered as much of my personal history as I cared to share with him, and I suppose he did the same with me. As it turned out, we had many things in common. He had not always been a swaggering seaman but rather had spent a few years in Manhattan working for a large, anonymous, quadruple-named advertising corporation. Ruffin worked his way up to one of the top writing desks, turning out award-winning, account-gathering campaigns that earned him embarrassingly large sums of money. He admitted to being the author of some of the most famous commercials in the industry. Remember those *great* Volkswagen commercials in the early sixties—back when the Bug was really a sensational car? Or the original Alka-Seltzer ads? Or even the first television push for new investor/clients for one of those sextuply named brokerage houses? Ruffin was indeed a bright guy.

Then he took up engineering till the Space Program went bust. He had been married then, caught his wife playing around with one of the other bright young men in the office, and did the only honorable thing. Extricating himself from the marriage and gathering up his wise decade's worth of investments, he told the aircraft company where they could shove it, moved to Annapolis, bought a

47

fine ship, and started a new life. And he loved it; you could just tell.

He was well read, creative, and industrious. The kind of friend I had always sought out but had found damned few of. But I think the occasion when I really knew that Ruffin was my friend was the night he casually mentioned something he had read in one of Loren Eiseley's books. Loren Eiseley, the late naturalist, philosopher, poet, essayist, and anthropologist, was easily my favorite writer. He is well known among the lettered eschelons of our culture, but sadly inglorious to most of society's minions. I think his first book, *The Immense Journey,* is the most magical, exhilarating, inspiring book I have ever read. In fact, I have for many years used the book as my own special "person barometer." I have several copies of the book, one of which I offer to friends and acquaintances I meet. When they return the book, I can tell by their reaction to it whether or not I really want to know them as friends.

So Ruffin was an all-right guy, and I felt pleased with myself that I had chosen such a fine captain. Everything was going so well that I had almost forgotten the purpose of the voyage. I had to, on occasion, in the privacy of my own cabin, dig out Durham Kent's journals to remind myself of their existence and the importance of the sea cruise. I had finally decided to share the entire matter with Ruffin, now that I had become familiar with him and knew he would understand my enthusiasm and share my zeal to discover one of the "fluxgates."

It was after the first bad storm, which we had on the fourteenth day out, that I decided to tell him the entire story.

SIX

IT WAS twenty-four days before we reached the approximate coordinates layed down in Kent's journals. The seas were high and the wind was getting a bite to it as winter tightened about the North Atlantic. Ruffin not only believed in the possibility of Kent's journals being fact, but he became possessed with a passion to discover the fluxgates that was, if anything, more powerful than my own. I had always imagined that I was doing it for the curiosity, for the *adventure* of it, but when I analyzed my own motives, I knew that it was more out of a sense of wanting to find out if a childhood fantasy could come true. I can remember as a small boy, closing a book by the paleontologist, Roy Chapman Andrews, and wishing—dear God *wishing* with all my soul—that somewhere, somewhere on the big, mysterious planet there was a secret place where the dinosaurs still foraged and thundered through steaming swamps and green forests. I remember wishing that there was a Neverland. An Oz. A Prester John. And a hundred other places.

That was my real reason. But Ruffin's was more mature than that. He *was* the soldier of fortune that I only thought I was. He as much as vowed that we would remain at sea until we did find an entrance into the fluxworlds.

And I thought for a while that perhaps we would indeed grow old upon *The Metamorphosis*. Even though we calculated and recalculated the data in Kent's journals, we found nothing out of the ordinary. I kept coming back to the journals' mention of the fluxgates being cyclic, of following some arcane pattern of openings and closings

49

that only Nemo claimed to have understood fully. What we were doing was simply staggering around the general geographic area. The odds of our being at the right place at the right time could be indeed staggering.

But whatever the odds were, we beat them. On our 101st day out, I was on deck, standing watch. The sun had set within the past hour, and the moon, which was appropriately (and possibly necessarily) full, had just begun its climb from the edge of the sea. I sat just outside the wheelhouse, leaning on one of the capstans, smoking a Carlton, watching the moonlight form this silvery, yellowy highway out across the water. If you looked at it just right, it became like a solid thing, a gangway into the world of the Mary Celeste and the Dutchman and all the other ghost ships that might not be so mysterious after all, if one considered the words of Durham Kent.

I was considering those very words as I scanned the horizon to the left and right of the moon's pathway, and that is when I saw it. At first it seemed like a great hyperbolic swell on the surface of the ocean. It was huge and gray, like a tumorous growth. As I watched, it grew larger until it threatened to blot out half the sky. It seemed to be swirling within itself, bubbling and roiling with great intensity.

And it was goddamned big.

Rushing to the quarterdeck hatch, I yelled for Ruffin, who came up the stairs within ten seconds, pulling a jacket over his clothes.

Both of us stood and watched the thing take a more definite form on our starboard side. It was probably three hundred meters across and getting bigger. As we steered closer to it I could see that it was not the solid shape that it first seemed to be, but rather a pearlescent mist. I stared into it by the light of the full moon and imagined the forces, the elements that wrestled within that faintly glowing mass—it was as if the very bonds and energies that held the universe together were fighting for dominance within the strange cloud, within the place where the very stuff of time itself mixed and flowed like pigments upon a palette.

"What do we do now?" I asked, not taking my eyes away from the slowly forming fluxgate.

"I don't know."

We were still about a thousand meters from the thing, but I began to sense that we were drifting against the direction of our billow, as if we were being drawn toward the gray mass.

"I mean, look, it looks like we found it," I said. "Do we sail into it, or what?" The words were hard coming out. My throat was so dry I thought I might choke if I tried to say anything else.

"Jesus Christ, I don't mind telling you, but I'm scared!" Ruffin moved behind me and checked the compass on the brass stand by the helm. "Hey, Bryan, come here, look at this."

I joined him and saw the needle of the complex navigational instrument spinning wildly. "Some kind of electromagnetic disturbance, huh?"

"No shit," he said. "I wonder what's causing it."

"Gee, I'd never guess," I said, feeling slightly giddy, on the verge of hysteria.

Looking away from me, Ruffin stared into the grayness to our right. Now it was closer, or larger, and its shape was changing from the swollen hemisphere into a kind of a torus configuration. A dimple had appeared on one side of the curved surface, and it grew larger, falling in upon itself and forming a smoothly contoured concavity. It was like a giant doughnut floating on its edge and sunk halfway into the water. I stared into the center of the torus; it looked like a gigantic funnel. The walls of the funnel started to glow with a faint green-yellow light; the glow began to pulsate like the ebb and flow of some great living creature.

"We're moving toward it!" Ruffin yelled. "It's caught us! It's sucking us in!"

He ran toward the bow of *The Metamorphosis,* and I followed him. A calm seemed to descend on me now, as if I knew that we need not be apprehensive about making a decision. The fluxgate—and I was positive now that that was what it was—was deciding for us. It had sensed us,

51

or its sheer titanic force had gathered us in. At any rate, we were sailing straight into its center.

As we drew closer, we started to hear the sound. It was like the wailing of the Sirens, about Circe's isle, and for a brief moment I wondered if perhaps it was a formation just like this one that had inspired the Grecian myths made famous in Homer's *Odyssey*. But as *The Metamorphosis* lapped closer to the pulsing formation, I heard the wailing sound slowly ooze into something else: a low frequency groaning, a sound of straining, of stress, of something wrong.

We were very close now—less than ten meters. Above the masts, the stars were winking out; below, the cradle-rock of the ocean was fast diminishing. The sound grew louder. *There is something wrong,* I thought. This thing was an aberration, a cosmic flaw, and we heard the sound of two universes rubbing, grating, edges. It roared over us now. Ruffin yelled something out to me, but I could only see his lips move in the pale green light. There was just the sound and then the faraway center of the torus, the grayness, illuminated by the green light.

I had the sensation of falling, as in a dream, from an impossible height . . .

SEVEN

THERE WAS a nothingness for an instant. A *blank* in my consciousness that left me cold and terrified, and afterward I thought that I had peered for a moment into the jaws of infinity itself. Then came a single, very loud cracking sound.

I blinked, and when I opened my eyes, *The Metamorphosis* was floating calmly in sunlit waters that were smooth and clear. Ruffin was still standing beside me, rubbing his eyes, shaking his head. Looking up, I noticed that the sky seemed several shades bluer, that the air was more humid, that the temperature was at least fifteen degrees warmer. The sun was lower on the horizon, and though I was still totally disoriented, it was probably in the western quadrant, because it did *not* look like a sunrise.

"You okay?" asked Ruffin.

I nodded, cleared my throat, slowly uncurled my fingers from their death grip on the ship's handrail. "Pretty scary when you're not used to it, I guess."

"No shit," said Ruffin. He scanned the horizon, saw nothing. "You think we really went through?"

"Who knows? We sure ran into something. Have any idea where we are? Something tells me this is definitely not the North Atlantic."

Ruffin walked away from the rail and checked his compass, slowly shook his head. "Not yet. I'll have to wait till sundown and get a fix on the stars. I've got some instruments belowdecks that should give a us a pretty fair idea of what's going on, where we are . . ."

I tugged at the neck of my turtleneck jersey. It was uncomfortably hot, and I shrugged out of it, feeling the warm dance of sunlight on my bare arms and neck. "We better change into something cooler," I said, still scanning the glasslike surface of the sea around us.

"Yeah, you go change first. I'll stay up here and keep watch," said Ruffin. "I don't think we should be too casual about things till we know exactly where we are."

"And *when* we are. . . ." I added, trying to smile but doing a decidedly half-assed job of it.

Belowdecks, I selected some jeans, a striped knit jersey and some low-cut deck shoes. Then I pulled out the logbook I had been keeping since the beginning of our voyage. The book, up till that point, had been filled with very short entries marking times, locations, and crisp, wry observations either on my own state of mind or on Ruffin's developing personality. I was convinced that we had indeed passed through one of the fluxgates, and I was impressed with the fairly good accuracy of old Durham Kent's calculations as to the location of the North Atlantic formation. I wanted to enter that thought into the log but felt that it would be best to wait until we had definite confirmation. How that proof might be discovered, I had no idea just then.

There were other preparations which I made at that time, which later proved to be fine examples of foresight. I checked my weapons in the bottom of the steamer trunk and packed it neatly with the ammunition, the survival kit, and some jungle boots in a flotation pak—an elongated, self-inflatable container of which Ruffin had many, used in the event of a very drastic emergency. Like abandoning ship. I put the pak near the entrance to my quarters, which in turn was directly next to the stairs leading to the main deck. Bringing the logbook up on deck with me, I relieved Ruffin at the rail.

He gave me his binoculars, glanced at the log, smiled, and went below.

The Metamorphosis was sailing northwesterly at about three knots, with a small catch of breeze in her sails. I moved over to the helm, checking the compass out of habit rather than out of function, much the way you glance continuously into the rearview mirror of your car.

54

It was an oddly reassuring habit that I would suppose many sailors fall into when cruising unknown waters. Every now and then I did a port and starboard scan of the area, then did a more extensive slow pan with the binoculars. The minutes passed and it was uneventful. It was as though we were the only living creatures on the entire planet.

That thought gave me some pause, and I stood rigidly for a moment sincerely hoping that I was wrong about *that*.

Ruffin was still belowdecks when I saw the thing in the water.

It was about two thousand meters off the starboard side, just below the surface, moving fairly quickly, definitely smoothly and in control. It was dark and it was *big*. At first, I almost passed over it with the binoculars, thinking it was just some coloration in the water caused by the reflection of a dark cloud or something like that. But then I noticed that it was moving, and that the sky was perfectly clear above it.

Ruffin's footsteps sounded on the stair behind me. "Derek, come here, quick! Look at this thing!"

As I pointed toward the large black shape looming beneath the surface, I noticed that it had veered slightly to its left and was slowly angling toward us.

Ruffin grabbed the binoculars and zeroed in on the thing. Without the glasses, I could not see it anywhere near as clearly, and my imagination filled in what I had lost without the lenses: a sleek, riveted craft, dark and silent, leisurely homing in for the kill. I anticipated my death with nothing short of rampaging panic—heart hammering in my chest, breath getting short and seemingly airless. Would it slice through our hull like cutting through a soft loaf of bread, or would a torpedo slip silkily from its submerged prow? Or perhaps some Victorian catapult of Greek fire would break the waves and hurl its phosphorescent death into—

Ruffin started laughing, and I thought: this is it. The torpedo is launched, headed for our midships and he is going hysterical on me.

"What the hell's the matter with you!"

Lowering the glasses, Ruffin turned and smiled. "Take a look," he said. "Go on, take a look . . ."

I took the binoculars and peered through the double lenses. I have always had a hell of a time using binoculars—the image seems to joggle and shake all over the place, and it *never* looks like that phony matte they use in movies and television. I fine-focused on the dark shape that was closing steadily on our position and was surprised to see that it had broken the surface. There was a large expanse of smooth blackness sliding through the water, gently curving back down—a whale, a very large whale. I followed its motion until its large flukes broke the surface, fanning out briefly before slapping the surface and disappearing.

"That thing had me petrified," I said. "Did you know what it was right away?"

"Yeah, practically. I've seen just about every kind of creature there is out here. You just had me stirred up for a second, that's all. Adrenalin and all that."

"What kind of whale was it?"

"Can't be sure. . . . it was a fairly good size, though. Sixty or seventy feet, I'd guess. Looked like a Greenland whale to me. Thought I saw part of the mouth and the really big head on it."

"Greenland? We can't be anywhere near Greenland," I said.

Ruffin smiled. "The Greenland whale used to be found all through the North Atlantic *and* the North Pacific all the way to the Beaufort Sea. There used to be *millions* of them. They're practically extinct now."

"You think that's where we are? The North Pacific?"

"Could be. The climate's right. If that was a Greenland, well that's a possibility. We'll know more when the stars come out."

"But if we are in the North Pacific, that means that we did it! That we passed through . . . something like a space warp."

"Oh, I've already considered that. Now we have to find out if we passed through *time* as well," said Ruffin, as he

56

took back the glasses, wrapped their strap, and replaced them in a watertight case "Look, let's get something to eat before it gets dark. I'll go down and start something up."

I nodded and Ruffin went below. I stood at the rail watching the sea, when all of a sudden the full realization of what was happening to us really took hold. It transcended the idea of simple adventure; it was a fantastic odyssey; a scientific investigation. Where were we? What would we do when we found out? I had no idea, and I suppose that was part of the thrill, part of the mystery and the appeal. It seemed like a long time till sunset.

Ruffin's instruments were precise navigational aides. When coupled with his charts, they gave us a very good idea of where we were, which was about three hundred miles west of the Aleutian chain. Conclusive proof, of course, that we had defied the laws of physics. Ruffin said that we were sailing through a large whaling territory, although in the twentieth century, the size and number of schools had been greatly diminished by modern whaling techniques.

We kept watches through the night and all the way through the next day and night. During that entire time we were totally alone, except for the whales, which we saw in great number. There were many Greenland whales that would pull alongside of *The Metamorphosis* and follow us for several hours; there were Grays, which were smaller than the Greenlands, but faster and more playful. There were also great fleets of dolphins that often surrounded our ship as if they sensed our harmless nature and wanted to keep us company in our lonely voyage.

I was on watch at about 8:00 on the morning of our third day in the North Pacific when I spotted the ship. It was about the same length as our own ship, but twice as wide, and its black hull looked even darker as it sailed out of the east behind the rising sun. In the glasses I could see that it was fully rigged, three masts, plus a big spanker. Hanging down from big, heavy-timbered davits were long, white, open boats—three to each side. As the ship sailed

57

closer to our position, I saw an American flag whipping furiously from the mizzenmast. By the time Ruffin came topside, the other ship was within hailing distance, and he stood up near the port bow waving back and forth at the visitor, which he immediately identified as a typical whaling vessel of the 1860's and 70's.

There came an answering bellow from somebody on the whaler, and I could see her crew make some adjustments to bring her about and pull along our port side. The name on the side was *The Progress*. The entire crew seemed to line the rail, obviously curious about the sleek lines of *The Metamorphosis*. Ruffin ahoyed them and bantered back and forth some nautical bullshit, finally inviting us both aboard the whaler. The captain of *The Progress* voiced his approval of this, instructed his crew to tie up our schooner, and extended a shaky-looking gangway across our rail.

Ruffin introduced us as a pair of Danish shipbuilders out on a shakedown cruise of an experimental ship design. That was pretty quick thinking—since Scandanavia had little contact with America at that time, and it was a culture that was politically neutral. The captain of the *The Progress* was a short, stocky, bowlegged man named Whitcomb Hancock. He had a squared-off face, neatly lined along the jaw with a red beard, bright blue eyes, and a mouth with three fourths of his teeth long since departed. He invited us below to his quarters, and I was immediately staggered by the stench which arose from the bowels of the ship. There was no evidence of whale flesh above, nor below, but I imagined that after years of flensing on the decks, the wood was permeated with the overpowering, fetid odor of decay and slaughter. If I could keep from passing out altogether, I hoped that I would eventually grow immune, if not accustomed, to the smell.

Captain Hancock's quarters were small and dark, and the ceiling was so low that Ruffin had to keep his head bowed to keep from rapping it sharply upon the crossbeams. Hancock seated himself behind a large chart desk, pulled out some dusty glasses and offered us some rum. We accepted and Ruffin said, "Skoal" (a nice touch, that).

"So where will ye be headed now, young gentlemen?" asked Hancock, genuinely interested.

"Down past the coast of Japan, through the Indian Ocean, Ceylon, Madagascar, the cape, and then the long haul up to Europe," said Derek calmly, as if he had anticipated the question.

"Been puttin' in at some pretty fair ports, I'll bet," said Hancock.

"Well, we stopped in San Francisco," I said, instantly wondering whether I had said the wrong thing. If this was indeed the 1860's, how developed was the West Coast? How different were things in this alternate universe? We would have to find out.

Hancock frowned. "That's a worthless pit. The devil'll be takin' it by and by, lad."

"Uh, yes, it was quite bad, wasn't it?" I said helplessly.

Ruffin changed the subject by asking the captain about his cruise, and we learned that *The Progress* was recently upon the North Pacific area, fresh around the Horn from Gloucester, Massachusetts, and had yet to join the New England fleet that was operating just northwest of our present position. During the conversation, Captain Hancock reminisced over previous expeditions into the icy waters north of us, and at one point mentioned leaving New England in the spring of '58. Ruffin and I both caught the reference and roughly computed our time to be approximately 1867 or 68. That would mean that the Civil War—if there had *been* a Civil War in this fluxworld—was probably over.

I chanced a reference about the war, asking if Hancock or any of his crew had ever been involved in it. I could sense Ruffin cringing at my boldness, but it did not seem to bother the crusty old captain.

"Damnation, no!" he said, pouring another dram of rum for himself. "The navy's got plenty of ships without dragging my vessel into that mess. Besides, it'll probably be over by the time we get back to port next year. I hear

59

tell of a new kind of gun they've invented in Philadelphia that's bringing the devil down on those filthy Rebs!"

News that the Civil War had not only occurred here, but was *still going on*, was a shock to my historical sense, but I remained outwardly calm, pretending to nod understandingly.

The conversation was allowed to drift back into more nautical topics, with Captain Hancock expressing a great interest in *The Metamorphosis*. He was incredulous that two men could crew such a large vessel on a globe-spanning shakedown. Derek spoke slowly and carefully as he explained modern sailing techniques as if they were freshly minted ideas from his inventor's brain. The captain was entranced by Ruffin's lectures and seemed to be buying our story with no problems looming. I sat there almost bursting to ask him more about the state of the world in this alternate existence, but Ruffin must have sensed this and kept signaling me with glances of his keenly expressive eyes to remain silent.

An hour passed, and as Hancock filled up on rum, his manner became less formal and more raucous. He started telling us stories of past expeditions—singling out singularly humorous or tragic incidents—of legends and of other strange phenomena of the sea. When he mentioned sea serpents, both Ruffin and I visibly became more attentive. I questioned him more about the sightings of strange creatures in these particular waters.

"Aye, lad," said Hancock. "There be some crews won't sail these waters because of the Ironback!"

"The 'Ironback,' what's that?" asked Ruffin.

"Meanest beast in all Creation!" said the captain. "I've heard tell that it comes up from the foulest depths in the darkest of nights. Big yellow eyes, churns up the sea a boil like Satan himself, comes straight at a vessel and rakes her hull with its back! Got big horny spikes on his back, tear up a wooden hull and take her to the bottom, that's what they say . . ."

"Have *you* ever seen Ironback, Captain?" I asked.

"One night I think I saw him lurking on the surface off the coast of Greenland . . ."

"Greenland? That's a long way from here, Captain," I said.

"Aye, and Ironback's a swift and powerful beast, sir."

"Then I suppose we should be on the lookout for such a creature," said Ruffin.

The captain nodded, and we let the conversation drift again so that he would not think we were taking an over-interest in his monster. Later, we were invited to share dinner at Captain Hancock's table, which proved to be a variable feast of dishes culled from the sea. Aside from a lack of imaginative spices, the fare was quite palatable. Afterward, Ruffin invited Captain Hancock and his first on board *The Metamorphosis,* which proved to be some-what of a mistake. The captain was utterly confused, and probably a bit fearful of the electronic gear in the main cabin, plus the "new materials," such as plastic, aluminum, and fiberglass that so much of our ship utilized. When we finally cast off from *The Progress,* I'm sure that Captain Whitcomb Hancock was convinced that Denmark was a plenty strange place.

Ruffin suggested that we head in a generally westerly direction toward Japan and away from the colder northern waters where the whaling fleets would be con-gregating. He had no idea what shipping lanes were in op-eration in this parallel world, but he assumed that the less contact we had with the natives, the less problems we would have explaining our presence. That all seemed fairly obvious to me, and I offered no logical objections.

I kept thinking about Captain Hancock's "Iron-back"—obviously *The Nautilus*—sliding silently some-where beneath us. Both Ruffin and I were inspired by the chance encounter with *The Progress*; we would hunt these waters until we found the submarine. As we sailed west of the whaling fleet position, I was surprised by the numbers of whales and dolphins we discovered. Ruffin's sonar gear was almost continuously pinging large schools of the great mammals. During the hours that I manned the console, I feared that even if we did chance upon *The Nautilus,* I would not be able to recognize the craft among the swarming schools. Ruffin had no such fears, however; he

61

claimed that a metallic ship would give off a totally different kind of echo and that the ping would be distinctly
metallic.

"Don't worry about it," he had said. "If there's anything down there, you'll hear it."

So why didn't I hear the torpedo? . . .

EIGHT

APPLIED PSYCHOLOGISTS, or "human engineers," as they like to call themselves, will tell you of a strange experimental discovery first noticed among personnel who must watch a monotonous display for extended periods of time. Loosely known as "the green light phenomenon," it was initially documented in studies of World War II radar operators who sat in front of their screens for eight- and four-hour shifts. The operators became so accustomed to the continuous sweep of their screen and the soothing green light of the background that the majority of them would fail to see blips or "bogeys" when they *did* appear on the screen. It was as if their minds were on autopilot and they were not recording what their eyes actually perceived. Their minds—hypnotized by the boring, repetitive display—tended to generalize a subconsciously "acceptable" set of perceptions, regardless of what the eye was actually seeing.

This is probably why, after almost three hours of the monotonous echoes and *pings* of whales, sharks, and other large marine creatures, I did not "hear" the distinctly metallic *pong* of the submarine, much less the gradually increasing keen of the torpedo which churned toward the midships of *The Metamorphosis*.

And so I was sitting at the console belowdeck—for some unknown reason thinking of how incredible it was that Beethoven had composed the Ninth Symphony after he had gone completely deaf—when Ruffin almost fell down the stairs in a state that can only be called panic-stricken.

"Jesus Christ! What the hell're you doing down here!? There's a torpedo coming straight at us!"

I vaguely heard his voice coming through the foam padding of the headphones, then he was grabbing me roughly by the shoulders, pulling me from the chair.

Before I could say anything, he was screaming to get abovedecks, then scrambling up the stairs. I followed him as fast as I could, still not sure what was going on, although I had heard something about the torpedo. I knew that I should have been as terrified as Ruffin, but there is that moment of confusion, of total bewilderment, that sometimes invades you at such crucial times. I knew that something terrible could be happening, but I could not, for the life of me, respond with the proper fear.

Rising above the hatch, Ruffin's strident voice broke through: "Come on! Get up here! Get moving!"

He was crowded into the deepest corner of the bow, huddled down, and I ran toward him, glancing off the starboard side just in time to catch a glimpse of a silvery, frothing shape burrowing in on us. I dove forward in midair and never touched the deck.

While I was briefly airborne, the explosion gutted *The Metamorphosis* right above the keel. The shocked air mass grabbed me and carried me up, over, and beyond the railing, and drove me into the sea like a fisherman's sinker. As I flailed my way to the surface, fighting the heavy drag of the wet clothing, I turned to see Ruffin's ship practically ripped in half and going down fast. Debris was scattered all around me—pieces of sail, masts, railing, pins, blocks, planks.

I screamed out Ruffin's name as I searched the wreckage. There was oil on the water from the ruptured diesel tanks; it was burning with a thick, acrid smoke. I couldn't see much of anything. The aft section of *The Metamorphosis* had already disappeared, and the bow had listed over, so that the sprit was almost in the water. I saw no trace of Ruffin.

A piece of ship floated by, and I grabbed on, pulling myself up surfer-fashion. Something told me that I should keep as little of myself down there for the sharks as possible. Things did not look good.

"Bryan! Bryan, you okay!?"

The sound of Ruffin's voice rose above the crackle of the burning oil, and I searched its source in the black clouds. "Yes! Yes!" was all I could shout, my breath coming in quick, strangling gasps.

"The bastard! The goddamned bastard!" he shouted, although I could still not locate him. He sounded fine, not hurt, I mean, and I felt relieved to know that.

As the bow slid into the sea, I saw a flash of yellow—the color of Ruffin's jacket—bob briefly up and down behind a swell, and I started paddling weakly toward that spot. Ruffin was hanging on a thick, white slab that had once been part of the main cabin's forward wall. The porthole and glass were still untouched in its center.

"You okay?" I shouted. "You all right?"

"The dirty mother! Goddamn him!" He could see me now and he was shouting directly at me.

As we paddled and drifted toward one another, I said, "Who? Who're you talking about?"

Ruffin reached out and pulled my flotsam abreast of his own. We reached out and held each other's belts. "Look at him!" Ruffin pointed off toward the east.

Looking in that direction, I saw the ill-defined hump of a great, dark shape, mostly submerged beneath the gently swelling waves. It was at most two hundred meters away. There were hints of windows, of railings and rivets, but only for a brief moment. As soon as I spotted the thing, it began to slide beneath the water.

"Nemo?" I asked dumbly.

"Who else? The bastard! He sank my ship."

"He tried to kill us." I shouted at him. "Screw the ship!"

The next few minutes were passed in a half-assed shouting match and argument. When we had finally vented our pent-up frustrations and leftover adrenalin, Ruffin collapsed flat on the section of planking and started laughing. Now I was positive he was going hysterical on me, and I had no idea what was going to happen next. Then he pushed himself up on his elbows and pointed to a spot behind me.

Turning, I saw the bulk of the ship's remains floating in

a scattered circle. Bobbing near the center of the debris was my steamer trunk, airtight and waterproof in a flotation collar, slowly drifting away from us. I paddled toward it, thinking of the weapons I had stashed there, and reached it without any trouble. At the same time, other debris was breaking the surface, including several of Ruffin's flotation paks—the international orange rubber standing out sharply against the darkly contrasting sea. I hoped that one of the paks that worked free of the sunken wreckage would contain my survival kit.

Ruffin gathered in two of the paks and started paddling toward me. "I think we've got some food in one of these."

"Speaking of food," I said, "what about sharks around here?"

"Haven't seen any, but they're supposed to be thick as thieves in this area."

"Gee, that's just great."

Half the day passed with the both of us hanging on to the trunk and flotation paks. One of them had some canned rations, which we scooped out with our fingers and ate. My hands and fingers would get cramped from clinging to the planking and the trunk, and I was forced to change hands every half hour or so. Our prospects for survival didn't look good at all, and I found myself thinking about the choices we had in dying. Not that any of them seemed attractive, but I was sure that I would opt for my Walther PPK before starvation or *megalodon aperitif.* Funny thing about the whole situation was the contemplation of my own death. I had always lived in great fear of dying. The whole "other side" question had always left me more than baffled, and the thought of me just not existing any longer left me in a great—if fleeting—depression.

But out here in the middle of the Pacific, surrounded by nothing except a few unseen sharks, staring death in the teeth, so to speak, I had no fear of it. Rather it was a resigned, and quite calm, acceptance. Man is supposed to be the most adaptable of creatures, and I guess he is.

We held on as the sun was heading down toward Japan. That's when *The Nautilus* showed up.

Ruffin noticed it first: a furious boiling in the sea to the east. The surface was bubbling and the turbulence broadcasted shock waves which tossed us about with indifference. I could see a great yellowish light beneath the surface, turning the water a brilliant lime green. Then the jagged sawtooth edge of its prow leapt from the sea like a monstrous predatory fish, slapping down the waves beneath like an iron fist.

The vessel was a hell of a lot bigger than I would have imagined. At least one hundred meters were visible above the surface. It sat silently watching us, less than fifty meters distant, its great yellow-white windows like eyes burning across the water. I wanted to cry out, to say something, anything, but the words wouldn't come out. The details of the submarine's construction were half shrouded in the evening light, but I could see the thick plates of its outer hull, the myriad rivets and seams of its armor. It was a frightening and formidable-looking ship.

There came a clanging sound as a hatch was sprung, and I saw several men clambering out onto the flat back of the sub, directly behind the conning tower which so greatly resembled the head of a nasty sea-creature. The men launched a boat and motored silently toward us.

"Lively now!" one of them shouted. "Steady now."

When they reached our position, no words were spoken. We were hauled in, our gear following us into the bottom of the launch. Oddly I felt equally relieved to see the trunk being saved as well as my own hide. The launch cut through the waves and notched itself neatly into the side of *The Nautilus*, we were helped out, led through the narrow hatch, and guided down to the first deck. There was no evidence of malice in the actions of the crew—all wearing the same dark blue, no-frill uniforms—and I saw no weapons among any of them.

We descended into a small chamber framed by bulkheads and steel walls, a metal deck, and some wall racks which held fire axes, harpoons, and other pieces of emergency equipment. I noticed that the workmanship,

67

the detail, and the design of everything was extremely fine. Everything gleamed from the polishing rag, from the obvious care in its maintenance.

A hatch in the opposite wall opened, through which another crewman stepped, followed by a short, muscular man wearing a finely tailored jacket. His eyes were a dark ocean-blue, and his strong jaw was emphasized by an expertly trimmed full-face beard. His nose was sharp and hawklike, his mouth wide but thin lipped.

I stood there dripping all over the deck, suddenly aware of how wet and uncomfortable I had been. The atmosphere inside the submarine was warm and dry and very habitable. My eyes locked into the bearded guy's, and he paused for a moment before approaching us. I took a quick look at Ruffin and saw that he was bristling, seething, and all that sort of thing. For a moment I thought he might spring at the man responsible for deepsixing *The Metamorphosis*.

Deciding that some kind of distraction was in order, I spoke: "Captain Nemo, I presume. . . ." I smiled, held out my hand.

The bearded man stiffened. "How the *hell* did you know *that?*"

"It's a long story, I'm afraid." I kept smiling.

"I'm sure it is." He broke into a smile. "But, we will have plenty of time to hear of it." He paused dramatically. "I am Captain Nemo, yes. And these are members of my crew. I suppose you know the name of my vessel?"

"The Nautilus, right?"

"Astounding! Incredible!" said Nemo, looking quickly about to his crew. "No one, other than the men on board this ship, could possibly know that! Who are you fellows, anyway?"

I smiled and looked at Ruffin, who was smiling, I think, in spite of himself. What I had seen of Nemo so far was not what I had expected, however. He presented none of the harsh, impregnable characteristics that I had Vernely associated with him. Instead, he seemed cheerful, gregarious, and extremely personable.

"There *is* one man who knows such things, besides us,

Captain," I said in my best Rod Serling voice. "His name is Durham Kent."

Nemo snapped his fingers and laughed. "Of course! Old Kent, of course! I think you gentlemen had better join me in my cabin after you've had a change of clothing. Are you hungry? I'll have some food served there."

He turned and climbed through the hatch, motioning lightly to his crew, and we were directed to descend the iron ladder to the next level of the submarine. We were taken into a small locker-room-like area, where a quartermaster's cage flanked the entrance to the chamber like a tollbooth. A beefy, red-faced guy sat behind the cage and issued us some standard crew uniforms, some socks, and underwear. It was all woven of cotton of extremely fine quality, and I noticed that all the buttons were of brass, bearing the scrolled monogram of the letter N.

After changing clothes, we were guided back through a long corridor that presumably ran down the center of the vessel. Everything was fashioned in iron or steel or brass, and there was a finely crafted aspect to everything down to the smallest valve or lever. The corridor was illuminated by electric lights—small translucent globes in brass fixtures of ornate design. There were paintings in gilt-edged frames along the walls of scenes reminiscent of Millet oils, sea scenes of William Turner, the misty landscapes of Corot; not exactly the type of decor you would expect in the average citizen's home, to say nothing of a submarine full of stouthearted men.

At the end of the corridor, we climbed a spiral staircase, entering an antechamber with hatches on three walls, entered the center one, and we were standing in the doorway of what appeared to be a typical Victorian parlor. Nemo was seated behind a hand-carved mahogany desk with a leather top. Bookcases lined both walls, a silver tea service stood nearby on a glass-topped cart, there was the great pipe organ at the end of the room—just like Verne had described it. The carpet was a lushly woven Persian of a maroon, blue, bone, black, and gold.

"Come in and sit down, gentlemen. Make yourselves comfortable," he said, smiling genuinely.

We did this, and he spoke again. "You took me by such surprise that I forgot to get your names. Please forgive me."

We introduced ourselves and waited for Nemo to reply. I knew that Ruffin wanted to know why we had been attacked, but he apparently felt that we should keep things easy as long as our host was in good spirits.

"So, Mr. Alexander, you say you know of Durham Kent?"

I nodded, looked at Ruffin, and began our story, from the discovery of Kent's journals through the torpedo attack and rescue. The tale required quite a bit of time, and it was interrupted by many questions, an offer of cigars, and snifters of brandy. Nemo was intensely interested in the details of our parallel earth. When I finished the tale, the captain sat back in his chair, posed as if deep in thought. "Yes, Kent was my first mate back then—almost ten years ago. He got into a scrap with my navigator, Mr. Holmes, and ended up killing him. I held a shipboard tribunal, and the sentence was that he be set adrift in the North Atlantic. Damnable luck, that. He must have known more of the cycles of the fluxgates than I had imagined. My fault, I guess." He paused, took a sip of brandy. "Tell me more about this Verne chap."

"Well, it seems like he made a reputation for himself by writing about you," I said.

"So I understand you. I'd like very much to see a copy of his work . . . what did you say it's called?"

"20,000 Leagues Under the Sea."

Nemo thought upon that for a moment, then: "Damn! That's an odd title, isn't it? That implies that the ocean is more than 40,000 miles in depths!"

"Yeah, I always thought that it was confusing. What Verne meant, though, was the distance traveled during the course of the book. *The Nautilus* cruised around the globe twice during the narrative."

Nemo waved me off with a swipe of his hand. "Ridiculous! And you say the book was popular?"

"Extremely. It was written almost a hundred years ago, and it is still read by hundreds of thousands of new read-

70

ers every year. You are a very famous literary figure," I said, toasting him with my brandy.

Nemo laughed at this remark, as would anyone told they are extremely famous. "I'd very much like to read the book of Verne's."

"If your men salvaged some of our things, I think I have a copy of it with me. I also have Kent's journals."

"Excellent, Alexander, excellent. I shall get to it straightaway." He paused and checked a silver pocket-watch. "We will be having dinner within the half hour. Would you gentlemen care to have something now, or would you prefer to dine with me?"

"I guess we can wait," said Ruffin. "Do we get some quarters, some place to get squared away?"

"Of course," said Nemo. "I've had my men secure two cabins on Three Deck. You can go there and prepare for dinner if you'd like."

Ruffin stood, seeming to be anxious to leave. "There's a lot I'd like to talk to you about," I said, standing by Ruffin's side.

Nemo nodded. "There will be ample time, I assure you."

We were guided from the parlor and led down a corridor and below two decks to a section of crew quarters. The rooms were small but extremely well designed and not uncomfortable. Everything was decorated in the Victorian style—studied elegance, but never at the cost of total functionalism. I liked it very much as a change from the chrome and plastic world from which I had fled.

Ruffin stood in the doorway to my room after our crew-member escort had departed. "This is weird, Bryan."

"Why do you say that?"

"How come you didn't say anything about the torpedo!?" Ruffin's face was hard and reflecting his irritation with me and the general situation. I knew that I could never know the anguish he must have felt at losing his ship. I wanted to say that I would replace *The Metamorphosis* when returned to our earth, but I knew it would not make things any better.

"I don't know," I said. "I'm not sure he's the one who did it . . . I guess."

"Why *not?*"

"I don't know yet. Just a hunch. Look, don't get so upset about it. I plan to clear things up later. Give us a little time to figure things out. Nemo doesn't seem like such a bad guy."

"I'm sure Attila had his nice moments, too."

"You don't mean that," I said, grinning as I unlocked the latches to my steamer trunk.

"Nah, I guess not. What you got in there?" Ruffin pointed to the trunk.

"Books, cigarettes, a couple of other things," I said, motioning all the way in to the cabin. "Close the door."

Ruffin eased into the room and shut the hatch. "What's the matter?"

"We've got this," I said pulling out the 9 mm handgun. "And this." I unwrapped the rifle.

"You know, that somehow makes me feel a little better. You're pretty smart for an English professor."

Smiling, I repacked my gear, picked up a copy of *20,000 Leagues,* locked the trunk. "Shall we dine, Mr. Ruffin?"

NINE

NEMO'S TABLE was tastefully set with a Wedgwood service and Belgian silver. The circular bay window with the irising shutters—just as Verne had described it—was opened, affording Ruffin and me a spectacular view of the sea at a depth of perhaps seven meters. The water was clear, the searchlights of *The Nautilus* illuminated the blue green sea and the occasional creature that passed close to the glass. There was an aspect of the scene that transcended peacefulness. In the sea there was an eternal silence, a natural balance of color and movement that was almost hypnotic in its subconscious appeal. There was something very Darwinian about it, and Jungian, too; it was as if the sea creatures were our primary archetypes—on the cellular as well as the psychological level.

We dined on a fantastic oyster chowder, langostino, the fillet of some large, unidentified, but extremely tasty, fish, and a pudding culled from the glandular extract of the anemone. There was also a vintage Chablis, and brandy afterward. Nemo offered us cigars especially cured and wrapped from kelp harvested in the China Sea, but I stuck to my Carltons—something which amused the captain greatly.

After the table had been cleared and the steward had departed, Nemo opened the conversation. "We don't get many visitors on *The Nautilus*. I can't tell you what an unusual experience this is."

"How long have you been at sea?" asked Ruffin.

"Seventeen years. *The Nautilus* was launched in April, 1853. I've made improvements in her design since then, of course, but she has been proved a very seaworthy vessel."

"Verne, through Kent, I suppose, wrote that you had given up the society of the land, that you were a misanthrope, dedicated to remain forever in the sea. Is that right?" I asked.

Nemo smiled. (He was quite a refined gentleman.) "Well, not exactly. I am a scientist first, an adventurer second, and misanthrope a distant third. I considered the unending voyage of *The Nautilus* to be a grand experiment rather than any great escape. There are other reasons for my voyage, which you'll probably learn of in time. But we will have plenty of that." Nemo paused and picked up Verne's novel, which I had placed at the edge of the table. "I must read this tonight. I am dying of curiosity, you know." He sipped from his brandy and emitted a gracious, controlled laughter.

"I can't blame you," I said.

"Did Verne write any other novels?" said Nemo.

I smiled. "Reams of them. One was a sequel to *20,000 Leagues*. Called *The Mysterious Island* . . . wasn't very good, but they did make a movie about it."

"*Movie?*"

"A form of entertainment in our . . . fluxworld, I guess you'd call it. Something like a kinescope. You have kinescopes here?"

Nemo nodded. "Little flickering pictures on photographic cards? Yes. They're terrible little trifles. I've always thought the process could be refined. Perhaps using a continuous loop of film, only positive instead of negative, and run them past a lens at a constant number of frames per second."

I laughed. "No kidding? Where'd you ever come up with that idea?"

"It came to me one afternoon while *The Nautilus* was on the surface exchanging and recirculating its air. I often think of inventions that I would like to try out. Never seem to get around to most of them." Nemo looked past up through the oval window where the aquamarine world flowed in silence. He looked a bit befuddled, somewhat regretful, and definitely eccentric.

"Let me let you in on a little secret, Captain," said Ruffin, pausing to draw in a prodigious breath on the kelp cigar. "That's just about what 'movies' are." He proceeded to explain the cinematic process in detail as Nemo sat in even greater stupefication, smiling dumbly every so often and nodding, as if he himself had often thought of doing it in similar fashion.

We all laughed a bit about the movie thing, then the conversation drifted back to the subject of Verne. Captain Nemo was extremely interested in the French author, and through our subsequent discussions, I learned some interesting things. Durham Kent must have been quite a fascinating companion and manservant to Verne, because he had provided the writer with material from Nemo's fluxworld for myriad novels. There actually *was* a fellow named Phileas Fogg in Nemo's world. A year before *The Nautilus* was launched, the English gentleman had become international news by traveling around the globe in sixty-seven days. Apparently Verne had believed that sixty seven days was too incredibly short a time for his readers to accept, and had lengthened it to the more agreeable eighty days. Or maybe he didn't like the extra syllable which disrupted the mellifluousness of his title. One cannot be certain of this. There also existed in this fluxworld a Baltimore Gun Club. When Nemo had entered the sea, the BGC was one of the most highly respected ballistics and ordnance research organizations in the world. There had been talk among many of the club's leaders, especially one of its board of directors, a chap named Barbicane, of designing a gun that could fire a projectile to the moon. But, as far as Nemo understood, the feat had never been attempted. Seems as if someone named Edison had carefully checked out all the data, ran the necessary calculations, and had advised Barbicane of the utter unfeasibility of the project. Orville Edison was the name as Nemo remembered it.

There was also an Arne Saknussen in this world. He had descended into a series of deep caves in Norway which led hundreds of miles into the earth. Contrary to Verne's *Journey to the Centre of the Earth,* Saknussen did not disappear forever beneath the surface but instead had returned to report to the Scandanavian Geological Congress of 1851 that there was nothing much, hundreds of miles down, but a lot of rock, some isolated pools of water, some lava, and some steam. And, as if in passing, old Saknussen had dismissed the idea of going to the center of the earth as patent nonsense.

Nemo kept us amused with tales such as this for hours. At one point he mentioned that he had been, earlier on in his life, a member of a scientific research facility in Philadelphia called The Weldon Institute. It had been founded by Cornelius Weldon, a famous American patriot, statesman, and inventor, whose brother-in-law, Benjamin Franklin, had been an export merchant in coonskin hats during the revolutionary war. For some reason, the name, Weldon Institute, the mere mention of the words, seemed to cause a change of expression and mood in Nemo. He did his best to conceal it, but I noticed the captain's discomfort, and never one to take advantage of a situation, I pushed forward.

"The Weldon Institute," I said, pretending to muse upon the words. "That sounds familiar."

"I suppose Mr. Verne recorded that obscure fact, also," said Nemo.

"Not in connection with you," I said. "But if my memory serves me, it was mentioned in a book called *Robur the Conqueror.*"

"The supercilious bastard!"

"Verne?" said Ruffin, leaning forward, surprised at Nemo's sudden change in mood.

"The fool!" said Nemo, stubbing out his cigar, sparking ashes out of the brass tray. "No, not Verne . . . *Robur.* Robur the *Conqueror!*"

"I take it that you know him?" I had to repress the urge to smile, fearing the results it might produce in our otherwise gracious host.

"Know him? Yes, gentlemen, I know him . . . all too

terribly well. He's a madman. Brilliant, but utterly mad. He's the one who sank your ship."

"What?" Ruffin sat up rigidly, billowing out the word with a thick blue cloud of smoke. "How do *you* know?"

"Take it easy, Derek," I said. Then turning to Nemo: "Are you sure?"

Nemo settled back in his chair, apparently calming himself. He closed his eyes for a moment, sighed, and nodded his head. "Oh quite. I saw him do it."

"Couldn't you have stopped him?" Ruffin was anything but calm at this point.

Nemo shook his head. "We were chasing him down when he came upon your vessel. He must have detected the presence of the electronic gear you were employing, and suspected that you were working in collusion with *The Nautilus*."

"Detect our gear?" said Ruffin. "He can *do* that?"

Nemo nodded. "Oh, of course. *The Nautilus* is also equipped with similar detection gear—something I've recently been developing so that I could locate *The Kraken*."

"*The Kraken?*" I said.

"Robur's submarine. That's what he calls it. You know the story of the Kraken?"

"A great sea-beast in Norse mythology, isn't it?" said Ruffin.

"Yes, that's the one." Nemo nodded gravely. There were lines etched upon his face that plainly told of the years waged against this fellow Robur. And in between the lines you could see the hate and frustration and obsession.

"I had been thinking that you had sunk us," said Ruffin.

"A torpedo took you in midships, Mr. Ruffin. My *Nautilus* does not have torpedoes." The captain did not seem to be upset by Ruffin's admission of suspicion.

"Are you still on his trail? Robur's, I mean." I looked at Nemo, trying to appear as concerned and sympathetic as possible.

"No. When we surfaced to rescue you, the dog escaped. But have no fear. I shall catch him again. It seems as if you gentlemen have come aboard at a most interesting time."

I recalled the old Chinese curse: "May you be born in interesting times." Now, I suspected that I would more fully understand the inherent wisdom in such Oriental apocrypha.

"Why is that?" said Ruffin.

"Because I now believe that the war I've waged against Robur is drawing to its inevitable end. When *The Nautilus* came upon your craft, I thought I finally had him. He was most fortunate this time, but he will have no more such nods from Lady Luck."

As Nemo spoke, there came to his eyes a great and terrible fire. It was a look I had seen several times before in my life—once in the eyes of an obvious madman who held me at gunpoint on a snowy Baltimore street corner demanding my wallet; again I had seen that look in the face of my grandfather, when he was on his deathbed and he told me how totally *pissed* he was at the cosmos for taking him away before he had a chance to accomplish all in life that he desired. Very different people, but it was the same look, believe me.

Nemo wanted Robur so badly that he could almost taste it. I could not imagine what could have set these two brilliant, but obviously eccentric, personalities against each other.

So I asked Nemo to tell me the whole story.

TEN

THE YEAR was 1845 in Nemo's fluxworld, and the location was Philadelphia, Pennsylvania. It was an exciting time to be alive if you happened to be a member of the Weldon Institute of Research and Technology—a large Gothic castle of red brick on Chestnut Street in the heart of the old city. Nemo was one of the youngest members of the Institute, barely twenty-five, and just finished his studies at Harvard, where he earned his advanced degrees in engineering.

Nemo's real name, by the way (he confessed this to us in utmost secrecy as we sat in his private chambers), was Percival Makepeace Goodenough. I think I now fully understand why he decided to make some changes upon that moniker. "Nemo" is a word stemming from Latin and other Indo-European root languages, which roughly translates into "no man" or "no name," depending upon which source you consult. Take your pick. But any way I figure it, it seems as though Nemo decided that no name at all was preferable to Percival Makepeace Goodenough.

Nemo's reputation as *Wunderkind* was already established when he joined the team of researchers and scientists at the Weldon Institute. By the age of twenty-five, he had designed and built a prototype steam engine that was the forerunner of the turbine; had devised a revolutionary calculating instrument that heralded a new era of navigation; had designed the largest suspension bridge then extant in the world in the Straights of Mackinac in northern Michigan; had submitted plans for a device that would utilize the mysterious emanations from the element radium in medical research. This last idea

79

was found impressive by all those who encountered it, but it was also little understood by anyone but Nemo, and he had not the inclination nor the time to construct the device himself.

This was because of his acceptance into the Institute, where the great project of the day was the construction of a flying machine. It was not to be a lighter-than-air aircraft, but a solid-body vehicle that would be strong enough and powerful enough to actually lift itself into the skies. Nemo was inspired by this seeming impossibility of this project, and he threw himself into the work with all his energy.

But there was also at the Weldon Institute at this time, a young scientist, aged thirty, by the name of Robert Burton, educated at Oxford, but a naturalized American citizen since the age of twenty-eight. Burton was, until the arrival of Nemo, the *enfant terrible,* the *bête noire* of the engineering world. He had made great progress in the fledgling field of electricity and the technology of storage cells. He had also developed several special metallurgical processes which served to strengthen the world's alloys by a factor of six.

It was Burton who had sparked the Weldon Institute into its airship project and it was through his almost fanatical public relations efforts that he was able to persuade some of the nation's wealthiest industrialists to contribute funds for the project. His personality could only be described as incendiary—either in topics of a scientific nature or on a strictly social level. It did not matter what Robert Burton was talking about; whatever the topic, he could not fail to stir some emotion or reaction in you. That reaction might be good or it might be bad, but it was guaranteed to be intense.

Burton had assumed control of the airship project by self-acclamation and was delegating, designing, inquiring, and controlling all matters when Nemo joined the Weldon team. Nemo brought no presuppositions with him concerning Burton, other than the generally accepted view that Burton was a kind of genius. Nemo was perfectly willing to cooperate with Burton to the fullest extent; in fact, Nemo admired the man's effusive brilliance. Sparks of creativity and energy seemed to fly from Burton's mind like steel at the grinding wheel. It was an infectious brilliance that inspired others working with Burton to press onward with ever-renewed vigor.

Models were designed, studied, and tested. Failure upon failure held back the team, but each day brought out some new improvement in either design or theory that led the Weldon team further along the road to self-powered flight. And it was during this time of trial-error-partial success that the Weldon team began to split into two distinct camps.

It seemed as if, to Nemo, there was a basic flaw in the principle of Burton's design, which involved the shape of the craft's hull. Burton assumed from the beginning that the main body of the ship would be in a very similar configuration as to that of the sailing ship, and that the mode of lift and propulsion would be from an altogether independent source. The current idea was a series of rotors all running in furious unison. But Nemo felt that this basic conception was working against the entire notion of *lift* and envisioned some esoteric and heretofore unknown hull design that would actually aid in the lift and propulsion of the craft.

Nemo, however, being a quiet, studious type, did not voice these feelings openly to Burton, fearing the fiery repercussions which might result. Instead, he contented himself to his private calculations and experiments in the privacy of his second-story flat on Walnut Street, sometimes working in the late hours of the night. As time passed and the flight experiments began to get bogged down (the $\frac{1}{20}$ scale models simply would not fly), Nemo began making his ideas known to several sympathetic colleagues at the Institute. When the associates did not scoff at Nemo's radical theories, he became bolstered up and convinced that he should approach Burton with his suggestions.

Burton was working in his private chambers on the top floor of the Weldon Building when Nemo confronted him, knocking on the door.

"Who is it?" Burton's voice was irritated, tired.

"Goodenough, sir. I'd like a few words with you if I may."

Burton opened the door, and Nemo stepped through into a room literally clogged with paraphernalia: drafting tables, lamps, a telescope, a calculator, reams and reams of paper, and hundreds of models in various stages of repair or construction. It was a baronial expression of cluttered genius. "I don't appreciate being disturbed when I'm up here, Goodenough."

"I fully realize that, sir, but I think I should speak to you about something. Something very important to you."

Burton eyed him with a more than suspicious glance but directed him to the only chair in the room, situated before a large, slanted drafting table. As Nemo sat down, Burton rushed over with a piece of cloth and hastily covered the plans upon which he had been working.

"Now, what is it, lad?"

Nemo paused, grating a bit on Burton's penchant for calling practically everyone "lad," with no respect to age, position, or professional standing. It seemed so absurd coming from someone scarcely older than Nemo himself. "It's about the airship," said Nemo, and he proceeded to explain to Burton the inherent flaws he detected in the theory and design of such a craft. Nemo spoke slowly, but without hesitation, adding each carefully wrought observation to the next, being extremely careful, considerate, and on occasion, too respectful.

Burton sat silently through the entire discourse, interrupting Nemo only at the times when he wished to clarify a point, but never to voice an objection. He sat nodding his head, never taking his eyes off the well-intentioned Nemo.

" . . . and those are basically the essential points of my observations, sir," Nemo finished up quietly. "What do you think?"

Burton paused for a moment, then began pacing about the crowded room, kneading his hands into one another, eyes darting from one point in the room to another. "I think you are a most bold fool!" he said finally, glowering at Nemo from the center of the room.

"What?"

"How can you interrupt me in my work, in my very *study*, mind you, to bother me with such claptrap!? Get out of here! And don't ever bother me about such nonsense again!"

Nemo sat calmly. Although he had not expected such an outburst, he felt qualified to deal with it rationally and competently. "It was not my desire to upset, sir."

"Well, please know that you have. Don't you think I have already contemplated the possibilities of which you speak? Don't you think that I have already worked out the calculations and found them unfeasible?"

Nemo sat for a moment, then decided to be truthful. "No, sir, I don't think you have."

This only further enraged Burton, who turned and picked up a small model of an early prototype ship and crushed its balsa wood hull in his hands, dashing it to the floor. "The insolence! Who in damnation do you think you are, Goodenough? I shall report this incident to the board of directors! I'll have you barred from the Institute, do you hear?"

"Yes, sir, I fully understand what you are saying, but I doubt if you can do any such thing."

"What?"

"I doubt if it is against the 'rules' of this fine establishment to even speak to the famous Robert Burton, much less disagree with him."

Burton paused in his raving, wiped some perspiration from his brow, pushed his hand through wild, wavy hair. Then turning slowly, he eyed Nemo cagily. "Have you mentioned these ideas to anyone else?"

Nemo knew immediately what the inventor/fanatic was thinking. "Yes, as a matter of fact, I have."

"Just as I thought. You're a sly one, aren't you, Goodenough?"

"I had never thought of myself as such, sir. Careful, perhaps; prudent, maybe; but never sly."

"But very insolent, I assure you. I asked you once to

leave, Goodenough, and you ignored me. I shall ask you again, and if you refuse me again, I shall take more drastic measures, Now please, leave me at once." Burton turned and threaded his way past the tables and stacks of oddment to the window which overlooked the downtown section of Philadelphia. He stood with his back to Nemo, waiting.

"Very well, sir," said Nemo, rising from his chair. "I am most sorry that I seem to have upset you. I had no idea that you were such a self-centered fathead. Goodbye."

Burton whirled about, with clenched fists that were knuckling into whiteness. If he had been closer to Nemo, it was possible that he may have attacked him. But hindered by the distance, and the fact that Nemo had already reached the door and opened it, Burton only stood rigidly, shaking and trembling with the pent-up fury of someone on the brink of becoming mentally unhinged.

It was not an inauspicious beginning for the rivalry that would continue to grow between the two men until, years later, it emerged as a festering open wound, flecked and lapped by pure hatred.

Nemo, ever more convinced of the errors in Burton's plans, did exactly what the half-mad inventor feared he might do. Under the name of Percival M. Goodenough, Nemo published several papers in the leading engineering journals of the day, which fully explained his own theories about heavier-than-air flight, about the principle of lifting bodies, and self-propulsion.

The papers created more than a small explosion of interest in the engineering world, especially among the members of the Weldon Institute itself. This became especially true when in the second paper, Nemo employed as a foil to his own aeronautical arguments the presumably faulty designs and logical snags in the personal designs and theories of Robert Burton.

It was at this point that, during the Institute's monthly assembly, Burton stood before the entire elite gathering and declared open warfare upon Nemo and any men who would follow his ideas. There was a great uproar of noise and confusion throughout the assembly hall, such as had never rocked the hallowed structure since its earliest beginnings. But the noisy public demonstration that sprang up among the hundred-odd members of the Institute was only a grim symbol of what was to follow. Almost immediately the members of Weldon split into two factions—those who continued to favor the designs and beliefs of Robert Burton, and those who felt that perhaps the young Percival Goodenough was on the proper course.

The result was injurious to the greater causes of the Weldon Institute itself, not only to their greatest project of constructing an aircraft, but also to the myriad smaller research projects and ongoing concerns. This was not apparent at first, but gradually it became clear that the Institute could rend itself apart at the seams if something were not done to reconcile the ever-widening rift that was appearing among the ranks of the members. It became more difficult to acquire funding and grants and even public support for the Institute's many works once the journalists of the world learned of the avowed rivalry between two of Weldon's most brilliant minds.

And this was further compounded by several mysterious events.

Nemo had taken to afternoon walks into the gardens that flanked Philadelphia's public library, and it was from there that he would sit for hours and watch the pigeons and gulls that placidly glided and soared and winged all about him. The atmosphere of the public park was immensely soothing to Nemo's troubled mind. The daily confusion and strife that seemed now to reign at the red brick Institute was so palpable that one could even sense it in the air, even when all was quiet and there were no heated arguments leaking above the transoms of the closed laboratory doors.

At the time, Nemo was grappling with the notion that birds flew despite the obvious lack of any great power source to propel them through the air. This flew (pardon the pun) in the face of Robert Burton's contention that the only way man would fly would be by building an enormous enough power source—enough to defy the combined factors of gravity, drag, mass, wind. Nemo was well aware of the lightness, the hollow bones, the aerodynamic shape of the bird, but this was not enough to compensate for the defiance of the laws of physics. The bird flew. It was that simple.

After many afternoons in the park, Nemo came upon the idea that there was something inherent in the very structure and operation of the bird's *wing* that held the secret to powered heavier-than-air flight.

In his laboratory, he began to study the morphology of the bird, every available species, to see if he could detect what it was that could be found in all of them that was consistent and necessary for flight. He became a part-time vivisectionist and biologist, adding to his already cyclopedic knowledge of the scientific world, and soon arrived at several alternate theories that had to be tested. Models were constructed, and he attempted to re-create the basic shape of the bird in various modes: paper, wood, wire, and metal. Although he was not successful, he felt instinctively that he was on the right track, and moved all his apparatus and papers to the Weldon Institute where he could share his views and modest discoveries with his sympathetic colleagues. Perhaps the combined efforts of many could pick up the new threads he had unraveled from the mystery and solve it.

But this was not to be.

News spread through the Institute of Nemo's new approach to the project, and just when many of the members expressed a renewed faith in the success of the project, a most curious and insidious happenstance occurred.

Some person or persons stole their way into the great Gothic edifice in the dead of night and thoroughly ransacked Nemo's laboratory and office. All his papers were heaped into the hearth and set ablaze; his instruments smashed; his models utterly destroyed; his books of tables and calculations also put to the fire. Years of work evaporated into the smoke and fury of several night-hours.

The Institute was of course horrified, and the finger of suspicion pointed immediately to Robert Burton. He had a convenient alibi to account for his time, but this did not rule out the possibility that he had hired simple, mindless thugs to do the job. It does not seem unlikely that one could find a man or two who would fairly leap at the chance to undo the work of someone so obviously more superior than themselves. The minds of small men are indeed small and ruled by the most petty of motivations.

This incident served to further divide the two camps within the Weldon Institute, and its board of directors found it terribly necessary to clear up the mystery of the vandalism as quickly as possible. The Philadelphia police were employed and backed by the urgings of several large industrial financiers (who had placed vast fortunes in both money and trust within the Institute) to solve the mystery.

It took less than a month of careful investigating to track down the perpetrators—two local, small-time criminals with long records of small-minded offenses, and a history of hiring out to whomever offered them a job. From there it was more difficult to establish a connection with Robert Burton, since both men—simpletons that they were—confessed that they had no idea as to the identity of either Robert Burton or Percival Goodenough. The pair of criminals were so simple-minded and so free of such notions as loyalty or devotion that whoever had hired them must have recognized this, and had been wise to remain anonymous. They described receiving a parcel from a man dressed in a hooded coat in an obscure alley and thus received half of the appointed sum. They received the other half of their money upon completion of the task.

All the evidence was circumstantial, and although it pointed directly at someone within the Institute who knew the precise location and contents of Nemo's offices, no concrete connection could be made with Robert Burton or his allies.

Nemo was faced with the almost impossible task of reconstructing his notes and plans. He was thus occupied for the next few months, while Robert Burton and his team of supporters succeeded in building a small, four-man prototype model of the Weldon airship. It was twenty feet in length, the body of which was a modified ketch, and sprouting from its decks like thinly petaled flowers were sixteen rotors arranged in rows of two, atop ten-foot shafts. The shafts were connected by a series of pinion gears and driveshafts and engaged by means of an ingenious differential clutch of Burton's design. The mode of power was a monstrous steam boiler which weighed many tons. The attempted launch was made outside of Philadelphia on the banks of the Delaware River, and the representatives of all the world's major newspapers were present for what Robert Burton had promised would be the greatest moment in the history of mankind.

The evening before, a young, impetuous reporter from the *Inquirer* had interviewed Percival Goodenough concerning the proposed flight of Burton's ship, which he had dubbed *The Osprey*. In the interview, which appeared in the morning papers on the day of the launch attempt, Goodenough was quoted as saying that *The Osprey* not only would *not* fly, but might prove dangerous to the four aeronauts aboard her. In the interview Goodenough had backed up his feelings with several sets of equations displaying the amount of force needed to move a given amount of mass, and contrasting it to the amount of motive force able to be generated by Burton's steam engine drive. "It was impossible," said Goodenough, "to lift *The Osprey*, and the equations prove it."

But the reporter chose not to print the equations under the rationalization that the general public would not understand them anyway. And so the article appeared with Goodenough sounding like a sour-grapes detractor of a great man. Such are the perils of talking to newspapermen.

A great crowd had gathered on the banks of the Delaware by 10:00 A.M. and all eyes were upon the odd-looking craft with the forest of propellers upon its deck. Vendors hawked foods in the throng; a brass band played Austrian marches; children ran between the stands of

88

adults, playing tag; women sat calmly with fans and parasols to ward off the late-September heat of the morning.

And *The Osprey* hunkered upon the greasy bank, chugging and belching and farting, its boilers and gears straining to build up the proper amounts of pressure and torque. Burton climbed aboard the vessel and stationed himself in its bow, standing like an animated figurehead from which vantage point he imagined that he would be able to salute the crowd as his ship lifted off in grand fashion and levitated above their astounded mass. His three crewmen descended into the hull, where the actual operation of the craft would be handled.

A soft breeze was blowing off the western bank when Burton gave the signal, and *The Osprey*'s engines began to clatter and hum with new strength and energy. For a moment all was static, and an eerie silence settled over the spectators. In the hazy, humid air, from a distance, Nemo watched the spectacle, and to him, for a moment, *The Osprey* seemed to swell and shudder. Its rotors whirred into invisibility as they ripped and bleated at the air; its hull began to vibrate, and great clouds of steam seeped from the seams in the wooden deck.

Nemo was momentarily blinded by the explosion which replaced the spot where *The Osprey* had a moment before rested. Some would later testify that the craft had actually lifted several feet off the ground before disintegrating, but this would be contested by other witnesses who must be considered equally reliable.

At any rate, Burton's ship was horribly destroyed, and burning fragments of wood and red-hot boiler plate rained down upon the panicked crowds and into the oily waters of the Delaware. The three crewmen were obliterated and not a trace of their remains was ever discovered, so great and furious was the explosion.

But Burton miraculously survived.

From his position at the point of the bow, he was instantly hurled through the air some one hundred thirty feet and slammed into the river, where a small schooner

89

was able to race to his rescue. He was dragged aboard, unconscious, broken of limb, and partially burned by the scalding steam, but he was undeniably alive.

The Weldon Institute was greatly embarrassed by the spectacular failure of *The Osprey,* and Burton's reputation suffered equally from the smears that erupted in the newspapers for several weeks to come. Reporters kept referring to the article in which Nemo had predicted the disaster, and when Burton emerged from the hospital, he took up the cry that his vessel had been sabotaged by no one other than Percival Goodenough.

The accusation rocked the scientific establishment and threw the reputation of the prestigious Weldon Institute into public disgrace. It was said that the accident had somehow affected Burton's mind, and that he had slipped across the thin line that often separates the genius from the psychopath. When Burton was well enough to return to Weldon, he was met with an aloofness, a restrained disposition, that the half-mad scientist could only interpret as the Institute's willingness to disenfranchise themselves from him.

Robert Burton countered this reaction with more accusations of Percival Goodenough, but there was, of course, no evidence to support such claims. As time passed, the members of the Weldon Institute cast their unanimous allegiance with Goodenough, and under an ensuing monthly assembly cast the resolution that Robert Burton be dismissed from the Institute permanently.

Burton was, to say the least, disturbed by this.

He arose from his seat in the assembly hall and railed at the body of learned gentlemen, then stormed to the podium. "Very well, you ignorant dogs! I will leave this place of infantile minds. You will never see Robert Burton again, but I promise you this: you will hear of his works, and you will feel his wrath. May you all go quietly to hell!"

And with those words, he left the stage, his left leg still stiff from his accident, giving his gait an awkward, somewhat tragic aspect.

It was almost a year later to the day before the members of the Weldon Institute heard again from Robert Burton. But much had taken place in his absence. Percival Goodenough resumed his work upon the airship project but was forced to abandon it when the Institute's financial backers abnegated their support. It seemed as if Burton's failure reinforced the current thinking that a true heavier-than-air aircraft was a physical impossibility. Although saddened by this swing in the temperament of the public, Goodenough continued to be the true scientist that he was and devoted his time and his boundless energies to new projects. He became acclaimed throughout the country as one of the most promising young men of his generation, and the memory of Robert Burton was fading from the minds of everyone.

Until one morning the members of the Institute arrived at their familiar quarters to find an enormous flag—at least it appeared to be a flag or pennant of some sort—draped across the roof and upper stories of the red brick building. The flag measured fifteen meters on the long side and ten on the short; it was a black background with a dazzling orange and gold sun in its center. The sun was surrounded by a random field of stars.

Upon investigation, the members learned from the night porter, whose quarters were in the basement of the building, that he had been awakened at approximately 4:00 A.M. by an odd noise. It sounded as if the sky was filled with a "fluttering thunder" that sent vibrations through the air which shook the very foundation of the old building. The man, obviously shaken by the experience, also reported hearing the sound of a trumpet being sounded in the cool of the night. The instrument blared out the raucous notes of unfamiliar fanfare.

There were some members of the Institute who thought the night porter had gone daft and would have dismissed the entire incident if they did not have the enormous flag to indicate something contrary.

If anyone suspected Robert Burton as the source of the mystery, they did not make their thoughts public. But

Percival Goodenough thought immediately of Burton, and recognized what the presence of the odd flag *atop* the Institute's building implied. He spent several days distracted by the omen, wondering if there would be any more strange occurrences that might possibly connect with Robert Burton. He feared that the flag incident was not an isolated one.

And he was correct.

Exactly a week later, the following telegram was received:

MEMBERS OF WELDON:
BE FOREWARNED THAT YOU SHALL REGRET THE ERRORS OF YOUR SORDID PAST. THE ALBATROSS SHALL SOON BE UPON YOU.

ROBUR THE CONQUEROR

The effect of which was to place the Institute in a state of confusion and fear. It was obvious that the name "Robur" referred to Robert Burton; but it was "the Conqueror" that had everyone stirred up. An attempt to trace the source of the telegram revealed that it had been sent from the main rail-station in Baltimore, and had been dictated by a tall, thin man in a tweed cape, pince-nez, and a gray beard . . . a description that did not fit Robert Burton at all.

There was also much talk of the meaning of the message itself. That it was a open threat, there was little doubt. That it was the ravings of a certifiable lunatic, there was much to support such a notion. But the real question was the meaning of the word *albatross*. Several members jumped upon the literary allusion to Coleridge's poem of the ancient mariner and the symbolic bird which he was cursed to wear upon his neck. These members said that perhaps the Weldon Institute was going to be publicly shamed—in some way made to face the world with some ignominy slung about its figurative neck. Although this seemed plausible, Percival Goodenough did not feel that it was the intention of the literal—rather than literary—mind of Robert Burton. *No*, thought

Goodenough, *the answer to the meaning of* The Albatross *is something far simpler*—although he feared that its manifestation might prove to be quite complex.

Exactly one week after the receipt of the telegram, an experimental steamship, *The Prospect,* while sailing proudly up the Delaware River toward her familiar berth near Franklin Crossing, was utterly destroyed. Fortunately there were five survivors among her crew, and they all reported the same phenomenon: just before *The Prospect* exploded, they all heard the sound of thunder and trumpet fanfare which seemed to be coming from *above* them. There had been great banks of evening fog and mist rolling across the river that evening, but two of the sailors claimed to have seen projectiles—some sort of missiles—falling from the sky and striking the deck of *The Prospect* with devastating results.

There was hardly time to consider the implications of this disaster before the timetable of events was accelerated. Percival Goodenough was convinced that it was Burton who had destroyed *The Prospect*—especially since that steamship had been designed and sanctioned by an earlier research project of the Weldon Institute. Goodenough was also convinced that Burton had performed the deed by means of an airship—or as Burton had always referred to his imagined craft, an *aeronef.*

On the morning after *The Prospect* disaster, Goodenough was debating whether or not to share his suspicions with his colleagues, when there came a great commotion outside the windows of the Institute's solid walls. The street was filled with an oddly terrifying mixture of sounds: the rising crescendo of voices crying out, screaming, gasping, and shouting; the roar of syncopated and continuous thunder; and the thin, crisp notes of a trumpet being sounded.

Rushing to the window, Goodenough peered out to see an incredible sight. Advancing upon the Institute from the east was a great, dark bulk, hanging in the sky like an impossibly large insect. It was a bloated, ungainly thing, its swollen body held aloft by an uncountable number of vertical shafts and propellers, all furiously churning and rip-

93

ping at the still morning air above Philadelphia. The craft's hull was vaguely cigar-shaped and possessed small propellers both fore and aft. The streets below were filled with frantic human traffic, running and surging like commingling currents of water, with no real apparent direction or purpose.

But the airship drove on above them as if they were beneath notice and drove steadfastly on toward the Institute. Goodenough stood his ground, his keenly trained eyes searching for evidence which might make the situation more clear, more understandable. Such is the curse of all men of science.

As the craft drew ever closer, Goodenough recognized a black pennant flying from an aft mast and noted the gold sun and the field of stars. He knew then that he stared into the colors of his delivering angel. Racing from the window, he retreated to the inner corridor, shouting passionately to his colleagues, imploring everyone to take shelter.

Even as he ran, concussions began to rock the upper stories of the old brick building. There was the sound of continuous thunder above his head as Goodenough half ran, half stumbled down the stairwell. In a moment the halls and wells were filled with anxious men running and falling and surging through the smoky mist of pulverized brick and mortar and plaster. The entire building was being blown apart, each level crumbling in upon itself.

Goodenough reached the street level, along with a large contingent of Weldon members, and was absorbed into the crush of fleeing spectators. From above, the black shape of Burton's *aeronef* rained down large explosive objects into the now-flaming ruin that had once been the proud headquarters of one of the world's finest centers of scientific research. The airship hovered precariously, defiantly, just above the wreckage, invulnerable to any and all manner of epithet hurled at it from the ground below. As the crowds pushed and seethed away from the area of destruction, a small force of Philadelphia police arrived and raised their handguns against the horrible ship in the sky. But their fusillade went unnoticed by the great airship, which continued to hang above the burning Institute, dutifully emptying its load of aerial bombs, apparently determined to remain in that position until there was not one stone left upon stone.

The spectacle continued for the greater part of an hour, despite the efforts of several naval vessels in port which vainly attempted to reposition their deck guns and fire upon the airship. The only effect of this folly was to hurl cannon shot in errant trajectories, into unfortunate sections of the city. Several residential neighborhoods were set ablaze during the incident, with great loss of life and property.

It was not until the entire city block which housed the Weldon Institute was a roiling black storm, which defied the efforts of two fire companies to control, that the destroying airship disappeared into the smoke and haze of the atmosphere above the grim scene. Witnesses close at hand reported hearing an increase in the noise level caused by its whirring rotors, a perceptible whining sound, as if the ship's engines were straining greatly, and then a gradual ascension of the craft until it was beyond view.

By week's end, all the papers of the Western Hemisphere had carried countless articles on the incredible devastation caused by the mysterious aircraft in the skies above Philadelphia. The loss of life had been quite staggering: of the ninety-two members of the Institute present at the time of the attack, only thirty-seven had survived. Of the Institute itself, nothing remained except for its special documents and records, wisely kept in Blaylock fireproof safes in the basement of the building. Everything else was either utterly destroyed or irretrievably damaged by fire, smoke, and water. For all practical purposes, the Weldon Institute had ceased to exist.

But this situation was, most fortunately, only temporary.

As a result of the great publicity of the bombing, pledges and grants poured in from corporations, financiers, and industries throughout the continent, and even from Europe—all promising great sums of money to rebuild the Weldon Institute and reoutfit its wondrous laboratories. Needless to say, this was a great relief to the surviving members of the Institute and its bereft board of directors; but it is a well-known fact that money is not a panacea to assuage all wounds.

Percival Goodenough knew and felt this with all his heart. No matter how much money poured in from across the globe, he knew that the Weldon Institute would never be as it had once been—not only because of the loss of some of its finest, most gifted members, but also because of the manner in which it had been destroyed. Although physically unhurt by the calamity, Goodenough bore grievous psychological scars from the experience. His entire personality underwent a slow, but inexorable, change. Gone was his light, airy step, his cheery conversational banter, his adolescentlike enthusiasm for anything new and curious. In its place there now resided the shadowy form of revenge, of brooding hate, and the single-mindedness that almost always leads to obsession.

It was as though Percival Goodenough felt personally responsible for the devastation laid to the Weldon Institute. If he had not antagonized the unbalanced Robert Burton, if he had not humiliated the demented man in public, if he had not . . .

But that no longer mattered. There was only one thing now, only one purpose in Goodenough's life that would ever consume with the passion previously channeled into basic research: the destruction of Robert Burton, now Robur the Conqueror.

Goodenough remained with the Institute during its phoenix days, until it had actually opened its new doors and had begun the semblance of operations once again. This time, precautions had been taken to arm the upper levels of the structure with the latest armaments, and to employ a highly trained security force which monitored all movement in and out of the building. Goodenough always thought sad thoughts when he passed before the security gates at the entrance to Weldon. It was a tragedy of true proportion when men could no longer trust their fellow men. Ah yes, Goodenough still harbored such danger-ously idealistic thoughts. But that was soon to fade away like mist rising off a morning pond.

All during this time, there came reports from around the globe of the appearance of Robur the Conqueror's aeronef which, announced to the world through a leaflet-drop in London, was called the *Albatross* (one little mys-tery cleared up to the satisfaction of utterly no one). The dark ship assumed the habit of dropping out of the sky at the most inopportune times—such as when a railroad shipment of precious metals or of bank notes was being carried from one financial center to the next; or when a munitions ship had just left the safety of its harbor and struck out upon the open, lonely sea; or when a ware-house or distributing center had recently stocked itself in a surplus of raw materials.

Robur became known as a pirate of the skies. His in-fernal craft would swoop down hawklike and pluck away whatever it was that he needed to augment the slowly building empire of hate and demented revenge that he ob-viously planned to wreak upon society.

There was a growing fear among the members of the Weldon Institute that Robur the Conqueror was only waiting until the Institute was totally rebuilt before he would once again strike from the sky. This was ap-parently in the minds of the insurance and brokerage houses of Philadelphia, because the Institute was unable to obtain any protection or liability coverage that would include another attack by the *Albatross*. In fact, there were some agents who actually wrote policies for Weldon that specifically mentioned and summarily excluded any damages incurred by Robur or his engine of destruction.

Spurred on by this development, plus his ever-growing desire to rid the world of Robert Burton's special brand of madness, Percival Goodenough contacted an old uni-versity colleague by the name of Impey Barbicane, who was now the chairman of a prestigious weapons research and application organization called the Baltimore Gun Club. Goodenough's proposal was clear and simple. He wished to obtain the expertise and cooperation of Barbicane's associates in the design and construction of what could only be termed an antiaircraft cannon.

Impey Barbicane, a tempestuous, iron-willed man, leaped at the opportunity to join in such a project. The resources of the Weldon Institute, the United States Army, and the City of Philadelphia were placed at the disposal of Barbicane and his men. With Goodenough supplying the calculations, the theoretical data, and the driving motivation, the Baltimore Gun Club soon produced several prototype models of the antiaircraft weapon. There was an urgency in the project which spurred everyone ahead, because the new Weldon Institute had been completed for several months and the members were all settled into its new quarters, going back to the business of being brilliant.

Robur could strike at any time.

The first two models of the new gun were dismal failures, and that only served to throw more fear into the backers of the project. The major problems were the weight and the mobility needed in such a weapon that could hurl shells into the air and strike a moving target with any acceptable accuracy and force. The mobility problem was solved to a marginal extent by Goodenough's idea of mounting the gun's carriage on a specially constructed railroad car; this design was later enhanced by the successful construction of a fully rotating, steam-assisted turret assembly that also raised and lowered the barrel with surprising quickness. Some of the Institute's experiments in metallurgy resulted in the application of new alloys that gave the gun strength and the lightness necessary to be able to swing the barrel about on its carriage with swiftness and accuracy.

The only insurmountable problem was the acquisition of targets upon which to practice and train a team of qualified gunners. There was, after all, only one *Albatross,* and when/if it ever arrived over the skies of Philadelphia, there would be no time for practice sessions.

Refinements in the design continued to be made as the members of Weldon remained vigilant, mostly under the dedicated motivation of Percival Goodenough. Time passed, but the morning eventually arrived which all of Philadelphia had feared and speculated upon.

Out of the east, with the rising sun as a blinding baffle upon its back, the *Albatross* blatted and thundered toward the center of Philadelphia. There was the idiotic sound of the trumpet, and the forces of the city were quickly mobilized against its formidable, but at least more familiar, foe.

Goodenough raced from his office down Walnut Street to the old rail yards where the Barbicane Gun (as it became known) rested in oiled readiness beneath nets of camouflage. He arrived at the spur just as the engine and its deadly cargo were reaching full steam; Jumping aboard, Goodenough gave the signal and Barbicane and his gun crew were racing through the center of the city toward the location of the Weldon Institute's newly risen towers of ivory.

If the *Albatross* noticed the strange train as it wormed its way through the urban labyrinth, it gave no indication, but drove steadily upon its most obvious target. It was imperative that the Barbicane Gun open up before its adversary reached its target. The great locomotive shuddered and thundered along at its very top velocity, until they were at last within the range of the long, black barrel.

The routes and positions of the three objects—the Institute, the *Albatross,* and the Gun—formed the corners of an equilateral triangle. Goodenough, from the cab of the locomotive, screamed encouragement at the gunnery team amidst the storm of soot and steam and smoke as they clattered across the city toward an intersection with the aeronef. Steam hydraulics powered the turret of the gun, while a team of two men cranked high-ratio gears that controlled the elevation of the barrel. At the breach was a platform that moved with the gun where the artillery was loaded and the spent shells ejected. The man who actually aimed and fired the weapon was suspended in a cagelike affair located one-third the distance up the barrel from the breach.

As the train reached its closest point to the Institute, its air brakes wheezed and its steel wheels slid across the rails, scraping and sparking, until the great mass of steel meshed to a halt. Above them the aeronef hovered and hung like a fulsome insect, fat and awkward. When it was less than thirty yards from the Institute, Barbicane gave orders to open fire. Elevations and latitudes were measured and the long, black barrel erupted with its first shell, which careened above the hull of the *Albatross* and miraculously threaded its way among the forest of propellor shafts. A miss.

If anyone aboard the aeronef noticed the attack, no caution or evasive action was taken. Instead the airship drove boldly toward its target, gaining altitude in expectation of another bombing attack. Barbicane's gunner readjusted their weapon, led the *Albatross* as a hunter would a flight of geese, and fired again.

This time a blossom of flame sprouted from the aft section, and the sky was briefly littered with smoking splinters. A great cry rose up from the thousands of spectators cramming the streets to watch the most fantastic battle in the history of mechanized man. As the smoke cleared, Goodenough saw the smashed remains of three propeller shafts smoldering above the deck of the aeronef. The aeronef itself seemed to be hovering with less stability, having acquired a rhythmic, swaying motion. The Barbicane crew reloaded and fired again, this time the shell striking the sailing-vessel-like bow, and although it was only a glancing blow, huge fragments of wood and cinder showered down from the sky.

More cheers from below, and the *Albatross* suddenly seemed to have lost its interest in the Weldon building. It labored slowly in the air, wheeling about, facing its most narrow profile toward the Barbicane Gun, then churning forward with a great whine of its engines and an increase in the whirl of its remaining propellers.

The narrow configuration and the rapid speed proved to be a formidable target for Barbicane's crew. Three more rounds were fired as the bulky target advanced, and

100

all three missed. As the *Albatross* passed directly over-head, a small load of aerial bombs was dropped, and they scattered about the locomotive, tearing up great sections of ties and rail, but missing the engine and its gun carriage. The crew reloaded as the aeronef fled eastward toward the water, the barrel cracked with a thunderous report, and several seconds later four more of the propeller shafts were blasted into flinders. Still hovering, but more slowly, more fitfully now, the *Albatross* limped away from the gun's position. Goodenough ordered the locomotive into reverse, and the train chugged back along its path roughly parallel to the escaping flight of Robur's ship. Another shot struck the aft section of the hull and started a small but tenacious fire on the decks. For the first time, Goodenough could see panicked crewman scurrying like rats above the decks.

Three more shells arced into the sky but did not find their mark, and soon the *Albatross* was out of the gun's range. But it was burning badly as it rotored out over the Delaware River and down its winding path to the sea. It was a triumph for the Weldon Institute and the Baltimore Gun Club, quite plainly.

Naval gunboats followed the limping, wobbling course of the stricken aeronef all the way to the Atlantic and some ten miles out in the open sea, until the flaming hulk finally fell from the sky and dashed itself to pieces in the choppy water. The naval ships pushed onward toward the site of the splashdown but found no trace of Robur or any of his crew among the flotsam of wreckage that littered the ocean's surface like autumn leaves.

This last bit of information greatly troubled Goodenough, and he was unable to enjoy completely the spectacular victory over the attacking *Albatross*. As long as there was no proof that Robur had gone down with his ship, it was not possible to assume that the dangerous madman was no longer a threat.

The years passed, and there was no evidence forthcoming to suggest that Robur the Conqueror still lived. The world fell back into its more familiar preoccupations of economics, politics, religion, and war. There were few men who still remembered the dreaded name of Robur, but one of them was Percival Makepeace Goodenough.

ELEVEN

THE HOUR WAS very late by the time Nemo had finished his story—at least as much of it as he felt like telling. I looked over at Derek Ruffin and saw that he was nodding, either under the influence of the brandy, the lateness, or maybe even the droning details of Nemo's narrative. Me, I was still alert and more intrigued than ever with the complications of Nemo's fluxworld.

"I hate to sound like an ungrateful boor, Captain," I said. "But, what happened after that?"

"I beg your pardon?"

"I mean, that was about seventeen years back, right? How did you get from there to . . . here?"

Nemo smiled and nodded. "Yes, that's true. Well, there is more, but it's getting late. We will have a long voyage together, gentlemen. Plenty of time for talk."

I was not sure I liked the sound of that, although it seemed completely cordial and without any semblance of threat. "Just a brief summary would be okay," I said after a pause. "You've really sparked my curiosity."

"Yes, I suppose I have. Very well, I remained on at the Institute only another half year. It seems as if the incident with Robur had changed me irrevocably. My heart was not in my work, if you can understand that. . . ."

"More than you'll ever know," I said. "There's hardly any of us who haven't had *that* feeling at some time or another."

Smiling politely, Nemo continued. "You, see, Alexander, I was convinced that Robur had survived! I knew it! It preyed on me until I could stand it no longer. I had to find out; so I gathered together my property, my stocks, and other investments and liquidated everything. I hired

103

away as many of my most trusted colleagues as I could, then set up a laboratory and a foundry on my family's land off the coast of Cape Cod. It was true, I *had* become weary of the world, and with the invention of *The Nautilus*, I found a way to achieve both my ends: be free of the ties of the land—its petty politics, and driving economics and social conventions—and more importantly, to be able to seek out Robur wherever he might be."

"Sounds like it was quite a risky chance," I said.

"Maybe, but I was proved right in the long run. Robur had obviously survived the destruction of the *Albatross*, and through the years, I confronted him or his works, but never to any final decision."

"How do you mean?"

"Robur tried to build another aircraft. He based himself in the mountains of Austria for a while. My men kept track of him. Spies, you know. But I'm sure he had his spies, too. He must have known that I was building *The Nautilus* . . . and then there were several attempts at sabotage."

"And let me guess, when Robur learned of your submarine, he started building one too, right?"

"Not immediately, no. It took him years to be convinced that his aeronautical theories were not tenable. He only turned to the sea recently—within the last few years. And of course, he knows nothing about the existence of the fluxgates. . . ."

I smiled, humoring him. "That is your secret alone."

"Yes, and I intend to keep it that way. The world at large is not ready for such knowledge. They can't keep one plane of existence in order, and I shudder to think what mankind would do with a multitude of worlds in which to flounder and fumble."

"Don't you have anything to do with the society of men any more?"

Nemo smiled this time. "Oh, occasionally, I suppose. I keep abreast of the world political situation as best I can. There's still that terrible Civil War going on in the States, you know."

"I learned a little about that from a whaling ship we

met," I said cautiously, remembering what the captain of *The Progress* had said about some sea monster named "Ironback."

"Whaling ship, eh? That's one of Robur's favorite targets. He loves to cut under their keels and split them open like mackerels. That's why *The Nautilus* is in these waters. It's a new season, and the chance of finding *The Kraken* in these waters is quite a good possibility." Nemo paused to light another cigar. "What about your own fluxworld? They have a Civil War?"

"Oh yes. Pretty bad mess. Brother against brother. Millions killed. But it only lasted until 1865."

"Most curious."

"Lee surrendered to Grant at Appomattox. There's quite a few good books out on the entire campaign."

Nemo laughed. "Grant? General Ulysses S. Grant?"

"Yeah, that's the one." I looked over at Ruffin to smile, but my companion had fallen asleep.

"That's interesting. General Grant was killed here in 1863, before Gettysburg. The story I've heard is that he fell into a ditch one night after some hard drinking. Lay there all night, as the story goes, and a team of horses carrying some cannon didn't see him as they passed by the camp in the hours before dawn. Rolled right over him."

I smiled, once more reminded of how the various twists and turns of the various fluxworlds wrought such changes in them. I wondered how many parallel worlds there actually were. The possibilities were infinite and equally fascinating.

We talked a bit more about the differences between our two worlds, but it was by then very late and even I was starting to get drowsy. When Nemo remarked upon Ruffin's falling asleep, I suggested that I take him back to our cabin and call it a night. The captain agreed, and I helped Ruffin to his feet as we took our leave.

As I struggled down the corridor, I could hear Nemo at his organ keyboard playing a Bach cantata.

TWELVE

THE NEXT DAY we were awakened quite early, despite the late session of the night before. I've always been used to running on short sleep, but it was a little rough on Derek, and he stumbled and grumbled down the steel corridor to the officer's mess where we dined on fried kelp and some kind of fish eggs and a delicious tea culled from some exotic strain of seaweed. The first mate was also present, along with some other crewmen that I had yet to meet. It was a congenial meal, although our conversation was not anywhere near as involved or as casual as it had been the night before with the captain.

I kept getting the feeling that the first mate, whose name was Bischoff—a name which befitted his thick-shouldered, bald-headed Germanic aspect—was suspicious of us, that he did not wholly trust us. This thought was not backed up by anything concrete; it was just that Bischoff's eyes seemed to belie his congeniality. There was a barrier just beyond his pupils through which I was unable to see. I decided that I would just keep a running check on this guy and make sure that I didn't do anything that he might think was untoward.

After breakfast, we received word that Nemo wished to see us on the bridge, and we joined him there by following the first mate through the corridors and up a spiral staircase several levels to the control room of the submarine.

Nemo was waiting for us there, dressed in a nicely tailored blazer with a scrolled "N" on the breast pocket. He wore gray slacks and a white turtleneck jersey. With his longish hair, his expertly trimmed beard, and flashing eyes, he looked more than impressive. It was no wonder

106

that despite his eccentricities and obsessions he had no trouble commanding the respect and the loyalty of his crew.

"Good morning, gentlemen. Did you dine well?" He executed an abbreviated bow.

"Oh yeah, it was fine," said Ruffin, and I agreed with a nod.

"Splendid," said Nemo. "And now I will escort you on a tour of *The Nautilus,* as I promised, and not unlike that of Verne's fictional version with Arronax and his valet . . . except for a *few* surprises, I hope."

Nemo beamed with pride. He looked, for a moment, like a young boy, about to show his friends a cherished toy.

But *The Nautilus* was no toy.

As we strolled about the deceptively spacious bridge, I could see that it was crammed with every conceivable instrument of the Victorian age of steam, and quite a few pieces that were from another age—the one that raced ahead in the brilliant mind of Nemo. There were actual consoles and banks of gauges with padded chairs for the four operators in the chamber. There was also a large stainless steel helm with auxiliary controls alongside, which provided a manual overide to the operators who manned their four stations in a small semicircle behind the helm. Directly in front of the helm were the two convex windows of thick glass that gave the appearance of luminous eyes to anyone who might see the ship lying restively on the surface of the night sea. Through these ports you could see the sloping prow of the vessel out to its armored and spiked tip, plus a good perspective of the depths off to each side. It was a well-designed command post, where a small number of men could control the ship with efficiency and comfort.

"What's this?" I asked, walking up to a series of gauges, surrounded by ornate pieces of brightwork. (Always there were the small touches, the signs that care and craftsmanship, as well as brilliance, went into the construction of the ship.)

"That tells us the amount of pressure being exerted per

square inch upon the surface of *The Nautilus*," said Bischoff curtly and matter-of-factly.

"And the one next to it gives the depth in feet, fathoms, and meters," said Nemo, indicating the design and calibration of the complex dial.

"How deep will she go?" asked Ruffin.

Nemo looked at him and grinned. "The answer to that question is moot, sir. I really don't know."

"What?"

Nemo laughed and looked at his crewmen, who shared in his joy. "Gentlemen, the deepest part of the earth's oceans which I have yet to discover, in *this* fluxworld at least, is in the Pacific—a place called the Marianas Trench. It lies almost 36,000 feet, or 6,000 fathoms beneath the surface. *The Nautilus* has traversed the bottom of that trench."

"And showing no signs of strain, I guess," I said.

"Precisely. And so, you see, I have no way of knowing how deep this ship will go. There is no place else that I have found to test her."

"What kind of hull design could you possibly have used to withstand the pressure of depths like that?" Ruffin seemed truly interested.

"The outer hull is alloyed steel of a formula of my own discovery back when I was still with the Institute. It is eight inches thick. The next layer is a honeycombing of aluminum and titanium that is another five inches thick. Then there lies a traditionally buttressed and bulkheaded medial hull of the same fine steel. Another thinner layer of honeycombing, and finally the inner hull and interior walls. This was meticulously worked out in theory and in applied experiments for almost two years before I was satisfied that this hull design would take me anywhere in the sea that I wished to go. So far, I have not been proved wrong." Nemo tapped upon the steel hull and it resounded dully. "Now these," he said, pointing to another set of instruments, "indicate our speed, pitch, drift, and the like. I have two large gyroscopes on a separate power cable, which keeps the vessel stable under any and all maneuvering. This gauge reports on the functioning of those gyroscopes and monitors any problems that may occur in their operation."

"This is so well thought out," said Ruffin. "So modern, it's amazing."

"Thank you, Mr. Ruffin, but you will notice that I have explained not even a fraction of the ship's capabilities. I have also been experimenting with electrics, radio waves, transponding techniques, and other methods of undersea navigation and detection." Nemo paused and indicated another set of instruments. "This is still in the experimental stages—in fact, I have been testing it out on this particular voyage."

"Where did you get such an appreciation of electronics—much of this stuff is far ahead of anything that people were working on in my world at a comparable time," I said, not really able to believe what Nemo was telling me.

The captain smiled. "I wish I could claim the credit for these innovations, gentlemen, but I must nod in the direction of my great rival, for it was he who was the genius when it came to electricity."

"Robur?"

"Precisely." Nemo sighed, shook his head, and directed us down the spiraling ladder to the main deck below.

"This floor, as you may have surmised by now, has most of the crew accommodations—a complement of thirty-five men—plus the galley, refrigeration and storage of all mess materials. There is also a full complement of recreational facilities off to the left. Just step through here, please."

We were guided through a bulkhead hatch and were immediately transported into the plush world of a Victorian men's club. The walls of the room were paneled in finely rubbed oak, trimmed in blond filigreed wainscoting, and accented by specially illuminated original oil paintings. Leaded-glass lamps were suspended from the ceiling, casting a warm, even light upon the thickly piled and woven maroon carpeting. There were carved, stuffed Elsworth chairs, reading lamps, spittoons, and ashtrays in every corner, plus two large gaming tables and a billiards table in the center of the room. Two members of the crew were engaged in a game of nine ball and paid our visit no notice.

"Beautiful," I said. "Excellent taste and design."

"Thank you, Alexander," said Nemo. "I have always believed that the morale and conduct of a crew is dependent upon the manner in which they are treated. My crew is very loyal to me, and I might add, quite content."

We left the period-piece parlor and entered the bluish gray confines of the submarine's corridor once again. As we passed down the hall, I saw everywhere the hallmarks of pride and craftsmanship, from the smallest, polished turnbuckle to the handles of cursory valves and spigots to the brass railings and handholds that were in such abundance on board. It seemed as if Nemo had thought of every contingency, and that he was a splendid human engineer—he had studied carefully the relationships between men and their tool/machine environments. The result was a finely crafted vessel that adapted superbly to the comfortable operation of its human occupants.

Afterward we inspected several of the crew's quarters, very similar to the chambers of Derek and myself, which is to say they were of efficient design but a shade on the Spartan side until each crew member decorated it to give it some personal warmth. I kept reminding myself that, after all, these guys did not sign on expecting it to be a cruise to Barbados.

We then descended to the next level of the submarine, which included the spacious chambers of Nemo, and a fantastic array of other wonders.

"In here," said Nemo, "is my laboratory. It is set up primarily for my studies of the sea and its creatures."

We entered a large, extremely well lit room that was lined with shelves and specimen bottles, most of them filled with rare examples of the marine world. Each bottle was carefully marked with the genus and species, the date collected, the location, and sundry other data. All were strapped onto the shelves to prevent them from being damaged by any turbulence from the sea. Nemo's careful eye for detail and contingency was everywhere. In the

110

center of the room were two large work tables, one with troughs and runners for dissection, plus a myriad of flasks, pipettes, distilling tubes, scales, gas burners, and several microscopes. The other table was covered with carefully indexed notebooks, reams of illustrations, meticulously drawn by hand, small boxes of file cards, and blotters and pens. Everything bore the mark of Captain Nemo, the scientist, the compleatist, the Renaissance Man.

"Were you always interested in the sea?" I asked as we perused the equipment and the facilities of the lab.

"Yes, I suppose I was. In my early years upon the cape, I spent almost all my available hours either on its beaches or on its surface in small dinghys. My affairs with the physical sciences and the Institute were but a brief interruption in what has been a lifelong love affair, I fear. It was only after the disastrous incidents in Philadelphia that I realized that I should return to what I loved best throughout my life." Nemo's voice grew softer for a moment as he seemed to recollect the long-ago days of his youth. He cleared his throat and continued. "I was always fascinated by the creatures of the sea, and there were times when I would be drifting off Nantucket, peering down into the brackish green depths, that I would envy those slipping, silent beasts of the sea. I wished to be like them in their world of eternal silence and cool and dark. With *The Nautilus*, I have finally joined them."

Ruffin and I nodded perfunctorily as Nemo continued talking. He seemed to be slipping into a small, but deeply felt, reverie, and felt that it was necessary to unburden thoughts that he had obviously carried far away in his "heart of hearts," to borrow an apt phrase from Conrad.

"Did you know that I used *Tursiops truncatus* as my model for the construction of *The Nautilus?*" said the captain in a burst of enthusiasm as he turned from a pile of drawings by his desk.

"What's that, the dolphin, right?" asked Ruffin.

"Yes, the bottle-nosed dolphin," said Nemo. "One of the most maneuverable, graceful creatures in the sea. And quite intelligent, too. I've often suspected that I could devise a way to communicate with them if I put my mind to it. With my early detection gear, I've frequently listened to them communicating amongst themselves. Fascinating! Clicks and whistles and staccato shrieks, it's beautiful to hear them! The whales communicate too, you know."

Ruffin nodded. "Yes, there're some scientists from our world, they've carried out lots of experiments with the aquatic mammals. There's even a few guys who claim that the dolphins are more intelligent than man."

"Really!" cried Nemo, pausing, considering such a notion. Then he smiled. "You know, gentlemen . . . they might be correct. When I think of the chaos that man has created for himself since climbing down from the trees, perhaps the dolphins and the whales were wise to remain beneath the quiet depths where they were alone with their thoughts and their simplest, most pleasurable instincts."

The captain seemed to be looking at a place that was far away from us as he spoke. If I hadn't felt that I was beginning to understand him, I would have thought that he was a bit on the other side of being crackers.

I tried to change the subject as we slowly walked toward the exit to the laboratory. "What did you think of Verne's incident with the giant squid?"

Nemo looked up and grinned. "Oh that. He rather romanticized it a bit, I'd say. Fairly accurate, though. I remember when that happened. Kent was aboard then. Your Mr. Verne lifted it whole cloth from Kent's recollection."

"Do the squid really get that big?" I asked.

"Some of them do, but you never see much of them. They're frightfully skittish and they seldom come anywhere *near* the surface. I've often thought that those poor creatures have evolved some sort of communication system, too."

"Oh yeah," I said, "I think I read something about oceanographers observing them and saying how they seemed to be able to glow and pulsate, change color . . . right?"

"Precisely," said Nemo. "I've seen them, the big ones

112

that is, several miles down, all huddling together along underwater canyons. If *The Nautilus* shuts down her running lights, you can see them, silky and pale, floating in the darkness, flashing colored messages across their trunks: blues and reds and oranges, all iridescent, like Chinese silk waving in a breeze. Beautiful."

"Are they dangerous?" I asked.

"Not usually. The one that Kent recalled was inadvertently rousted from its breeding ground when *The Nautilus* had a temporary power failure and we just plummeted right into its territory."

Nemo then directed us to another spiral staircase that led to the third and final level of the submarine. "And now, you will see the heart of *The Nautilus*," he said, ushering us below.

The first chamber which we descended upon was similar to that described by Verne through Kent—a simply designed, circular room with a hatch in the center of the floor. All around the walls were the familiar diving suits and brass helmets hanging on separate racks. "The suits with which you are already acquainted," said Nemo, brushing past them with an almost indifferent wave of his arm. I almost got the impression that he was a bit put out with Verne for having stolen some of his fire.

He directed us through another bulkhead door and down a long, dimly lit corridor. We passed several closed hatches, which Nemo paused to open briefly. He showed us their interiors which contained workshops, filled with all manner of tool, both manual and powered. There were electric ovens, forges, crucibles and kilns, torches and tanks, valves and regulators, generators, and devices which defied recognition. It was like a vast storehouse of clutter and wonder, and just looking at it made me admire this strange captain even more.

"But this is nothing," said Nemo, as if he could read my thoughts. "You should see the workshops and labs at my home base. Ah! There is a place where a man can work! But come, I must still show my most magnificent achievement. This way please."

He indicated further passage down the corridor from

113

which I could now feel the thrumming vibrations of the vessel's great engines churning and driving, filling the steel and the air with a steady hum. We arrived at a hatch that was sealed in the center of the floor in a small antechamber. Leaning down, Nemo slowly unwound the wheel lock, and as the door swung open I could see its immense thickness.

"Lead shielding," he said slowly. "Look below, Alexander, and tell me if you recognize anything."

Peering through the hatch, I saw yet another chamber, although it was located behind a depth of leaded glass of a thickness I couldn't determine. In the center of the chamber was a cube, perhaps a meter on a side, with black rods crisscrossing and passing through the cube. Also from its sides ran three thick conduits which all converged and ran aft toward the sounds of the engines. What I was looking at was a simple, but obviously efficient, nuclear reactor.

"You have fission power?" I could only look at him, while feeling like a child marveling at his father's great strength.

"I knew that you would recognize it," said Nemo. "It heats distilled seawater which, when turned to steam, drives a turbine, which provides torque and power and electricity for all my needs."

"This is impossible," said Ruffin. "The technology of your era—it doesn't provide for something like this. *Does* it, Bryan?" He looked at me.

"Yeah, it does. As long as you've got the fissionable materials. Everything else could be made from existing technologies. Don't you remember that spate of articles in the college journals about how anyone could make a nuclear bomb in his basement with a little plutonium?"

Ruffin nodded.

"A nuclear bomb?" asked Nemo.

"Unfortunately, yes," I said.

"I've been working on the calculations and theories that would give rise to an explosive variation of the reactor," said Nemo. "But I am puzzled about the notion that a chain-reaction process would eventually stop. Isn't it possible that the atmosphere itself could go on reacting, exploding as it were, until the entire planet was consumed?"

"You know, when the scientists of my age exploded the first atomic device, there were those among them that feared exactly that," I said.

"And still they went ahead with the experiment?"

"There was only one way to find out, wasn't there?"

"Mankind is truly mad," said Nemo.

Ruffin shook his head. "You're just finding that out?"

Nemo smiled sadly. "No, my friend, Ruffin. Certainly not, especially since I fear that we shall all be counted among their number."

There was an awkward moment of silence as we all regarded each other, feeling as if maybe we had walked back to the ballroom floor with our flies unzipped.

Nemo broke the silence. "But come now and see the engines themselves."

We were led through an anterior bulkhead into the engine room itself, where five crewmen monitored gauges and supervised the smooth operation of the double driveshaft, slung with massive counterbalances, flywheels, and bearings. The air was filled with the almost solid sound of moving steel. There was the smell of machine oil and graphite and human sweat; it was an elemental mixture of odors and sounds that permeated me with a sensation of power. There is, I think, a certain beauty in the appreciation of a superbly functioning machine; there is something in that beauty that sparks the mind. But maybe that's just a perverted romantic view of the Industrial Revolution, yes? In any case, the engine room of *The Nautilus* held some kind of primal appeal for me.

As we were escorted from the engine room, Nemo continued to speak. "The rest of the vessel is devoted to storage, ballast tanks, air tank reservoirs, and defense systems."

"What about armaments?" asked Ruffin as we passed through the corridor toward the spiral case leading upward. "I haven't seen a thing."

Nemo grinned coyly. "There is a concealed 70 mm

115

cannon, designed by none other than Barbicane himself, which may be elevated above deck just behind the command bridge. It uses incendiary shells and an improvement on Greek fire—jellied petrochemicals."

"Napalm," I said, cringing inwardly at the thought of what such a weapon would do to the wooden ships of Nemo's time.

"What's that?" said the captain.

"That's the name for it in my time. We used refined gasoline—a highly volatile petrochemical—in a colloidal suspension. Nasty stuff."

"So have my experiments with it verified. I truly hope that I shall only need to use it but once in my life," said Nemo. He looked away from me, but I could feel the years of obsession smoldering within him.

As we climbed the staircase, he continued to talk. "There is also a more complex version of the electric gun, which Verne ascribed to my divers, affixed in the prow of The Nautilus. Its range is considerable and it has the effect of burning out steel plate of thicknesses up to eight inches."

"Why no torpedoes?" I asked.

"I considered their deployment, but they seem so primitive to me. The reliability factor is 50 percent at best, and I usually strive for higher efficiencies than that. No, gentlemen, in my quest for The Kraken I am confident in the weapons that I have on hand. Although I admit to experimenting with several new offensive tools . . ."

"Such as?" Ruffin pressed him as we entered the level where the crew's quarters, including our own, were located.

"The field of subsonics and resonance factors intrigues me," said the captain. "So does the idea of concentrating heat energy into a tight beam. I have been conducting some interesting experiments in both fields at my home base."

"Where's that?" I said nonchalantly.

Nemo wheeled on me, his charming smiles and idiosyncratic grins now gone. "I'm sorry, Alexander, but I can't tell you that."

116

The statement was flat and to the point. I got the message.

I was going to change the subject, when Nemo spoke once again. "It's odd when you consider the turns our tour and conversation have taken, but everything seems loosely connected, related even."

"What do you mean?" I said, noticing that he had led us quietly down the corridor to the entrance to my quarters.

"All the talk about weapons and strategy and location . . . if I did not know better to the contrary, I would suspect you of being an accomplice to my embittered enemy!"

Ruffin and I exchanged quick glances. "What's that?" I said slowly.

"Think of it, Alexander. I am in the midst of tracking down *The Kraken,* when a mysterious surface vessel appears upon the scene. I know from my instruments that this odd vessel contains electric instruments and sophisticated engines. I know that this ship is no invention or extension of my own technologies, and I can think of only one other who could be capable of such things. Ergo, you are of Robur's camp, and I am being lured into an ingenious trap."

"Trap!" Ruffin started to smile nervously, as if to dispel the very logical extrapolations of the captain. I turned and saw Bischoff, the burly first mate, emerge from the inner shadows of my quarters, and for the first time, I started to get a bit uptight. These guys weren't fooling around.

"Please, Mr. Ruffin, allow me to continue. And so when I saw your ship blown to smithereens by the retreating *Kraken,* I was at first astonished, until I realized that one such as Robur is not beyond such Byzantine methods to achieve his ends. Could he not have purposely blown up his own surface ship for the express purpose of forcing my humanitarian instincts upon myself? Could he not have done such a thing, knowing full well that I would give up my chase to rescue innocent survivors of his foul deed?"

I nodded my head. "Yeah, I guess he could have done that . . . but he didn't, believe me."

"Oh, it's not necessary to believe you, Alexander. I have already checked things out for myself. While we were at dinner, I had Bischoff throroughly check through the belongings you hauled aboard. As much as I wished to discount your story of passing through one of the fluxgates, I was convinced of it when I received the book of Verne which you mentioned so obligingly, and after I had inspected the weapons—yes, the weapons—which you secreted aboard my vessel."

"Listen, I didn't secret them aboard. They just happened to be stored in that chest and things that we were able to salvage from the wreckage, that's all."

He waved me off into silence.

"No need to explain, Alexander. Coincidences abound in this universe. I understand. I am convinced that the weapons, the rifle and the handgun, could not have been produced by the technology of my fluxworld. I know that my own forges could not duplicate such steel, nor could my machine shop achieve the tolerances exhibited in that rifle. Oddly enough, those guns—something that would have convinced a lesser man than myself of your evil intentions—have vindicated you."

It was just at that moment that I lapsed into one of those rapid-fire, revelation-hitting-you-in-an-instant kind of thoughts. I realized that my personality had changed drastically in the few days that I had been in the presence of Nemo. I mean, when I seriously considered him and all his eccentric affectations, I saw him as a semilikable, odd kind of chap whom if I had met him at a cocktail party or at a bus stop, I would have ceased paying attention to after a few Bloody Marys or crosstown shuttles, respectively.

But somehow, on board *The Nautilus,* on board *his* vessel, Nemo seemed to become much more than what he seemed. I found myself deferring to him, respecting him, actually tempering my somewhat abrasive, forceful personality so that I was a more gracious and tolerable guest. There were few people who had that kind of effect on me,

118

an effect powerful enough to either consciously or unconsciously elicit a change in my usual demeanor. I realized that Nemo was a more powerful man than I had at first outwardly suspected; he was wise and lucid and preceptive—as well as a bit insane.

THIRTEEN

AFTER THAT little scene, Nemo left us to our quarters, saying that we would be soon leaving the North Pacific heading south through Polynesia and eventually around the cape. He invited us to lunch in his chambers later on in the day and begged his leave so that he could devote a few hours to some private study.

I went in and sat on the edge of my bunk, eyeing the sea-stained steamer trunk that Nemo's men had so efficiently gone through. "That was some kind of little confrontation, wasn't it?" I said to Ruffin who was standing silently just inside the door to the cabin.

"No shit. You know, the way he treated us right from the start . . . I never had any *idea* that he might have thought we were with Robur."

"You think *I* did?"

"He's a lot more sly than I gave him credit for," said Ruffin.

"Yeah, I was just thinking the same thing."

Ruffin balanced himself on the edge of the washbasin. "Have you given much thought to how dangerous this whole scene might be?"

"I've been starting to think about that, too." I tried to laugh but didn't do a very good job of it.

Ruffin went on. "I mean, he's serious about boffing this Robur guy, right? And what about that atomic pile downstairs? Christ, are we safe with that thing around?"

"I don't know . . ."

"You don't know! Shit, Bryan, you're the physicist, and *you* don't know?"

"Look, I didn't get a chance to inspect the thing, you
120

know? It *appeared* to be okay. There really isn't much to them if you understand what you're doing."

"I can't believe it, anyway," said Ruffin, wringing his hands together. "Atomic energy in the world of 1870 . . . it's crazy! It's impossible! I don't give a shit how smart he is. . . . How in hell did he ever stumble upon nuclear physics?"

"I meant to ask him about it when he showed us that reactor, but I just didn't get around to it. He kept talking so fast and moving us along that I just didn't get into it. I'll ask him though, don't worry about that."

"You'll probably get some kind of long-winded answer too. The man can talk, that's for sure."

I grinned, but I knew that most of what Nemo had to say was worth listening to. "Yeah, but there's still a *lot* of things I want to ask him about. I mean, think of where we *are*, Derek! Think of it! We're in a parallel universe, an . . . alternate earth! It's crazy, it's unthinkable, yet we're here. It's so natural, so real, that I forget about it most of the time. We've got to ask him about the fluxgate business. It's got to be one of the most fantastic discoveries of all time."

"Sure, sure, Professor, but there's something else I think we should ask him about."

"What's that?" I said.

"Like when is he going to take us through one of those gates of his and get us back to the good old U.S.A. that we all know and love?"

"Oh yeah, that. You know, I've noticed that he hasn't even come close to mentioning anything like that. But I don't know, I've been so caught up in the discovery of this whole thing that I haven't really thought much about getting back."

"Well, *I* have. Somehow the thought of spending the rest of my life chasing around some kook in a tin can doesn't excite me, you know what I mean?"

"Yeah, I get you."

Ruffin stood up and started pacing within the small confines of the cabin. "And there's another thing I've been thinking about. Didn't Kent or you or somebody say

121

something about time flowing at different speeds in the alternate worlds?"

"I think so, yeah, that makes sense."

"Well, Christ, don't you see what that means? The longer we stay in this . . . this dimension, or whatever it is, the more time in our own world is *ripping* by! I don't know what the conversion table would be, but think about it a minute. If Verne picked up this guy Kent around 1860—*our* time—and Nemo said that Kent was exiled to the boat ten years ago—*his* time—then that means that our alternate world, our dimension, is flowing at a rate that's *ten* times faster than Nemo's. Even if we only stayed in this place six years, almost everybody we know would be dead and gone back in our own . . . our own earth."

"Yeah, I've been thinking about that," I said slowly.

"You've been *thinking* about it?!? Well, doesn't it bother you? I mean, is that all you've been doing is *thinking* about it?"

"Huh?" I knew what Ruffin was getting at, but for some perverse reason I felt like stringing him along for a bit.

"Bryan, what the hell is with you?"

I laughed. "Hey, take it easy, will you? I was just kidding. Look, I *know* we can't stay here very long. We'll have to talk to him about getting us back. I know that. Finding those journals of Kent's and then wanting to find out, I mean *really* find out, if they were true . . . well, that was the real joy in this whole adventure."

"Oh yeah . . . so now what?"

"So now, I find that I'm fascinated with old Nemo and I'd love to see him get his man, but I know that I should be getting back to the 'real' world, the good old U.S.A., as you so aptly phrased it."

Ruffin smiled. "Well, thanks. I was starting to get a little worried about you there for a while."

"Nothing to worry about. I understood what you were getting at."

"It just that things seemed to be happening so fast there

122

for a while. Too much information coming in too quickly, if you know what I mean."

I nodded and leaned back on my cot, feeling very exhausted even though it was still midday.

Ruffin stood up. "Well, listen, I think I'm going to go above, take another look around the bridge, watch the water, or something. You want to come along?"

I shook my head. "Nah, I think I'll rest. I've some more thinking to do."

Ruffin grinned again. "Hmmm, that might be dangerous. Okay, I'm getting out of here. Between you and Nemo, I don't know who's worse." He turned and left the cabin, his boots echoing along the steel corridor.

I lay there for a moment staring at the cold walls of the room, rehashing Ruffin's conversation. My friend was right. We *did* have to get out of here. We had about as much place in this world as a digital watch on George Washington's arm. Fascinating as it all was, we just didn't fit. Things in Nemo's world were tantalizingly close enough to our own so that we were often lured into a false sense of security, but when I thought about it, I knew that it was a "bad thing" for us to even consider staying here for very long. I began to appreciate fully how much of a prisoner Verne's fictional passengers must have felt aboard his *Nautilus*.

Yes, I thought, *there are going to be some interesting things to discuss over lunch.*

But I didn't know at that point that our meal schedule was about to be rudely interrupted.

FOURTEEN

THERE CAME echoing through the submarine the most godawful noise I'd ever heard. It sounded like a cross between some saurian in its death agonies and those buzzer alarms with which General Electric insists upon waking you up. It had to be some kind of Klaxon or alarm, and I quickly sprang from my cot and raced up the corridor.

When I reached the spiral staircase leading upward, I noticed several members of the crew moving stoically and perfunctorily toward their stations, and I was reminded of all those World War II sea movies. I guess sailors really *do* look like that.

Stopping the last fellow going belowdecks, I asked him what was happening.

"*The Kraken,* sir. Bridge's spotted her, and we're giving chase." The man in the dark blue turtleneck and trousers turned and scurried down the stairway.

I went in the opposite direction, arriving in the bridge to see Ruffin, Nemo, Bischoff, and the usual operators at their stations. Through the bubble-eye glass I could see the underneath surface of the sea as *The Nautilus* angled upward toward it.

"Steady now," said Nemo. "Start leveling off. That's it."

The operators labored over their controls and the first mate eased levers in front of the helm, playing them as if they were a finely tuned instrument. I could feel subtle changes in the motion of the submarine as we broke the surface and became somewhat at the mercy of the ocean swells and wind.

The sky was gray and low-slung, dark clouds crept along the horizon. Far ahead was an array of black specks bobbing and frequently disappearing behind furrows in the churning sea.

"What's that out there?" I asked, since everyone's attention seemed to be focused on the tiny objects in the distance.

"Whaling fleet," said Nemo.

"And Robur's out there too somewhere?"

"It's most likely. Our instruments detect a large metallic object. It can be nothing save *The Kraken*." Nemo reached above him and brought a retractable scope into play. Focusing it, he peered through the left eye-port of *The Nautilus*.

"Steady as she goes now. Full speed, Mr. Bischoff."

"What are you going to do?" I asked.

Nemo turned from the glass and looked at me. His face was grim, etched with years of case-hardened determination. "I'm going to seek out my enemy, Alexander."

"Do you see him yet?" I peered through the port and saw that the whaling ships were no longer black smears on the sea but were resolving themselves into distinct shapes. The sea curled away from our prow in ever-unfurling curtains. *The Nautilus* had surprising speed.

"No, he's probably submerged, probably playing games with those poor whalers."

"Games?"

"He sinks them," said Bischoff.

"Why?" I asked, straining to see what was ahead for us.

"For the sheer, mad pleasure of it," said Nemo. "God knows why he does it, man! Did I not say that he is a madman?" Nemo paused and asked for soundings from one of his operators. After digesting the data, he said, "Take her to port, Mr. Bischoff, five points, easy now . . . that's it, steady now. How's that, Mr. Gray?"

Gray, the operator of the detection console, nodded. "We're closing, Captain."

"You've found him?" I asked.

"He's accelerating, sir," said Gray.

Suddenly there was a blossom of orange and red, an

125

ugly stain billowing upward in the sea and sky. "God be cursed!" cried Nemo. "He's taken one of them!"

To the starboard side of our prow I could see the flaming hulk of one of the wooden ships. As we drew ever closer, I could see the cinders and fragments of burning wood still drifting down like black flakes into the sea. The ship burned furiously, since it was probably filled to the waterline with whale parts, blubber, and easily combustible whale oil. Several men tried to launch longboats, while others simply streamed over the gunwales and into the churning waters. Two of the other whalings ships hove and came as close to the burning wreck as they could without risking their own rigging set aflame or fouled in the smoking, toppling masts.

As the survivors were dragged aboard, the stricken whaler listed cruelly to her starboard side and slipped beneath the whitecaps. I could almost hear the burning oil and wood hissing and boiling as they were snuffed out, could almost hear the anguished cries of men at the mercy of the cruel waters.

"The bastard," said Ruffin. "They're helpless against him!"

"Hard to the port side," said Nemo. "Take her down two fathoms!"

The crew leaned into Nemo's commands, and the submarine turned to avoid the rescue mission of the two whaling ships to slip unseen beneath the chaos. When the maneuver was completed, only a small fraction of the command bridge peeped above the surface, only the upper arches of the eye-shaped windows burned white from the light of the sky. Everything else was bathed in murky blueness.

My attention was fixed upon the windows. A dark shape loomed ahead of us in the depths. "What's that there!? Look!"

Nemo laughed. "That," he said, as *The Nautilus* glided past an enormous black hulk, "is a cetacean, Alexander. A whale."

Several members of the crew grinned, and I felt like an ass. As the submarine grew closer to the great sea mammal, I could see the furrowed ridges of its great body, its tapering length, and eventually its streamlined flukes.

"A rorqual," said Nemo nonchalantly. *"Balaenoptera physalus,* the 'fin whale,' as they call it in these waters. It's quite plentiful and can get to be of considerable size. Biggest in the world except for the Great Blues."

"Did he see us?" I asked, wondering what it would be like for us to go careening into one of the monsters.

"Oh, yes, of course, Alexander," said Nemo. "The whale is a most intelligent creature. He recognizes *The Nautilus* for what it is, and he righteously stays clear of us."

I continued to watch our progress through the water and presently saw other whales slithering out of our path. Then they became so plentiful that they practically obscured my vision of anything else. Christ, they were filling up the sea! No wonder the whaling ships were collected in these waters. It was like shooting fish in a barrel.

"Got a new fix, sir," said crewman Gray. "I think he spotted us."

"Take her down, Mr. Bischoff. Ahead full," said Nemo. "Give me a new heading, Mr. Gray."

"Twenty-seven, mark nine. Range, twelve hundred yards, sir."

I stood behind the men, watching intently as Ruffin eased back to stand by me. The deck took a steep slant as the submarine plunged downward. I could feel a tension beginning at the back of my neck, and it tightened like a fist, spreading pain up into my head to my temples. I realized that my jaws were clamped tightly shut, and there was a metallic taste in my mouth.

The view through the windows was startlingly clear and as *The Nautilus* cleared the school of whales, I could see smaller fish and other creatures of the sea whip past our view, indicating the speed of our descent.

"Directly ahead of us, sir," said Gray. "He's turning to give us a stand!"

"Turn on the electric fencing," said Nemo, and someone reached to throw some levers on one of the control consoles.

127

"What's that?" I asked impulsively, even though I knew that the beginning of a battle was no time to be in the way.

Nemo fielded the question calmly, never taking his attention away from the eye-port. "The outer hull of the vessel can be electrified, Alexander. It serves as a partial protective net against *The Kraken's* torpedoes, which are electrically powered, and may be able to explode the warheads prematurely."

No one spoke for several minutes as *The Nautilus* struggled to close the gap on its prey. I watched through the dark, swirling sea, waiting for a glimpse of Robur's ship. The waiting was the worst part. If we had been suffering through a pitched battle it would have been preferable to the silence and the smell of men's sweat and fear thickly all about me.

"We should be within visual range, now," said Gray.

Everyone was scanning the sea around, looking for some sign of the enemy craft. To our starboard side I could see a vast undersea peak rising up as we plunged past it. The peak gave way to a long jagged ridge that slopped off into darkness. Along the sides of the ridge long strands of seaweed waved and swayed like fingers reaching out to us.

"There he is," said Nemo. Pointing to a spot somewhere beyond and slightly above the ridge.

I strained to see as Nemo studied our prey through his scope, and presently saw Robur's ship. It was long and slender, more streamlined than *The Nautilus,* and probably not as spacious. The prow tapered down to a flat, mantalike head, with fins that gradually diminished into the contours of the hull. One third of the way back the dorsal side, there was a rakelike conning tower, then the lines were unbroken until the aft section displayed diving planes and a meshed section which protected her screws. Its hull gleamed dully in the semidarkness and suggested that it was fabricated of some kind of aluminum alloy, although I doubted it. At any rate, it was a much brighter target than the steel blue plating of *The Nautilus'* hull.

No one spoke as our vessel closed the distance to *The*

Kraken, which seemed to hover tantalizingly just above the undersea ridge that passed our starboard side. As we drew closer I noticed that the conning tower of Robur's ship seemed to be moving, actually rotating, like the turret on a modern tank. I mentioned this to Nemo and he confirmed this, saying that Robur fired his torpedoes from the conning tower, and that the turret design afforded much greater maneuverability and firepower.

"Alert the electric-gun crew, Mr. Bischoff," said Nemo. "Hard to port, ten degrees. Now!"

Just as he said this, as if acting upon some warrior's instinct, I saw a spout of bubbles issue from the face of *The Kraken's* conning tower, and as our vessel banked left and slightly down, I saw the lumbering, but deadly, torpedo slip past our starboard flank.

"Now, bring her up fifteen degrees."

The Nautilus angled upward so that we were passing above our enemy's aft section at a declination that would force him to roll over on his side in order to fire upon us. It was a good tactical move that would buy time for Nemo as he put his own attack plan into operation.

When we were directly overhead, Nemo lashed out another set of maneuvers, and suddenly the submarine was diving down upon the still-motionless *Kraken* like a falcon with its wings tucked and its talons extended. We were no more than three hundred meters away as we dove at a sixty-degree angle, everyone holding on to handrails and grips for support.

"Gun crew, aim and fire," said Nemo calmly.

It was a daring, almost suicidal strategy. No one spoke, could speak, I'd guess, as we hurtled downward. As I watched, the dark blue water was laced with a bright bluish-yellow light, and a bolt of electric energy flashed from our prow. It struck several degrees to the starboard side of *The Kraken,* exploding the undersea ridge in a storm of swirling sand and debris. Robur's vessel rocked from the concussion, and *The Nautilus* was buffeted as it sliced through the shock waves and threatened to cleave the enemy like a knife through bread.

We came so close that I could count the torpedo tube
129

openings on its conning tower, the number of rivets in its armor plate. I braced myself for the impact, still, curiously, not thinking about my impending death—something I'd always thought I would in such a situation.

"Blow ballast tanks five and six, take her up and starboard ten degrees." Nemo spoke calmly once again, and the submarine responded to his commands like a thoroughbred on the final turn.

There was a vicious change in direction and the G forces ripped at my stomach. I hung on to a handhold, watching *The Kraken* disappear from the glass eye-port as we ripped away from the collision course. "Jesus Christ!" screamed Ruffin as he lost his grip on a handrail and slid violently across the deck. I reached out to catch him, but he slid by like a hocky puck going into the net.

"Range and position, Mr. Gray," said Nemo as the submarine easily righted itself.

"He's moving off, sir. Two thousand meters, turning slowly. Twenty-one degrees port."

Nemo calculated quickly to himself and issued new commands. *The Nautilus* crew responded immediately, and we were diving again for another attack run.

"Torpedoes coming, sounds like two, maybe three."

"Evasive action ten degrees, dorsal hook."

A few seconds of silence as everyone waited. "Two of them passed us, sir," said Gray, still listening to his headset. "The other one's getting—"

The concussion rocked us like a gigantic sledge. Even the operators were thrown from their chairs, and the submarine started listing to the starboard side.

Nemo scrambled to his feet, urging everyone else to their stations. There was a gash over his left eye, and a generous streamer of blood colored his cheekbone, getting lost in his beard. "Get a damage report, Mr. Bischoff," he said, and the first mate rushed, almost threw himself, down the spiral ladder.

"Regain course. Handle as she may, gentlemen. Gun crew, ready!"

More slowly now, *The Nautilus,* veered back into its descent, and as we cleared the ridge, I could see *The*

Kraken far below, nestled at the bottom of the undersea canyon, half-protected by an outcropping of rock. There was a fusillade of bubbles as two more torpedoes were launched from its conning tower. Everyone watched them corkscrew upward, but it was obvious that their course was awry and that they wouldn't touch us.

"Gun crew, aim and fire when ready," said Nemo.

Again the sea brightened in front of us, and for an instant it looked as if somebody had strung neon tubing across the distance between us and the enemy. Blue yellow bolts probed into the shadowed undersea canyon. The first struck the outcropping and severed it from the face of the cliff. A giant fragment cascaded down upon *The Kraken,* reaching it just as the second electric bolt struck its port-side diving planes. There was a brilliant bluewhite flash, and the image of a shimmering halo surrounding the enemy vessel's conning tower burned my retinas like a strobe light.

"Good shot," said Nemo in a low, guttural voice. "A glancing blow, but that should slow him up for a while." Then louder: "Hard to starboard, take her up fifteen degrees and level off."

Bischoff appeared in the stairwell, soaked in sea foam and smelling of machine oil. "Ballast tank Three ruptured. Number One gyro damaged. Electric gun is going out—generator freezing up. Dorsal rudder inoperative."

"Hull damage?" said Nemo.

"Three crew quarters above ballast tank show stress signs. I've had them sealed off and buttressed. Gyro needs to be checked before we can attempt to repair it. I wouldn't trust it till we can have a look at it."

Nemo nodded. "Shut down gyroscope one," he said to one of the operators, who immediately threw two levers on his board.

"All right, that's going to cut down on our maneuverability. Make us too vulnerable. We must disengage, Mr. Bischoff."

"Aye, sir," said the first mate, assuming command in the bridge and directing the operators.

Nemo walked away from his command post and pulled

131

an undersea atlas from a nook by the navigator's table. approached him as he flipped through the thick pages.

"Where're we going now?"

Nemo looked up at me. There was a sadness, a resignation, in his eyes. "We go home. For a while. This campaign has been halted temporarily."

"How long will it take?"

"That depends on many things, Mr. Alexander. I don't know yet." He stopped at the pages he had been searching for, and his attention was snapped away from me. After a few consultations and checks upon the table charts he spoke to the helmsmen. "Take a southwesterly heading. Hard to port, then follow the sea bottom. I want a twenty-four-hour watch on the ballast tank area. All reports of stress come immediately to me."

Nemo walked back to the eye-port and stared into the depths. "Status on the enemy, Mr. Gray?"

"He's laying in, sir. Might be waiting for us to make a move."

"Undoubtedly. All right, get her underweigh."

There was a lurching motion as the submarine's engine drove us through the water. If there was any difficulty in controlling movement, I could not tell, although the operators and Bischoff all seemed to be extremely well occupied. No one spoke for a few minutes as The Nautilus slid silently from the protective ridge of the undersea canyon, following its contours deeper and deeper into the indigo waters.

"He's following us, sir," said Gray.

"Closing?"

"No, sir, holding at four thousand meters."

"Any signs of damage or impairment?"

"Hard to say at this distance, sir."

Nemo paused, slowly tapping a fist into his left hand. "Take evasive action, Mr. Bischoff."

The crew responded, and The Nautilus went through a controlled series of dives, combined with pitch and yaw maneuvers that would require any pursuer to duplicate them. The loss of the number one gyroscope and the dorsal rudder did not help even a little bit.

"Still holding at four thousand," said Gray after five minutes had passed in tense silence.

"What do you think he's doing?" I asked.

Nemo seemed to be lost in thought, gradually coming out of it to stare at me mutely. ". . . Good question, Mr. Alexander. He may be partially disabled . . . or he may be playing some sort of game. It's obvious that he intends to remain on our tail."

"But why?" said Ruffin. "Why doesn't he close in for the kill?"

"He may not be able to do that. Or if he knows we're hurting," I said, "maybe he wants to follow us back to the home base where we must go if we are going to make repairs."

Nemo nodded. "Yes, I've considered that. No, if Robur thought he could finish me off, he would be on us like a hawk. If he can't, it would be of almost equal importance that he discover my home base." The captain turned away from us and consulted his navigational charts again. Then to Bischoff: "Take us down the canyon to the Caroline Divide. Compute a course through the Trench. He can't follow us there."

Bischoff nodded and started immediately to the task. Nemo regarded us again. "All right, gentlemen, there's nothing else we can do here. Shall we dine?"

Ruffin and I agreed and prepared to leave the bridge, while Nemo issued some final instructions that he be notified instantly if *The Kraken* were to attempt any change in position or possible strategy.

I walked down the corridor toward Nemo's chambers, wondering what we would be doing even twenty-four hours from that moment. There was a good possibility that we could all be settling down to a few centuries of slow-cured brine-pickling if Robur got lucky with another torpedo attack. Suddenly all my questions seemed inconsequential, and I found myself wondering about more vital matters—like my young and virile body.

When we reached Nemo's chambers, the table was already set, although there was no sign of his steward. The

133

captain directed us to our chairs as he leaned over and pulled the summons rope that would bring us our lunch.

"How do you know *The Kraken* can't follow us down?" asked Ruffin.

Nemo chuckled politely. "Mr. Ruffin, this is not the first time I have encountered that madman. We have faced each other all over the seven seas. We are both aware of the capabilities of each other's vessel."

"How do you find each other?" I asked. "I mean, it's a lot of ocean, you know."

Nemo smiled. "There are several reasons. First, Robur is a very predictable creature. He has a predilection for certain crimes, in certain geographic locales. By keeping a line on the Continent, I am able to trace the trail of his atrocities with a fair percentage of accuracy and encounter him in those locales. In addition, you must remember that he is the only metallic object of any size within the seas. That makes his detection more easily accomplished."

"Does he have any ways of detecting you, or predicting the movements of *The Nautilus?*" I asked.

Nemo paused as the hatch at the end of the room opened and an elderly man dressed in whites entered pushing a sterling silver serving cart. "Aah, we dine now. . . . Thank you, Valery," he said to the man who courteously nodded and began placing the steaming plates before us.

Nemo ignored my question as he meticulously described each of the ocean delicacies. It was a favorite quirk of his, and he seemed to get a special delight in seeing our reactions to the unexpectedly *haute cuisine*.

While Ruffin marveled over the anemone souffle, I studied the face of our server. There was something about his sharp, pointed features that looked familiar, but I could not pin it down. He looked vaguely like someone I knew, but the name, the place, escaped me. The man looked up and noticed that I was staring at him. I thought for an instant a similar flash of recognition flared behind his eyes, but it quickly passed to be replaced by a look of indifference.

Then the man was gone, and Nemo was lifting his

wineglass in mock toast. "May we survive to fight another day!"

We joined him in his toast with as much gusto as we could manage under the circumstances, and began the meal.

"What was that you were asking me, Alexander?" Nemo's eyes bored into me with the casual intensity that was his hallmark.

"Oh, I was just wondering if he has any ways of predicting the movements of *The Nautilus*. Robur, I mean."

Nemo paused to sip some wine. "That's an interesting question. I, of course, do not know for certain. It is quite obvious that he has some degree of electric sophistication, probably on the level of *The Nautilus*. But there *have* been times in the past when he seemed to encounter me on more than the off chance."

"So you don't know?"

"Not really. Why do you ask?" He looked at me intently.

"I'm not sure. I was just thinking that it's a little odd that you two can seem to find each other so easily . . . so conveniently."

Nemo smiled. "Yes, it is odd, isn't it." He seemed to think upon those words, as was also his custom. It was probably one of his most valuable assets—he never discarded any notion out of hand, but rather took the time to weigh it and evaluate it on its own merits. "But I don't think it's a primary concern of ours at this time. First we must successfully elude the enemy, return to my headquarters, and make the needed repairs."

No one spoke for several minutes, preferring to concentrate on the delicate flavors of the meal. I kept thinking back to the face of the chef, or steward, or whoever it was who had served us. There was something about that guy that was bothering me, but I couldn't place it. I sat there in silence, sipping some tea with a Carlton, but nothing would come to me.

Nemo interrupted me and my thoughts. "After the meal, I think it would be advisable for you two to remain in your cabins until we have dealt with the present situation. It will be safer there, and you will not be in anyone's way."

"I'd like to help, if I could," said Ruffin.

"You could, Mr. Ruffin, if you were properly trained. But I don't think this is either the time or the place." He smiled graciously, but both Ruffin and I knew that we had been effectively put down.

"I was wondering about something else," I said, anxious to break the awkward silence that followed Nemo's words. "Derek and I were talking about your atomic reactor, and I never did get the chance to ask you much about it . . ."

Nemo's eyebrow's arched for an instant as he drew deeply on his cigar. "What is it that you wish to know, Mr. Alexander?"

"Quite simply, how in hell did you ever come up with it? I mean, is there anybody on the Continent, or America that's been working on it? What was your original source of . . . inspiration, I guess that's the right word?"

Nemo smiled. "It is a very long story, Mr. Alexander, and I would prefer to show you how I came upon it, rather than merely tell you. In fact, I was planning to give a very special tour of a most interesting region of the globe. However, my enemy interrupted my intentions."

"Tour?"

"Yes, but no matter. It seems that we will be forced to travel that region at any rate. And so you will soon understand."

"That'll put us ahead of where I am now, because I don't know what you're talking about."

Laughing, Nemo flicked his ashes into a large brass tray. "I would be extremely surprised if you did, Mr. Alexander. But don't worry. Everything will become eminently clear, in its due time."

I could hardly wait.

FIFTEEN

AFTER WE FINISHED dining and had been "escorted" to our cabins by one of Nemo's men, I had the feeling that I would hear the outer door click shut and that we would be prisoners just like old Arronax et al. But there was no click, and as I eased into my bunk for a moment of rest. I found myself thinking about my fear of flying and my contempt for doing things in which I had little or no control of the total situation. But here I was in one of the most uncontrollable sets of circumstances I'd ever encountered, and it wasn't gnawing at me like I knew it should be.

If this was soldier-of-fortune-ing, I decided that I had had about enough. Thoughts flashed through my head. Did I really give a damn where Nemo got his idea for nuclear power? Did I really care if he finally zapped old crazy Robur? Christ, I didn't *know*. And I always liked to know what was going on in my head. I always liked to have things straight in my head, and in this submarine, in some alternate reality, involved with men who were maybe a little too brilliant for their own good, I didn't feel like I had much of anything straight.

As I lay on the bunk, I started thinking of all those green trees in Brattleboro, and how they would be turning into all the fire colors come September. Walking down the shaded autumn streets, a person could come to terms with himself, with his little piece of the cosmos, and how he fit into it. I started thinking of what I would do up there if/when I ever returned. I had always liked building things. Perhaps I could do some cabinetmaking, just on weekends, in a small shop. Special orders for friends and things like that. I'd always wanted to try my hand at some

137

acting, too. There were probably lots of community theaters in the area, and if there weren't, I would just build one, that's all. Then there were those classical guitar lessons . . .

I had to get out of here.

I must have fallen off to sleep, a state brought on by a combination of the afternoon wine, the stress, and probably the unconscious desire simply to escape from all my current problems.

The knock on the door rang me awake with a start, and before I could get up, I saw one of the crewmen poke his head inside.

"The captain would like to see you in his chambers, Mr. Alexander."

"Okay, be right there. You have to wait for me?"

The man shook his head, and I waved him off, stumbled to the washbasin, and slapped some cold water on my face. I needed a shave, but I didn't feel like fooling with it. My long hair was in need of some good old twentieth-century-American dandruff shampoo, and I was again reminded of how attached I was to my own time and place in the universe. I also thought about how nice it would be to see a woman once again. I was frankly getting tired of seeing these serious, lantern-jawed sailors all the time.

Leaving the cabin, I saw some of the crew walking haggardly back to their bunks. There must have been a change of shift going on, but I assumed that we were still on battle alert, or whatever Nemo chose to call it.

He was waiting for me—if you want to call it that—at the brass-piped organ at the far end of his chambers. I stood in the door for a moment listening to him as he swayed ever so slightly to the left-hand counterpoint of what sounded like one of Bach's toccatas—although I could not place it, knowing only that it was *not* the overly famous horror-flick favorite, the one in D minor.

Nemo must have sensed my presence, because he stopped at the end of a quiet right-hand passage and turned slowly around on the stool. "You slept well?"

"How did you know I was sleeping?"

"My crewman reported to me, that's all." The captain paused. "There's no need to be so full of anxiety, Mr. Alexander. I have recent reports that Robur's vessel was indeed damaged in the engagement. He is having great difficulty keeping pace with us, and as soon as we enter the Trench, he will be totally unable to follow us."

"When is that supposed to happen?" I said, taking a seat on a pleated, silk-brocaded couch.

"Quite soon, that's why I called you here. You are about to witness a spectacle of nature that few men have had the good grace to encounter."

"The deeps," I said in a half-question.

Nemo nodded and walked to the iris window, which was at the moment closed. He reached for a lever behind a curtain, and the great circular window opened from the center outward as the armored panels were retracted. I could see nothing beyond the thick glass—a combination of the reflected interior room light and the utter blackness of the sea beyond it. Throwing another switch Nemo watched me as powerful floodlights that rimmed the exterior of the window burst on, cutting into the darkness and then banishing it for a range of perhaps fifty meters.

Below us I could vaguely make out the passing crags and peaks of undersea formations.

"The Marianas Trench, Mr. Alexander. A pathway into the deepest, most vile territory on the entire planet. Seven miles beneath the surface."

"How deep are we now?"

"Perhaps three miles."

"And Robur is still with us?"

Nemo shook his head. "No, he should be reaching his limits just about now." He grinned to himself, nodded in a small, personal way, as if acknowledging his own craftiness.

I peered into the ghostly illuminated world beyond the glass. Beyond the diffused range of the floods the depths threatened to close in like a fist upon the fragile sphere of light. I could sense the immensity that lay beyond our vision, the incredible pressure that spawned the night-world creatures of the Trench. Slowly, *The Nautilus* descended. As I stood there at the window, flickering, insubstantial shapes began to appear just at the farthest reaches of our light.

"We are attracting them," said Nemo. "They will be hesitant at first. They have few visitors down here as big as us, except for the occasional sperm whale or giant squid. But they are always hungry and they will come to us."

I continued to watch the cruel terrain pass infrequently beneath the glow of the lamps. There was nothing else, except the murkily illuminated sea and the shapes just beyond. Then something darted past us. I caught a fleeting glimpse of eyes and teeth. How diverse was nature and its cruel stepchild, evolution. What was it that stirred within some ancestral fish to spurn the upper ocean levels and retreat through the millennia to the empty cavern of the ocean floor? I knew that there was no plant life at these depths, and so there was only one food supply available: each other.

Soon other creatures wandered briefly into the lights: things that seemed to be parodies of real fish, like grotesque cartoons or caricatures from the mist of nightmare. There was one basic plan down here: eat—and everything that writhed and slithered through this dark sea conformed to that plan in the most obvious ways. Monstrously oversized mouths, studded with razorlike rows of teeth. Their eyes were flat like pools of spilled cream, dull and without the slightest trace of emotion or sentience. Most of them were at least 50 percent head and mouth, and many carried hideous, stalklike appendages from which dangled luminescent palps of flesh. It was like a man walking a dark street, carrying a lantern ahead of him at arm's length.

The deeper *The Nautilus*, the more bold and populous were the creatures. They floated by with eerie slowness, keeping pace with our dive and seeming to stare right into my eyes. They were natural swimming and eating machines—nothing less, nothing more. Their design was so frighteningly clear that it made me pause to consider how cold and indifferent the natural world can be. I mean, I agree with Thoreau and all those fellows who love it so dearly, but when you've seen these things down here, you have to wonder about the whole Scheme of Things. Man, in his "wisdom," likes to venerate himself, in light of his exalted position among the lesser creatures, because he can think and reason and feel ethical. But are there really any ethics in the natural world? There aren't any down here, I know that. I can *feel* that.

Nemo wants to devour Robur; and vice versa.

The things out there want to eat each other. When I think about it, there isn't really much difference.

"What do you think?" asked Nemo as the nightmares peered in at us.

I told him what had been passing through my mind, and he laughed politely. "Yes, I've often thought similar things about us. When I was at the Institute there were biologists who were urging the launching of expeditionary ships to dredge the depths because they believed that it was down here that the 'stuff' of Creation would be found—that primordial ooze that contained the secret and the essence of life. But they were wrong, Mr. Alexander. There is no creation down her. Only death, and the end of things."

We both stood silently for a moment as I watched the unending parade of the bizarre slip past us. The variety of shapes and experimental designs of the creatures was staggering and unclassifiable. There were animals down here that would never feel the sun's touch upon them, never have their bellies slit for the biologist's scalpel. They were as fascinating as they were frightening, and I had a hard time keeping my eyes off the damned things.

"Thousands of years ago much of this was closer to the surface. Hundreds of thousands, hundreds of millions, actually." Nemo gestured outward into the depths. "The planet is constantly changing, Mr. Alexander. Our passages upon it are brief and quite meaningless in the long run."

I felt like telling him about the nuclear power plants and the water pollution and the Air Quality Index and the

141

deterioration of the ozone layer because of our wish to smell nice and all that sort of thing. That might change his mind a little about how brief and meaningless our passages are. *No, Captain,* I thought, *we are quickly coming to the point where we could screw things up quite nicely for many thousands of years, thank you.*

Nemo started speaking again but was interrupted by a call on the ship's tube phones. "Excuse me, Mr. Alexander," was all he said, then walked over to the phones. He listened to the message, obviously from the bridge, issued some curt instructions in reply, then returned to where I was still standing. "We shall soon be approaching a very interesting archeological site. It will be there that I may answer all your questions."

"What about Robur?"

"He gave up the chase about an hour ago. We will be leaving the Trench now, and heading toward a point in the Equatorial Pacific that will be most instructional. Would you like some brandy?"

"Yeah, that sounds good."

Nemo sent for a steward, who in turn brought us snifters and a cut-glass decanter on a silver tray. When the man had departed and we had silently toasted one another and sipped the fiery, amber liquid, I looked up after his passage.

"He's not the same fellow that served us lunch, is he?"

"No, that's the regular steward. At lunch, he had been called to a battle station." Nemo looked at me, obviously curious as to my interest in the steward.

"Who was the guy that brought us lunch?"

"That was Valery. The chef and chief steward."

I wanted to tell him that the man looked achingly familiar to me but thought better of it. "Valery? That his first name, or last?"

"His name is Emile Valery, Mr. Alexander. He has been a member of my crew for almost two years, having signed him off a steamer in Reykjavík. Now, would you mind telling me what your sudden interest in my crew is all about?" Nemo sipped from his brandy glass, peering at me suspiciously through its curving glass.

142

"I can't explain it right now. I'm sorry, Captain. Just a funny thought I had, that's all. I'd like to check it out more thoroughly before I bother you with it."

"Very well, Mr. Alexander. Most curious, I must say." He looked past me through the window. "Ah, we are ascending. Soon they will be gone."

Turning, I looked out into the dark waters, where our floods now seemed to extend a sphere of pale light somewhat farther. The deep-sea horrors were fewer now, and less grotesque, if there can be such a qualified state of existence. "How long before we reach our . . . uh, next stop on the tour?"

"Within the hour, I should hope. Why?"

"There's something I'd like to check in my cabin. I'll be back in a few minutes. If that's all right with you, that is."

Nemo smiled and finished off his brandy. "Of course, Mr. Alexander, of course. I shall be expecting you."

I nodded and left the chambers. *Valery!* No wonder the man's face seemed familiar. I was sure that I had seen it before.

I followed the central corridor, looking for the hatch which would take me into the kitchen . . . and I wasn't the least bit hungry, either.

SIXTEEN

THE GALLEY, like everything else aboard the submarine, was a superior piece of forethought and design. Every available volume of space, every corner, every nook, was being used to full capacity. And, of course, everything was clean. The brightwork and brass, the porcelain and zinc, all shined from long hours of pride-filled polishing. There was a long counter-top constructed of laminated woods of alternating stripes of light and dark, and I imagined the trees which provided them were probably some dense, hard species only found on small islands off the coast of East Africa. Everywhere, the galley revealed Nemo's taste for exotically functional material and design.

As I entered the room, a steward was standing at the far end of the counter top with a large, flat blade, expertly dicing and trimming some kind of bright red seaweed. He looked up at me diffidently, then returned quickly to his work.

"Excuse me," I said, "but have you seen Mr. Valery?"

"He's in the back, dressing today's catch." The steward jerked his head toward a small door in the left corner.

I nodded and pushed through the door to see Valery sorting through a mound of sea creatures all carelessly stacked at the end of a porcelain sink and trough. The walls of the small room were covered with various cutting instruments, scrapers, cleaners, veiners, nets, and sieves. There was a large cannister into which entrails and other undesirable parts were flung with indifference.

Valery was working over a cephalopod the size of a football as I approached him. He appeared to be about forty-five, although his neck was thick and his shoulders sloped with defined musculature. His brown hair was thin

144

and wispy, combed straight back beyond a freckled, forehead. He wore small Franklin glasses that magnified his squinty, yellow brown eyes. He had a nose like a hawk's beak and a bloodless pair of thin lips. I had seen that face before.

"Hello," I said genially, trying to disarm the not unsuspicious look he shot at me before returning to the dissecting job at hand. "Never been back through here, and I was curious to see who was responsible for all the fine dishes we've been getting."

Valery grunted a noncommittal reply and continued to cut and flense.

"Listen, I'd like to talk to you for a moment."

"Talk."

"Mr. Valery, do you know who I am."

"Name's Alexander, ain't it?"

"Yes, does that name mean anything to you?" I stared at him, watching his eyes, his hands, to see if there was any gesture or change in his body language that might give him away.

He shrugged. "Should it?"

"Do you know what I'm doing aboard this vessel?"

"Shipwrecked. The captain saved you. That's all I know."

"Somehow, I don't think that's quite right, Mr. Valery."

The man turned to face me, holding a nasty-looking blade close by his side. His small eyes glared behind the octagonal lenses. "What are you talking about, huh?"

"You must know that my friend and I came through one of the time gates, the fluxgates, you must know about that . . ." I gambled that he did indeed know, since I had never really discussed the whole phenomenon with Nemo, and thus did not actually know how much any of the crew knew or understood about the cross-dimensional travel.

"Oh, that? Yes, I know." He turned back to the dressing of the squid, expertly opening its belly in one stroke, flicking his wrists several times while inside the creature, and squeezing its tail. The entrails slipped out

145

soundlessly, and he scooped them up and into the cannister.

As he reached for a spiny crustacean, I spoke again. "The captain tells me you signed on about two years ago, that right?"

"Mm-hmm."

"Where did you learn to cook such fantastic seafood dishes anyway?"

"I always been close to the sea. Just picked it up."

"What are you hiding, Valery? What are you afraid of?" I waited until he turned around, always one eye upon his knife, and noticed that his hands had begun to tremble slightly.

The old man threw down the knife and wiped his hands on his long, spattered apron. "I was afraid you would know. As soon as I heard about you coming on board. I knew what had happened. I recognized the Alexander name. You're one of them from Agatha's side, aren't you?"

He looked at me and I nodded slowly. Although I had not spent much time back at my aunt's place in Brattleboro, I did remember a large oil portrait in the drawing room. It was a portrait of a dashing young man in his twenties, wearing a yachtman's blues and white cap. It was Valery Rochemont, just after his marriage to Agatha.

"Everyone always believed you were dead." I said.

"I wanted them to. When I found those books of Kent's, I knew I had found a way to get out of that sterile, frigging life I'd been born into."

"Books? There was more than one?"

"There was the diary, then there were logbooks, rutters—they would have called them. Plots and positions and lots of data on the fluxgates." He paused, removed his glasses, and rubbed his eyes. "What year is it back there? How is Agatha?"

"Funny that you should ask," I said, then telling him the year. "And Agatha just died. I was the lone heir. That's how I found the stuff from Kent."

He drew in a breath, as if expelling the weight and

146

thickness of years of repressed guilt and anguish. "Ah, Aggie, I'm sorry for you. How old was she?"

"Close to eighty, I think."

Valery sighed. "Well, she lived a good life. My insurance policies must have taken care of that, at least."

"Why didn't you ever go back?"

Valery smiled. "Didn't want to! I was born too late, son. I didn't belong in the twentieth century!"

"Does Nemo know who you really are?" I leaned against the porcelain sink, careful not to sink my hands into something slimy.

"Hell no! He doesn't know a thing. That's why I didn't want to talk to you! You won't tell him, will you?" His voice changed markedly, and there was a pleading inflection that he did not try to hide. I couldn't understand why he would be so upset about Nemo knowing his origins.

"What's so terrible about that?" I pressed him.

The man licked his lips, and his eyes darted about the room, toward the door where the steward labored just beyond. "It's just that I think he would be upset to know that I lied to him."

"Lied? What'd you tell him?"

"When I signed with him at Reykjavík, I knew that he would be there. It was one of his yearly stops for supplies and crew replacement when necessary. That was in Kent's books. He had all the regular hangouts and procedures down in there. I knew right where to go."

"So you wanted to find Nemo?"

He looked at me. "Didn't *you?*"

"Well, you've got me there." I paused and looked at my uncle, Valery Rochemont, New England rich boy and antiquarian, and a closet adventurer. He still looked like his young-man portrait, in spite of the gray at his temples and a few wrinkles. He had been so haughty and defensive and was now reduced to acting like a little boy caught in some school-yard scheme. And yet, there seemed to be something else about him that was still not altogether up front. His small eyes, partially concealed behind the distorting lenses of the Franklin glasses, seemed to be darting and gleaming with other secrets.

"I don't know, Uncle," I said cheerily. "I think Nemo would be delighted to know that I had a relative aboard."

"No, please, Bryan . . . can I call you Bryan? . . . don't tell him! I beg you, don't!" He reached out and grabbed my shoulders. There was plenty of power in his hands.

"I don't know, Uncle. Your reasons don't seem to hold much water. You still keeping something from me?"

"No! no! I swear it!" He swallowed with some difficulty and looked away from me as he swore. A bad sign, that.

"Then what the hell are you so excited about?"

Exhaling roughly, slumping his shoulders, he turned away from me and returned to his work. "I don't know . . . I don't know. I'm just getting to be a crazy old man, I guess. It's been good on this ship, Bryan. I just don't want to foul things up for myself."

He would not look at me but continued working perfunctorily and without his previous verve. It was as though he had given up trying to convince me of whatever it was that he feared, and that he was leaving his fate in my hands. It was an impressive performance, but I was not sure I was going for it. Having been involved in con jobs, and people who were purporting to be things they were not, practically all my life in the academic world, I was not so easily prepared to accept his limply thrown line.

"Well, I don't see how you'd be doing that, Uncle. I really don't. But give me a few days to think about it, okay?" I turned to go, and he called my name.

"Yes?"

"Bryan, I never really knew you years ago. You were just another baby in that big family of hers. I . . . I never payed much attention to that kind of shit. . . . Maybe if we have some time, I can explain myself. For leaving the way I did. I guess the family really hated me for it." He wiped nervously at his jaw with his sleeve.

"I really couldn't tell you about that," I said, smiling. "I was never close with the family either. By the time I ever got any news as to what anybody was doing, it was

148

usually a year or two after it had happened. I never payed much attention to that shit either."

Valery managed a small laugh that was so obviously forced. I saluted him and eased out of the small room and past the steward, who was now stirring and seasoning an enormous cauldron of a wondrous-smelling soup.

There was no one in the corridors between the galley and the crew quarters, so I made my way quickly to Derek's cabin. Knocking on the door, I heard him stir and muffle out a desultory "Yeah!?"

"Bryan. Open up."

The latch clicked and I stepped inside. "Listen, I got something unbelievable to tell you," I said, taking my customary seat on the edge of the washbasin.

"Nemo's a robot," he said.

"Better than that. Dig."

Then I had expained the entire familial connection, filling in the missing years, the calculations would prove that Valery was indeed my missing uncle.

"I wonder why he didn't want Nemo to know who he was?" said Ruffin.

"I don't know. Seems like paranoia is an acceptable social custom around here. But I'll tell you something— relative or not, I don't trust the bastard."

"Why not? He hasn't done anything wrong, has he?"

I shook my head. "No, of course not. But I just have hunches about people, you know. Some people you see and you can instantly like them, trust them, feel comfortable about them, right?"

"Yeah, sure. Happens like that sometimes."

"And then there are others that are just creeps, plain and simple. I mean, you can look at them and know they just crawled out from under their private rock."

"And that's Uncle Valery?"

"Is it ever." I lit up a Carlton, studied the curling smoke, took a deep drag.

"What you gonna do? Tell Nemo?"

"I don't know. Not yet, I don't think. Maybe I'll just keep an eye on him and see how *he* reacts to *my* knowing

149

about him. If I'm right and there is something funny about him, he might get nervous and tip his hand."

"You know where his cabin is?"

"No, but I can find that out easy enough. I think I'll snoop around his kitchen a little bit, too."

"Yeah," said Ruffin, grinning. "Just don't get caught by him or anybody else. Nemo might not like the idea of you sneaking around his submarine, you know."

"I know. Listen, I'm supposed to meet him about now in his chambers. Says he has something surprising or 'interesting' to show us. Wanna come?"

"Why not? I assume that 'the enemy' has been successfully eluded?"

"That's what the man said."

"Okay, lead the way."

SEVENTEEN

"WELCOME, gentlemen," said Nemo. "You are almost exactly on schedule." He gestured us to a couch which had been placed almost directly in front of the iris window.

Checking his pocket watch, Nemo pointed outward into the deep blue depths. An occasional fish slithered past the glass, either glancing at us in cold ignorance, or completing its passage with no notice of us at all. *The Nautilus'* floodlamps burned far and wide through the serene waters, and I estimated our depth to be less than three thousand fathoms.

"No, look carefully, please, off to the left, as we approach, and you will see an unusual geological formation," said Nemo.

Both of us leaned forward and studied the gradually enlargening vista of undersea cliffs. We were approaching what appeared to be a vast underwater plain, which was sliced off at one end like a mesa in the Southwest desert. The top of the mesa stretched out into the diffuse, obscuring distance beyond the power of the ship's lamps, and there was no way to estimate its size, other than to admit that it was damned big. But as *The Nautilus* banked slowly in toward the formation, I realized that it was terrifyingly huge, dwarfing even the greatest of the desert mesas. The front face of it was easily one thousand feet high. The closer we came the more detail was revealed. Great crevices raced across the plain's surface like frozen portraits of summer lightning. There were large fractures along the face of the cliff from which lava flows, arrested halfway down their hot slide, hung like wax from a cold candle.

"What is it?" I asked, truly having trouble recognizing it.

"It is the remains of what was once a gigantic alluvial plain. The face of that cliff was once half of an immense canyon that was cut to the sea at this point. There was a great river that flowed through this continent that lies buried here."

"Continent?" said Derek. "What continent?"

"*Lemuria* was the inhabitants' own name for it. Legend had it that it was a lost land connecting Madagascar with Sumatra. But that was incorrect, due to the ancients' misconceptions concerning geography. Its actual location is in the South Central Pacific."

"Lemuria," I said. "What happened to it?"

"A great cataclysm, long, long ago dislodged the entire land mass from its tectonic shelf. Volcanic reaction followed and the entire continent slid into the sea."

"How long ago?" I asked, now studying the details of the ravaged undersea cliffs. As we grew ever closer I could see that surfaces that appeared smooth from a great distance were in reality jagged and ripped, split, as if by great forces.

"I have calculated the event as taking place approximately 20,000 years ago," said Nemo. "It is most interesting to note that—"

The bosun's horn sounded on Nemo's tube phone, and he left us for a moment to consult with its caller. Nodding his head several times, he replaced the receiver in its cradle and returned to us. "We are prepared to enter the undersea canyon, gentlemen. Please accompany me to the bridge."

The thought of taking a crippled submarine down into the rocky, knife-edged gorges of the immense plain in front of us sounded like insanity, and I'm sure that Ruffin was thinking similar thoughts, but neither of us had enough hair to say anything. So far, Nemo had demonstrated that he knew what he was talking about. I guess I was beginning to trust him, especially since there was nothing I could do to dissuade him from his own plans anyway.

There was the usual complement of operators on the bridge, plus Bischoff, the first mate. From the eye-ports, I could see that the submarine had shifted direction and was heading straight toward the sheer face of the cliff wall. As we approached, I could see massive cracks and fissures running vertically all the way to the topmost edge. Seemingly small, these fissures were actually hundreds of feet across.

Nemo stood before us, whispering orders and course corrections as his great vessel eased closer to the remains of Lemuria.

"You shall see soon what a great discovery I made almost ten years ago. Watch, now."

One of the fissures now yawned before us, and the submarine bisected its walls and dove downward at a slight angle. The powerful prow lamps lanced into the dark waters, bouncing off the scarred, glazed walls. There were no marine life present here, no sign of plant life, nothing. It was as barren as the surface of the moon. We glided onward for almost fifteen minutes before anyone moved or spoke. Then one of the operators mumbled something to Nemo, which I couldn't catch.

"Very well, engines at one-quarter. Steady as she goes. Now, gentlemen . . . just slightly to the starboard, if you will."

Derek and I leaned into the right eye-port and followed the tracks of the floodlamps. Down below, I could see that the canyon walls had gradually widened and tapered away from us, and we were entering what appeared to be a gigantic underground cavern, although flooded with the ocean all the way to the top. The far walls of the cavernous place were unseeable, but I couldn't help feeling swallowed up in something so vast.

"What's that?" Ruffin pointed downward. "Looks like a city!"

"It most certainly is," said Nemo, smiling openly.

I stared outward into the illuminated depths and was reminded of approaching the sprawl of Los Angeles on an

153

afternoon flight. Spread out below like an Oriental carpet lay the ruins of what must have been a spectacular city. Great structures, geometric oddities and monoliths, all half-crumbled or snapped off as if by the stroke of some capricious hand, lay strewn over the intricate network of roadways and elevated ramps that resembled the subways and tram systems of Chicago and old New York. It was not the stereotypical ancient-city layout that you see in the books on lost civilizations but instead was a modern, expertly planned megalopolis. It was as if Manhattan had been engulfed by a *tsunami* and buried permanently under a thousand fathoms.

"Lemuria once held hundreds of cities like the one you see below. By some serendipitous stroke of nature, this one city was held partially intact during the cataclysm. Its name was Khynas," said Nemo, as *The Nautilus* descended even lower, so that we were cruising just above the ravaged tops of some of the city's largest buildings. As we looked from such a close distance I could see that the construction resembled modern techniques of concrete, reinforced steel, glass, and plastic. Hard to accept, but that's what things looked like.

"You said 20,000 years ago," I said. "This city was alive and thriving *20,000 years* ago!?"

Nemo nodded his head. "It is a secret of the ages, Mr. Alexander. I and my men have investigated the ruins and records found within Khynas. There can be no doubt."

"But it's almost impossible. How did they achieve such a civilization so early on in—"

"Mr. Alexander, the earth is five billion years old. Man's presence is now ascribed to be somewhere more than two million. What is 20,000 years in one direction or another? A few seconds in the geologic hour? Surely nothing more."

I shook my head and continued to stare down into the green and ghostly city. There was evidence of complex transportation systems, airports, great promenades, avenues, rivers, and bridge systems.

"What caused the cataclysm?" asked Ruffin.

"The Lemurians' chief source of power at the time of

154

their end was atomic fission," said Nemo. "When I first came upon the ruins, I was completely baffled by apparatus and the power systems that fed their obviously electrical networks."

"*That's* how you came upon the reactor for *The Nautilus*," I said. "I'd been meaning to ask you about all this."

Nemo grinned through his beard. "Undoubtedly," he said. "Yes, but it took almost two years of rigorous investigation before I was able to understand the principles behind their research and application. Khynas is still my source of radioactive fuel for *The Nautilus*. Almost a year was required to crack their written language, and I am no cryptanalyst. But they were meticulous record-keepers. Their libraries and research facilities were crammed with material, all logically coded, classified, and indexed. I only had to find the proper keys and the kingdom belonged to me."

"How did you get in there. How was anything preserved?" I asked.

"I used the diving suits which your Monsieur Verne so perfectly described in his foolish novel," said Nemo with a bit of unveiled sarcasm. "As for the preservation of records, the Lemurians were a people full of forethought and grateful nods toward posterity. I discovered vast underground vaults and sheltered areas that remained watertight despite the catastrophe. There are still areas of this city which remain unknown to me, preserved and waiting by means of the vaults and natural air-pockets which formed when this piece of the continent slid into the sea and was pinched between the two occluding land masses that we passed through."

"You still haven't explained what happened to them," said Ruffin.

"There was much in their literature about the dangers of atomic fission, and the possible disasters that could occur if one of their reactors were to fail. There is little room for error in an atomic fission reactor of the size necessary to power an entire city," said Nemo.

"Yeah, I'm aware of that," I said. "We've got them in our own culture, and they're dangerous as hell. Especially when you consider how they're being manipulated and controlled by an industrial complex that cannot afford to shut them down, or even make them safe."

Nemo smiled. "Yes, politics and economics have always been comfortable sleeping partners, haven't they? At any rate, the Lemurians were attempting to switch over to a unique type of power source. In their era, the part of the earth was highly active geologically. There were rich veins of volcanic activity, and several direct trunk lines into the magma itself . . ."

"Geothermal energy," said Ruffin.

"Yes, I suppose that *is* quite a good term for it," said Nemo. "Your culture is very talented in that regard—inventing catchy phrases and names for things."

"Well, I guess it's better to be remembered for *something*, rather than pass into complete oblivion," I said.

Ruffin laughed, and Nemo cleared his throat to continue. "At any rate, Mr. Alexander, the Lemurians were attempting to tap this wealth of energy that surged and seethed beneath their continent. They attempted drilling, but the depths were too great, and there was only one way of doing it: they devised explosive devises of unbelievable power, unlocked by the energy contained within the atomic structure."

I grinned sorrowfully, shaking my head. "Yeah, I think we're familiar with that kind of thing, too."

"This is starting to sound very familiar," said Ruffin. "What did they do, forget about the energy project and decide to throw these bombs at each other instead?"

Nemo shook his head. "Oh no, they never dreamed that these terrible devices should be used for warfare."

"Well, that puts them one up on us, at least," I said.

Nemo questioned my comment, and I gave him a short lecture on our world's propensity for overkill, Hiroshima *mon amour,* and the special Pentagonian argot of megatonnage, rads, and saturation megadeaths.

Nemo shook his head, rubbed his beard. "Hardly seems civilized," was all he said before continuing. "And so, the Lemurians began a series of experiments in which they detonated their atomic devices at successively greater depths beneath the continent. Their intent was to create vast underground chambers to contain the magma, then sink shafts into the areas, heat steam, and power generators."

"But they set their charges a little too deep, right?" said Ruffin.

"Precisely. There were tectonic faults, deep beneath the continent, that could not be detected from the surface. By the time they were discovered, it was too late. The explosions set off a series of geologic chain reactions that altered the face of this entire hemisphere. I would imagine that they all perished in the heat and rage of a single night."

"Incredible," I said to no one in particular. There was silence for a while as everyone let Nemo's epitaph linger in the control room.

Nemo used this opportunity to give additional commands to his crew. *The Nautilus* responded by descending lower into the sunken ruins of the city of Khynas, gliding past shaken, encrusted hulks that had once been great monolithic buildings, bridges, and elevated roadways. The resemblance to modern America was almost chilling at this proximity.

"I will be sending out a detail to collect some atomic fuel, gentlemen. Would you like to accompany them?" Nemo looked at us quietly.

The thought of roaming around in the ancient city struck me at once as very appealing, but also very hazardous. I had never used scuba equipment in my life, and I was positive that whatever Nemo had devised was nowhere near as sophisticated as modern regulators and tanks. I told Nemo about my inexperience in underwater survival, and he smiled, looking on to Ruffin.

"I've done a lot of diving," said my friend. "What the hell, I'll give it a try."

"The option is entirely yours," said the captain to me. "But I assure that it is quite safe. I will accompany both of you, and neither of you will be required to take part in the actual operation."

I heard myself agreeing to the proposition, partially out

157

of fear of losing respect in Nemo's eyes, and partially because I knew I'd kick myself later for passing up such a chance to do some of that adventuring I once dreamed about.

Funny thing is: once adventure is staring you in the face, you don't find yourself dreaming about it anymore.

As *The Nautilus* snaked lazily through the remains of Khynas, Nemo and Bischoff led us down to the diving lock chambers where other members of the fuel collection team were already suiting up.

The diving suits themselves were made of a thick and unyielding India rubber—nothing like the elastic, pliable materials that petroleum research had provided in our own culture. My particular suit was a loose-fitting affair that had me perspiring freely before I had the thing completely sealed up. Apparently Nemo had never considered the scuba principle of letting a thin layer of water enter the suit around the body, thereby setting up a layer of insulating material which warmed from body heat and prevented great loss of body fluid. The helmet was heavy brass, cast from one solid piece. The face plate was thick and somewhat distorting around the edges and prevented much peripheral vision. As it was locked upon its fittings at my neck, I felt like I was being shucked into an iron maiden. My gloves were equally stiff and not designed for a lot of manual dexterity, but the boots were the worst part—sold blocks of lead that made movement in the open air almost impossible. When they finally dropped me into the diving chamber I had to be lifted and eased over the edge, much to the amusement of the rest of the crew—including Ruffin. Some friend he was.

As I slipped into the water I had the sensation of falling slowly, as if in a dream, then gradually touching down upon the rocky, sand-strewn bottom. I discovered that the boots were no longer the impediments I imagined. In fact, they served as a center-of-gravity base, which allowed me to remain erect and stabilized with little effort. The air tank on my back also served to keep me upright because of its natural buoyancy, and I found that by leaning forward and extending my legs I could walk through the currentless water without expending a lot of wasted energy. The more practice in movement, the more accustomed I became to the exercise, and I began to appreciate Nemo's design of the awkward-looking diving suit. Once you were in the water, the balance and the carefully conceived arrayment of equipment, weights, and counterweights made movement as efficient as possible.

I walked over to Ruffin, who had already settled into the silty bottom, and waited for Nemo to join us. His suit was distinguished from everyone else by two characteristics: while all of us wore a utilitarian brown color, Nemo's was a much lighter tan, and there was a scrolled letter "N" embossed on each side of his helmet very similar to the designs on football helmets.

Looking around, I saw that we were standing in what once must have been a grand avenue of commerce and traffic. The buildings, in various stages of decay, lined the open space as far into the distance as the prow lamps of *The Nautilus* could probe. As I stood peering into the murky, swirling waters, I felt someone come up to my left side and touch my helmet. It was Nemo, adjusting something above my head. Instantly, a small beam of light lanced out from above, and I knew that he had turned on my electric lamp, miner-style.

He motioned Ruffin and me to follow him, and we slogged along in a foot-soldier-through-thick-mud fashion down the avenue, away from the direction of the fuel collection crew, toward a great, low-slung building. Nemo directed us through a set of large double doors, and we were soon inside what looked like an aircraft hangar. The cantilevered, girder-reinforced roof of the structure had collapsed in a majority of the interior and folded in upon itself like an accordion tossed into a corner. But among the wreckage, I could see great machines, stanchions, superstructures, and scaffolding. Enmeshed in the twisted mass of one of the scaffolds was the half-finished hull of some kind of aircraft.

It was about the size of a contemporary jet fighter, although I could not tell what kind of engines it had been designed for, since that part of the fuselage had never been completed. It looked very much like some kind of insect rather than a conventional plane. Its wings were thin, exotically curved, and similar to the design of hang gliders.

Nemo gamboled lightly about the base of the aircraft, pointing out its various features through complex pieces of pantomime, then approached me and placed his helmet next to mine. His voice, though muffled somewhat, resonated into my helmet through the conductivity of the metallic helmets in contact.

"Notice the design of the wings," he said. "It was principles like that that I had conceived when still working with Burton. This is the proof that *I* was correct, and that he was wrong!"

Nemo broke contact before I could reply, and I was left with my own thoughts again. I was amused that even in the wake of discoveries such as the Lemurian mastery of flight Nemo was inclined to interpret things in terms of his own ego.

The next hour was spent in a silent, watery tour of the ruins of the region where *The Nautilus* had descended. It was apparently some kind of industrial area which was fed by an intricate system of slipways, trams, rails, ramps, and roadways. I saw oddly designed vehicles that were seemingly the principal mode of transport. Most of these were reduced to the barest of skeletal remains or transformed through silicafication processes into eerie sculptures which mimicked the work of long-dead craftsmen. We passed through what may have passed for a steel foundry, and I imagined the remnants of tin mills, roller bearing machines, ingots, furnaces, and converters. At times, as we trudged in slow motion through the broken city, I imagined that I was being watched by the dead eyes of the beings of this place. How strange a thing is time that I could be violating such lost and private domains and never imagine the thousands of years and millions of lives that produced what is now only a silent tomb. The men who walked these same streets as I were long since reduced to molecular nothingness, and yet the

160

city still remained, as it probably would continue long after I was similarly departed.

I began to feel grateful that our air supplies were running short, as Nemo signaled that we must return to the ship. Despite the physical exertion of pushing slowly through the watery graveyard, I found that I was becoming psychologically fatigued. The unending catalog of twisted relics and monuments to fallen people was, frankly, depressing the hell of out me. I was told that this was the end waiting for all of us, and then I was told again, and again. And I now felt that the message had been accepted without qualification on my part.

The radioactive fuel had already been loaded aboard and presumably crated off to the engine room, where Nemo's crew would integrate it into the submarine's power system. I imagined that it was all a rather tricky business, and I was thankful not to be a part of the procedure. I made a mental note to ask the good captain how extensive was his knowledge of radiation poisoning. No sense being paranoid unless it was going to be beneficial, right?

When we had been hauled into the diving chamber, unsuited, and sent through a most gratefully accepted shower, I changed and followed Ruffin and Nemo back along the corridor to his private quarters. Once we arrived, the conversation was naturally filled with references to the ruins of Khynas, and Nemo described what we had seen, defining it, in his usual loquacious fashion. His knowledge of the lost civilization was extensive and demonstrated years of intense, dedicated research, but there was a detached quality to his narrative, a coldness that occluded what I imagined would be the natural enthusiasm of a real archeologist, a true discoverer of time's greatest secrets.

But with Nemo, it seemed, everything was defined and interpreted through the functions and needs of his own persona. The ancient city of the Lemurians was *his*, so he implied, as he fancifully recounted other marvels he had uncovered or deciphered in their records. The secrets of their scientists, belonged to him alone, and the thought of

161

ever sharing this knowledge with the outside world was so unthinkable that I'm sure it had never occurred to him.

I felt like challenging him on his feelings because I was tired from the underwater trek and because I was depressed by what I had seen, and because I was put off by his cavalier attitude toward what I saw as grave-robbing. But as I sat listening to him lecture on, I realized that I was just being a romantic ass, and that Nemo's phlegmatic approach to the dead civilization was far more practical and quite expected of any card-carrying social Darwinist such as himself.

The conversation was interrupted by the entrance of First Mate Bischoff, who excused himself and immediately addressed the captain. "The fuel is loaded, sir, and I've completed the damage control report."

"Which is?" Nemo reached across his desk and selected a tightly rolled cigar, wet it with his tongue, fired it with a wood match.

Bischoff remained rigid and attentive, his whole body kind of locking up like some kid getting ready to recite a grade-school poem. "Gyro's definitely out. Bearings been crushed. We keep running her and she'll shake herself to pieces. Can't fix it out here, I don't figure. The electric gun is also gone—needs a new generator. Outer hull damage will hold till reach base. Dorsal rudder also out. But Grollier says he might be able to rig some kind of control on her."

"Tell him to try, but not to attempt putting it into operation till I've been down to inspect his work. I don't want him doing more harm than good to whatever control we still have left. You recommend returning to base as soon as possible, that right?"

"Aye, sir."

"Very well, secure for surface activity. We'll ship as soon as I've plotted out the course."

Bischoff nodded, backed off, and left the room. I looked up at the captain and waited until I had his attention. "Where's 'base'?" I asked.

"A long way from here, I'm afraid." Nemo walked to the iris window, peered out at blue green silence.

162

"How long will it take to get there?" Ruffin turned and directed the question at him.

"By conventional methods, it would be about three weeks . . . but," said the captain, turning to regard us with his cold eyes, "I don't think we shall be conventional in this case."

"What're you talking about?" I said.

Turning to face both of us, Nemo smiled. "You surprise me, Mr. Alexander. You really surprise me sometimes. Surely you haven't forgotten the means by which you arrived in our world?"

"The fluxgate? You can use them?"

"Of course. It can get quite complicated, but the travel is almost instantaneous from place to place. Besides, I'm sure you will find it quite interesting."

Interesting. One of the good captain's favorite words. The thing was, he was usually right.

EIGHTEEN

NEMO CALLED it the "Secret Sea."

Actually it was an apparently limitless number of "secret" seas, all splashing upon the shores of an infinite number of parallel earths. In the years since Nemo had discovered the gateways, he had explored no fewer than thirty of the alternate universes.

As with the discovery of atomic power, Nemo's knowledge of the system of dimensional pathways was garnered from the stored records of the Lemurians. Those ancient people had been aware of the parallel worlds for centuries through their rich, colorful catalog of legends and mythology. But it had only been within the last century before their demise that the Lemurians had begun to codify their legends and investigate them scientifically.

Nemo explained to us in great (and boringly lecturous) detail how he had first come upon the vaults which contained the accumulated date upon the fluxworlds, as they were called by the Lemurians. When he had finished his long narrative, I was able to retain all the salient facts, which I'll recount here without the excess expository baggage so dear to the captain's heart.

To begin with, there are fixed sets of coordinates all about the earth where the dimensional pathways are known to open and close. The timetable of these myriad time/space portals are also rigidly fixed, but following a complicated pattern that can only be determined if one can compute the earth's position in space and time as it orbits the sun. Simply viewed, it is like an immense network of subway tunnels burrowing from one parallel world to another, with certain rules attached: (1) your train only runs at certain times during the cyclic year, (2) your train only runs in one direction—i.e., you may pass through a portal, but you cannot pass back through the same one, (3) you cannot take a train from one Earth to *any* of the other Earths—i.e., only certain parallel worlds connect directly, such as Earth^1 with Earth^2, and Earth^2 with Earth^3. This would mean that in order to travel from Earth^1 to Earth^3, one would have to first pass through Earth^2. Taking this a bit further, Earth^{32} may connect with Earth^{17}, but Earth^{17} may not connect with Earth^{32}. In this case you might have to go first to Earth^{25}, which happens to have a connecting portal running back to Earth ^{32}, which, if you can recall, is where you originally wanted to return.

Listen, I said this could be complicated.

It had taken Nemo years of earnest research, but he had succeeded in keeping a complex log of his own personal explorations, plus appended logs and charts of previous Lemurian expeditions. The result was a kind of road map of the fluxgate system, which provided him with times and routes from various worlds to another.

His current plan was to pass into three different parallel worlds, each having various related interconnecting fluxgates, which would eventually deposit him back in his own world in very close proximity to his secret base—the location of which, by the way, he again declined to reveal.

He attempted to keep the entire system of dimensional travel a personal matter, allowing his crew only to know that it existed and that their captain knew how to utilize it. I really had no idea how much Bischoff or any of the other lieutenants knew of the system, but I kept thinking back to Durham Kent, who definitely understood the world of the Secret Sea, if not how to fully take advantage of it. In addition, I felt that security aboard the submarine was not what I would call "tight," therefore it was possible that Nemo's secrets were not as personal as he thought.

There was something bothering me about the whole scene. Not just the use of the dimensional gates—that seemed plausible enough, in view of what we know about other impossibilities like black holes, gravity wells, quarks, and quasars, and even tachyons—but rather, the way Robur at times seemed to know where Nemo was going to be. The captain was willing to pass it off to his own genius at being able to predict Robur's movements, but I was beginning to doubt it.

The Captain unceremoniously asked us to leave his chambers while he worked out the course through the fluxgates (I don't like that term for the gateways, but that *is* what he called them). *The Nautilus,* in the meantime, had surfaced in south equatorial waters, replenishing its air tanks, flushing out bilge, and refitting and cleaning as best it could. Ruffin and I decided to go abovedecks and get some sunshine and fresh air.

We were standing against the armor plate of the bridge, just behind the eyelike ports looking aft. There were several crewmen elevating the sub's cannon onto the deck through a pair of ingeniously designed trapdoors. The gun was a deep blue-black and it gleamed with machine oil and graphite polish. The men inspected the weapon meticulously and ran it through a series of sighting and aiming maneuvers until satisfied that it would be action-ready if the situation arose. There was a watch posted fore and aft, both armed with binoculars and scanning the horizon.

While we were standing there, feeling the warm, salty air and sun cavort about our pale faces, I noticed my secret Uncle Valery emerge from the aft hatch with one of his stewards. Both of them had large cannisters, which I presumed was garbage of some sort.

"That's funny," I said to Derek, who was idly watching the gun crew.

"What's that?"

"Those two at the end of the deck. The chef, Valery, and the other guy." I pointed to them. Valery caught my gesture out of the corner of his eye, and I thought I noticed him tense for a moment before emptying his cannister over the side.

"Yeah, what about them?"

"Don't you think it's funny that they would come topside to dump garbage when they have a pressurized chute in the galley to eject all that shit?" I looked over at the two men, who had finished their chore and were scrambling belowdecks—Valery a bit too hastily, I thought.

"Yeah, it does seem a little funny. But why not? I mean, maybe they just wanted some fresh air, or something." Derek was in one of his lackadaisical moods and didn't feel much like thinking.

"Then how come they didn't stay on deck awhile. They seemed to me like they were in a pretty big hurry to get below."

Derek shrugged his shoulders.

Since it was then obvious that he was not going to play Watson to my Holmes, I eased away from the bridge, walked cheerily past the gun crew, and stood at the far edge of the deck, where I could see what it was that had been scuttled over the side.

The swells and waves lapping against the hull had already dispersed a lot of it. It was the usual assortment of kitchen scraps: peelings, skins, feet, claws, heads, entrails, bones, roots and stalks from various seaweeds. It was all fanning out, flopping and slopping across the surface, some of it already sinking out of sight, some of it being snatched by scavenging fish. Just as I was about to turn back, feeling foolish at my unspoken hunch, I thought I saw something floating amongst the trash. Something bobbed and flipped, catching a glint of sunlight. Something metallic. Spinning around, I strained to see it again, but the distance was growing greater with each second and the swell of the sea was also catching the sun's light and occasionally throwing it back to me. Whatever it was that I might have seen was gone.

Ruffin was watching me as I returned. "What's the matter?"

"Nothing. I thought I saw something, that's all."

"Like what?"

"I don't know. Didn't really see it."

Ruffin pointed to the gun. "Hey, you take a good look at that thing?"

"Huh?"

"The gun. It's a hell of a mean looker. Bet it could

167

match up against anything they had in World War I." He smiled, obviously in admiration of Nemo and Gun Club friends.

"Yeah, I guess so." I stared out to sea in the direction of Uncle Valery's garbage.

"Hey, what's with you?" said Derek, tapping me on the arm.

"Oh, nothing. Never mind. Listen, I think I'm going below for a while. See you later, okay?"

Ruffin nodded and returned to his daydreaming, probably of taking on a few of the Kaiser's finest regiments with Nemo's toy.

I climbed below and headed for the galley. Valery was there, scrubbing and polishing the counter tops, trying to look exceedingly busy when I arrived.

"Hello, Uncle," I said cheerfully.

"Shut up! There might be someone around!" His face was flushed, and his eyes seemed glazed behind his glasses.

"Maybe there is," I said, moving close to him. "Tell me something, Unk. How come you were upstairs chucking garbage when you could have just shoved it in this thing here?" I pointed to the hatch and wheel lock which led to the ejection chute.

He didn't say anything but continued to stare at me, breathing deeply in an attempt to remain calm. I gave the wheel lock a spin, lifted the bar and opened the hatch. A nasty fish-market odor leaped out and slapped me, but I stared into the darkness of the chute. It was big enough to roll a basketball down, but not much bigger. On the inner seam of the hatch there was a small button, like the one that turns off your refrigerator light when you shut the door.

"What's this for?" I asked, holding my finger over the button.

Valery said nothing.

I shrugged and pushed it, instantly hearing the metallic whir of an electric motor further down in the darkness of the shaft. I kept the button depressed and the motor continued for another minute or so. I knew that I had heard

168

a similar sound in my own kitchen many times. The motor suddenly stopped. Probably an automatic cutoff.

"Well, Unk, that's sounds like some kind of disposal, doesn't it? Did they have those back home before you left? You know, a set of whirling blades to chop up anything that passed through? Nemo's a bright guy, isn't he? Thinks of everything, that captain. No, sir, we sure wouldn't want the garbage chute getting clogged up and fouling the pressure or the ejection process, would we?"

"What do you want?" Valery managed to say.

"I want to know what it was you had to throw over the side that you didn't want sliced up in this chute?"

"Nothing! I don't know what you're talking about!"

"What were you doing topside with garbage then?"

"I just wanted to get some air, that's all. A change of pace! Ask my steward. We always go up when we surface."

I smiled. "Oh, I'm sure you do. What do you have, little bottles with messages in them?" I paused. *No, it's probably something more sophisticated than that,* I thought. *Better wait, though, till I have more to go on.* "Maybe I should see the captain about this, what do you say?"

"I say you'd better get out of here right now, Mr. Alexander."

I looked at his expression and saw that it had changed drastically. His pinched features now were veined with a pent-up fury that suggested that reason was leaving him. If you push a nasty critter into a corner, he has no recourse but to bare his ugly fangs at you. I nodded and backed out of the galley, thinking a sudden paranoid thought: *this bastard could poison me!*

Walking back down the corridor toward the ladder, I fought to keep my fantasies under control, but the image of myself seated at the captain's table, delicately savoring a mollusk truffle in wine sauce, then suddenly writhing in the death agonies of cyanide seasoning, kept recurring. The thought of going without food for the rest of the voyage did not seem feasible, but I may have pushed my uncle far enough to do something rash.

But only if he was guilty of something rash.

I knew that I would have to find out, and damned fast.

By late afternoon, Nemo had the deck cleared, and we were once more submerged and heading southwest toward a rendezvous with a fluxgate. I sat in my cabin, getting hungry, and wondering what to do next. I wanted to tell Derek about the conversation in the galley and I wanted to get a look around my uncle's cabin, and the galley too. I would need help and a lot of luck to keep from getting caught. It would have been easier if I had known what I was looking for. But of course, I didn't.

I was thinking this thing over when Nemo sent a man down to summon me to the bridge. I followed him down the corridor and up to the command section, where Derek had already joined the captain and the usual bunch. From the main ports I could see that we were submerged, but only slightly below the surface. Our running lights were down, and the soft glow of the sun upon the sea's ceiling was like milky glass. The sea itself was a brilliant blue-green, and there were thousands of tropical fish schooling all about us. It was a beautiful, kinetic display of color and movement, like something that Matisse or Miro would have done if they had been into abstract filmmaking.

Nemo nodded my arrival just as he was ordering the ship to surface. The navigator announced our position in the usual number-and-degree jargon that meant nothing to me, and Bischoff stood by the helm like a cellist in an orchestra, ready to begin. *The Nautilus* broke the surface just far enough so that its eyes were above the water, alligator-style. Nemo checked his watch and announced the time until visual contact should be made.

Everyone was silent and staring straight ahead into the gathering orange smear of a tropical sunset. I was not conscious of how much time passed before we saw it, and I felt a shudder pass through me just like the first time Derek and I had found the one that had brought us here. Directly ahead, less than fifty meters, I could see the thing materializing out of the invisible dusk-light. An enormous

170

torus, on edge, swirling in its own gray light like the fluctuating light that waxed within mother-of-pearl.

"All ahead full," said Nemo, and the submarine surged forward perceptibly.

Even within the thick, insulated hull of *The Nautilus* I could hear that familiar sound—the sound of universes rubbing edges, the sound of Nature groaning at the incredible forces that were rending and grabbing at her seams. The center of the torus coalesced now into a more substantial form. This fluxgate seemed larger than the first one I had seen. It pulsed and swelled, seeming to grow even larger as we approached, and it looked like it could have taken a 747 without batting an eye. The center glowed with the eerie green light, and we headed straight for its center. The groaning sound increased. No one spoke. *The Nautilus* moved forward, was enveloped.

No sound. Grayness swarmed at the ports, as if trying to get in at us. The sunset, the sky, even the sea itself, seemed to disappear for an instant. Then a single sharp vibration through the hull, and I remembered the popping sound that had accompanied the passage of *The Metamorphosis*.

The vaguely doughnut-shaped configuration of the gate was gone, and we were sailing in the open sea. The sky above us was an ugly smear of brownish gray that stretched in every direction, and the sea was unbelievably calm.

"Where are we?" I asked, breaking the silence. I was suddenly aware of men breathing, coughing, moving about in their seats, of the vessel's running sounds.

Nemo stared calmly at the bleak sea, then turned to me. "I've only been to this world once, Mr. Alexander, and I did not wish to come back."

I looked out at the scene again. There was no sun, but only a greatly diffused light that was weak and feeble and seemingly clouded by some thick, but unseen, particulate.

"Geographically," Nemo continued, "we are near the west coast of Australia. In time, I have no way of placing us, although it appears that we are either in this earth's

171

far future or its dim past. At any rate, we are in a time when there are no discernible signs of life."

Looking at the utter bleakness ahead of us, I could well believe Nemo's assessment of things. The sea itself was a gray almost solid-looking color. There was no transparency, no sense of movement or flowing, other than the wake which *The Nautilus* cut as it glided half-submerged.

"The outside temperature is fifty-one degrees centigrade. The hull will be soon absorbing this heat, and we will become quite uncomfortable unless we descend rather soon," said Nemo. "The air, as I tested it on the previous passage here, is quite unbreathable, being largely carbon dioxide, ammonia, and some nitrous sulfides. It is a dead world."

I looked out once again before the submarine began its descent away from the nothingness that this earth had become, and wondered how far away from my own century this had been. I tried to imagine what we had done to ourselves to lay such an irrevocable disaster on the planet. The thought kept hitting me that if things looked even this bad in the center of the oceans, how horribly devastating must it have appeared on the continents themselves.

When I mentioned this to Nemo, he shook his head sadly, dramatically. "I too wondered about that, Alexander. So much so that I took a survey crew, clothed in our diving gear, ashore to the east of our present position."

"And what did you find?"

"That was the shock of it, you see," said Nemo, looking through the port as the prow dipped and slipped beneath the murky surface, starting off as if revisualizing his memories. "There was nothing to find. We found *nothing*. No trace of man, of life. Not a tree. Not a bird. Not even geologic life. The land was as flat as a tabletop, and just as smooth. Everything was covered with a glassy, slick substance that was hard as a diamond. Where we put ashore this condition stretched endlessly in every direction. It was as though something had melted everything down and then let it cool in a flat, placid pool."

"How long do we stay here?" I asked. "And is it safe?"

"We will cruise from this position to our next fluxgate location. The distance versus time will be a little over two hours, plus a wait at the proper location for close to another hour. As for how safe this particular world may be, I have no idea."

Nemo paused to consult some navigational charts and leave some careful instructions with the bridge crew, then headed for the spiral ladder. "I'm going below, gentlemen. You may join me for dinner in approximately one hour, if you'd like."

The thought of dinner set my teeth on edge, but I smiled and nodded to him, wondering what would come next.

NINETEEN

EITHER MY Uncle Valery had nothing to hide, or he simply had not yet thought to poison me. In either event, I survived dinner in Nemo's chamber with nothing more than a quiet buzz from too much brandy. Nemo talked about the Secret Sea and offered several theories as to how and why it existed, and some ruminations as to the force behind the entire mechanism. It was all quite fascinating, although there was nothing that struck me as being wildly original in his thinking, in terms of what the modern physicists of my own world were talking about every day during their coffee breaks. When you sit down and realize how insignificant the whole damn planet is, in view of the entire universe, it really should not surprise you that *anything* is not only possible, but is probably *happening* somewhere in the vastness of things.

But Nemo had never spoken to any of the more way-out physicists that drank coffee with me at Irvine, and I suppose I should not fault him. He refused to tell us what awaited us in the next fluxworld on our schedule, only saying that it would be far more lively than the present one. After we had passed two hours at his table, I excused myself, saying I was going to do some reading in my cabin—but actually I intended to do some skulking around.

By the time I reached the galley, it was all but locked up and Uncle Valery was nowhere to be seen. There was one crewman in the center of the room swabbing the floors. I waved at him easily and asked if he had seen Valery about. The man shook his head and suggested that he may be in his cabin.

All right, I thought. *Do you go get your Walther PPK*

and threaten to add some nine-millimeter holes to your uncle's physiology? Or do you just stumble in and hope that he doesn't kill you for being such an obvious ass? It was not much of a choice, really, and I decided to go and get my handgun, with a slightly altered plan in mind.

Now, before I go any further, I think I should tell you that I am not a violent person. Oh, I like my games of ice hockey and football, and even an occasional boxing match, but that is all vicarious stuff. I may have an aggressive, forceful personality, but I think that is more intimidation than anything else. I don't like to be physically abusive to anything except cockroaches (and then I can be *very* abusive). The thought of shooting someone, except in self-defense, croggles the mind, as does the very thing that I decided I must do to poor Uncle Valery: hit him over the head hard enough to render him quite unconscious, but not anywhere near that awful state we call dead.

Now think about this. As with most acts of physical skill, I would think that smacking someone on the back of the head with a blunt object just forcefully enough to black them out, but not to injure them seriously, would take lots of practice. I would think that one would have to acquire the right "touch," the confident sweep of the arm, the delicate flick of the wrist at the moment of impact, the all-important follow-through.

And I, of course, had none of these skills.

But there I was, walking slowly up the deserted corridor in the crew section, counting the doors, till I came to Valery's. Inside my shirt was the handgun, a slim, efficiently designed weapon, with a dense, if not terribly heavy, handgrip. The blunt, flat butt of the grip would do an adequate job, given the right placement and force of the blow. Even then I winced as I thought about the actual impact. But I kept telling myself *not* to think about it. Just do it.

Hefting the gun in my hand, checking to see that the safety was on and that I would not accidentally shoot myself while kiboshing my uncle, I practiced a few short, strong downward strokes. I tried not to imagine the sick-

ening thud that would emanate from the sudden connection of steel to scalp as I drew in a deep breath and
knocked authoritatively on Valery's door.

"Yes?"

"Captain wishes to see you immediately, Mr. Valery." I
spoke through the sleeve of my shirt, at least an octave
lower than usual.

"One moment, please." Now I hoped that he wasn't
pausing to get one of his kitchen knives.

But before I could worry about this, he was unlatching
the door. I stepped back quickly, away from his line of
sight. Silence. Both of us freezing. "Hello?" said my
uncle. "Who's there?"

I said nothing, held my breath, kept my weaponed
hand upraised, ready.

"Hello?" said Valery, and he foolishly stuck his head
and shoulders through the door, thankfully looking in the
opposite direction.

I conked him a glancing blow just below the occipital
lobe, wincing myself as I thought about what I was doing.
The follow-through was passable, and Valery stumbled
forward, obviously dazed, but not down for the count. I
knew what I must do, since he would be soon turning his
dumb face toward the direction of his attack.

Another deft whack on the back of his head, this time
more solid but benefiting from a flick of my wrist to give
it some English. He dropped like a sack of gravel and lay
just as still. Dropping down I felt for his carotid artery
and felt it jumping slowly but with plenty of strength. The
back of his head was a bit damp from the first blow which
probably cut him more than anything else. There was already a lump growing from the second blow that would
be of baseball proportions. But he was out cold and that's
what I needed.

Dragging him quickly back into the cabin, I dropped
him on his bunk, shut the door, and locked it. There was
a small closet, a set of cabinets and drawers built flush
into the wall, and a small footlocker under his bunk. If I
didn't find anything in any of those things, there was no
place else to look.

The closet had the expected complement of uniforms, some extra pairs of boots, a pea jacket, and a monstrously heavy parka, and a few extra shirts. I checked for secret panels, compartments, cracks or crevices, but the place was all riveted and welded tight. The set of drawers also yielded a lot of the expected things like socks, underwear, scarves, gloves, some extra pairs of trousers. Plus the usual "junk drawer" with trinkets, timepieces, pocketknives, mementos, photographs, jewelry, notepads, etc. There was quite a mound of the stuff, and though I sifted through it quickly, I was fairly sure that it was inconsequential material.

That left only the footlocker, and it was locked with two separate locks. I searched Valery's supine body and found no keys. Back to the junk drawer—hadn't I seen some keys in with all that mess? Yes, I had. On a small gold ring, along with what looked like some charms that Agatha might have once given him, were two keys that looked right.

They were indeed right, and the footlocker opened as easily as a suitcase. It was practically empty, except for several large, heavily bound books that looked like ledgers, plus a folio-sized leather-bound volume that looked like a companion volume to the Durham Kent journal back at Aunt Agatha's. I thumbed through it and learned quickly that it was a log of *The Nautilus*, obviously kept by Kent, and obviously unknown to Nemo. Various dates were underlined, indicating times when Nemo had used or explored a fluxgate, plus information describing the alternate world briefly, and exact times and geographic coordinates. It was apparent that Nemo's Secret Sea was not so secret after all. There was an appendix section which contained columns of calculations and graphs. At first they made little sense to me, except for places where Kent had apparently gone back, reconsidered things, and had scribbled in marginal emendations. After scanning some of these, it looked as though Kent had been trying to piece out the grand cycle of the fluxgates, as Nemo had done with the help of the Lemurian records. From the seeming complexity of the cycle it did not seem possible that Kent could have accomplished much, and from the looks of his notes, he did not.

At best, my Uncle Valery knew the locations and times of some of the fluxgates but had little or no idea as to how they fit into the entire cycle. Still, this was invaluable information on its own. I hefted the book in my hands. My first thought was to take it to Nemo and see what the good captain would do with it. But that might be tipping my hand too early. As far as I could tell, Valery had no way of knowing who tapped him on the back of the head—although I was sure that he would more than suspect me.

Upon thought of my uncle, I turned to check on him. He was sleeping peacefully in his bunk, and the lump on the back of his head had grown to orange-sized proportions.

Returning the logbook to the locker, I picked up one of the bound books. There was no writing on the cover, and the inside pages were filled with small columns of print that seemed to be meaningless. I studied them for awhile, checking to see if the whole book was filled likewise, and it was. There were no actual words; just columns, rows, and letter groups. I had never seen a code book before, but this sure looked like what I had always thought a code book would look like.

Code book. Immediately I looked over at my slumbering relative and thought: spy.

Didn't Nemo mention that both he and Robur had employed spies over the years? Of course, and who would be a perfect spy? Someone with no connection in Nemo's world—someone, like my uncle, who would arouse little or no suspicion. But how could my uncle have hooked up with Robur first? If Kent's journals mentioned Reykjavík as an infrequent stop in Nemo's travels, why did not Uncle Valery just tell Robur this, and let *The Kraken* lay in wait off the coast of Iceland? There was obviously more to the story than that, assuming that my Uncle Valery was indeed the spy I was making him up to be.

Of course there was more. If Uncle Valery was sending messages in code, he must have some means of transmitting them. He had no radio or telegraph in the room. I was fairly sure of that. Besides, Nemo's detection equipment would almost certainly be able to pick up the operation of any clandestine gear on board the ship. The garbage dumping was the only way I could think of that made sense, especially in view of Unk's great irritation at my questioning him about it. My original thought about messages in bottles came back to me, but I could not imagine Robur agreeing to anything so crude and chancy. The way I would do it would be to have lots of message containers, all holding the same message in case some were lost or failed to function, and set them adrift with some kind of low frequency radio beacon that would bleep like hell until Robur tracked it down and picked it up.

That all seemed logical to me, and I would try to figure on that as a strong possibility until something came up to contradict the idea. I was aware, of course, not to ignore contrary evidence just because it did not fit my pet theory. If I had a quarter for every scientist guilty of *that* crime . . .

All right, so I would start looking for things that might be flotation beacons. I put the code books back into the locker, flipped shut the lid, and slid it back into its original place under the bunk. The keys I replaced in the general disorder of the junk drawer. I checked about the room to insure that there was no sign of my intrusion, pulled Valery off the bunk, and arranged him on the floor as he had fallen back into his room, then eased quietly and unseen out of there.

I went back down to the galley to see what was up and discovered that the steward had finished cleaning up and it was secured—as they say on ships—but not locked. Opening the hatchlike door, I slipped inside and turned on two of the small work-lamps over the counter area. Everything was so incredibly neat that I feared poking around too thoroughly for not knowing how and where to replace everything. I figured that if Valery was working alone, he would not keep any curious-looking equipment in any obvious places, so I decided I should first check

179

the more secret areas. There were drawers and cabinets all over the place, plus small pantries, sliding panels, shelves, nooks, and yes, even some crannies. And all were filled with pots, pans, and all manner of utensil. It was going to be a long, and noisy, search.

Each area had to be studied first, then each item carefully removed and eventually replaced quietly, and exactly in its prior position. After almost two hours, I had not covered half of the possible hiding places when I discovered a small canvas bag stuffed behind a screw-on plate which provided access to the plumbing under the porcelain sink where Valery cleaned each day's catch. Opening the canvas, I found five objects roughly the size of family-size coffee cans. Each one was damned heavy, probably due to the power cell each one would need. I could hardly believe how dead-on I had been, and felt very good about things at that point. The bottom of the thing unhooked bayonet-style, and I examined it closely in the dim light. There were rubber seals around the edges to keep out seawater, and the bottom had enough space to roll up a good-sized piece of paper. There was also a small switch inside, which I assumed would start the thing transmitting its pickup signal.

Unlike the books and the log, I decided I had better keep these, if not take them straight to the captain. I replaced the thing in the sack with the others and began screwing the plate back over the plumbing access, when I heard footsteps. Behind me.

"I figured you would come here," said Uncle Valery.

He was standing in the entrance between the galley and the catch room. His shoulders were hunched up, and his arms hung down menacingly. In his right hand he held a curved utensil with a mean-looking hook at the end. I had no idea what kitchen job it was intended to do, but I knew that Unk had just thought of a new use for it.

"*Why* are you doing it, Unk?"

"You wouldn't understand," he said, taking a step closer to me. I was still hunched down by the side of the sink.

"Try me," I said, wondering whether I should get up

and reach for my Walther, or simply heave the heavy sack at his feet.

"Nephew!" he said loudly. "You're no relative of mine! You're from *her* side, not mine. She always did have a bunch of self-righteous bastards in that family. I couldn't stand it! She was always *right*. Her and all her damned New England tradition! Well, the hell with it all. That's why I left that insufferable place and that's why I'll never go back!"

He took another step toward me and raised his weaponed hand.

"Wait a minute, Unk . . ."

"And stop calling me 'Unk'!" He lunged forward just as I let go with the sack.

It dumbbelled through the air and caught him around the knees. Falling forward, he slashed out with the knife, which swished past my cheek so closely that I was certain he'd cut me and that I simply felt no pain from so clean an incision. He was scrambling to his knees, trying to crawl at me, when I had the Walther in my hand. Swinging hard at that curved thing, I caught his wrist with the heaviest part of the gun, and he whelped in pain. The hook clattered to the floor, and my uncle lunged again, butting his forehead against mine. Pain flickered across my eyes, and I thought I was going to pass out, but his hands were getting around my throat by then and I figured that this would not be such a fine idea. He was damned strong for his size and age, and I didn't have much time. His eyes were level with mine, and they were red and yellow and glassy. He was breathing hard and half drooling, half spitting with anger as he tried to strangle me, all the while muttering how he was going to kill me, *kill* me.

I still had the handgun, and while something told me to jam it into his gut and just squeeze off a few, I couldn't do it. Instead I swung down hard with whatever strength I had left and caught him on the back of the head once again. The pain must have been incredibly bad, because he screamed like a pig being cut open at the slaughter-house. Even *I* could feel it, it seemed. His hands went limp at my throat, and I realized that I was able to breathe again. I rolled to the side and he slumped off me. I think I had seen him unconscious more than I had when he was awake, and he was getting to look a lot better to me with his eyes all rolled toward the top of his head. Leaning against the side of the sink, I let the adrenalin/epinephrine-high wash through me, waiting for my heart to stop its furious clatter, for my breath to get regulated, for my hands to stop shaking.

But before I could do that, there were more footsteps. Lights were flicked on, and before I could stand up, there was one of the crew standing in the door with big, bald Bischoff right behind him.

Realizing that I still held the handgun, I eased it down to the deck, smiling gamely. "You'd better get the captain," I said.

"What the hell's going on?" said the first mate, who stepped forward and knelt over the very still form of my uncle. "You kill him?"

"I don't think so. He attacked me. I was just defending myself. Listen, would you please get Nemo?"

Bischoff turned and nodded at the crewman, who disappeared from the doorway, his boots slapping quickly down the steel corridor.

"What about you? You all right?" Bischoff looked at me squarely, then down at the Walther. "Carry that all the time?"

"What the hell is this, Twenty Questions?" My throat ached every time I talked, and I didn't feel like talking anyway.

"What's Twenty Questions?"

"That's twenty-one," I said.

"You making a joke at me, or something?" Bischoff glared at me.

"Who me? No, of course not. Where'd you get that idea?"

So we both stared at each other for a few minutes, me not knowing why I was being so hostile to a guy just being efficient and conscientious, and Bischoff probably

182

wondering why he shouldn't just smash me and get it over with.

We were both interrupted from our wonderings by Nemo's *basso profundo*. "Would you like to give me an explanation for all this, Mr. Alexander?"

I looked up to see the captain, plus two additional crewmen and Derek, all crowding into the small room.

TWENTY

MY TIMING had been bad. Before I could even begin to explain things, *The Nautilus* was scheduled to pass into the next fluxworld in accordance with Nemo's complex routing system back to his base. Despite my warnings that what I had to tell him might change his plans, he insisted on supervising the passage while Derek and I were held under armed guard in his chambers.

We passed a half hour in silence until Nemo returned. He dispatched the crewmen but kept them posted outside the closed entrance, and settled back to listen to my story.

By the time I had finished, Nemo was examining the flotation beacon closely, and scarcely paying attention to my concluding remarks.

"I hardly know what to say, Alexander. It all seems so unlikely. What are your uncle's motives for all this?" Nemo placed the beacon on his serving table, reached for a cigar, and lit it.

"I don't know, he wouldn't tell me."

"Perhaps he'll tell me," said Nemo, as he looked once again at the beacon, then glancing at the log and code books which he had sent his crew to pick up in Valery's cabin. "It's funny, Alexander, but I *never* believed that blood was thicker than water. Apparently you don't either."

I laughed. "Well, he was hardly a relative I ever knew, much less felt close to. But I guess what it comes down to is that I believe *you*, that Robur is the . . . uh, bad guy, as we say."

"Yes," Nemo said, smiling. "The bad guy. That's good, I like that."

"But what I was wondering about is the beacon that he probably threw over with the garbage," I said. "If Robur picks it up, he's going to know where we're going to come out, right?"

"Possibly. It depends on many factors," said Nemo. "I will have to study Kent's old log to see how accurate and extensive is his knowledge of the 'gates. Secondly, I must interrogate Valery and discover if he indeed disclosed our present plans. And thirdly, I must compute the amount of time it will take Robur to reach our base by conventional sea routes."

Ruffin cleared his throat. "That's *if* Robur's traveling by conventional sea routes . . ."

Nemo sat bolt-upright in his parlor chair. "Good lord, man! You don't suggest that Robur knows of the Secret Sea!?"

"It's possible," I said. "How long has Valery been with you? I would almost bet on him telling Robur about it."

"Yes, of course he would," said Nemo. "But Valery could not possibly know enough, even from Kent's logs, to direct Robur safely through the various 'gates. Only a madman would attempt to pass through the 'gates without a complete knowledge of their workings and destinations. You could be lost forever!"

"But he *is* crazy, isn't he?" said Ruffin.

"Oh yes, Burton's mad all right. Mad as a hatter!"

"Another thing," I said, trying to be specific and conscientious, but not intending to get the good captain any more upset than he already was. "How many people besides you know the exact location of this 'base' we're heading to? What I mean is, could my uncle have sent Robur there in the first place?"

"No, that's impossible," said Nemo. "Of course, that's impossible. The only men who know the location of the base are myself and Bischoff. Kent never knew it—it was established long after he'd been cut adrift. It would not be in his journals or logs for that reason."

"What about somebody using the constellations to map it out?" said Ruffin. "You know, the sextant and all that.

I'm sure a good sailor could do it, and Bryan's uncle was an avid yachtsman, right, Bryan?"

I nodded my head.

"No, gentlemen," said Nemo, allowing a small grin. "That is also impossible."

"Why?"

"Because there are no stars, no constellations above my base."

I frowned for a moment. "Undersea? A cavern or something like that?"

"Yes, Alexander. Something like that." He crushed out his cigar in a silver tray. Exhaled slowly, calmingly.

"Then if Robur *can't* be steaming along by conventional routes to meet you at your base, then what is it that Valery could have told him in that beacon we're all so sure he tossed over the side?" Ruffin spoke slowly, making sure that we both caught the drift of what he implied.

"You mean that he gave him directions through the 'gates?" Nemo glared at him.

"Maybe, I don't know," said Ruffin. "I'm just trying to cover every possibility, that's all. We've already concluded that Valery could not have directed him to your base of operations. *What is it* that he could have told him then?"

"Is it possible that *The Kraken* could be tailing us?" I asked.

" 'Tailing us,' Alexander? What does *that* mean?"

"Following us," I said. "Could Robur have followed us through the 'gates?"

Nemo paused for a moment, lost in thought; his eyes drifted to the iris window, which was for the moment closed. "That's a possibility I'd never considered. It all depends upon how long the 'gates remain open. They all vary, you know." He stood up, nodded curtly. "I must interrogate your uncle immediately. Excuse me, gentlemen. I shall meet with you presently on the bridge."

Nemo walked briskly to the door, gave some instructions to the two guards, who looked admittedly relieved, and disappeared with the captain down the hall. They were heading toward Valery's cabin.

186

"Hey, he never told us where we were headed now," said Ruffin.

"Oh, yeah, we forgot to ask him."

"You want to go up and see?"

I shrugged. "Why not?"

We left Nemo's chambers, closed the door behind us, and walked slowly toward the bridge. First Mate Bischoff, (coming from the opposite direction), joined us at the spiral ladder. He stood there silently appraising both of us for a moment, looking like some piece of Teutonic sculpture. Then his broad features were broken by an atypical smile. "I'm sorry," he said, fumbling for words that he obviously was unaccustomed to using. "The captain just explained things. . . . Sorry I was hard on you."

I smiled and tapped the big man on the shoulder. "Hey, that's all right. I guess I wasn't so civil myself."

Bischoff nodded, his smile now only a memory. "The captain says I should escort you to the bridge," he said.

I followed him up the ladder, with Ruffin, and asked him which fluxworld we were now traversing.

"A far sight better'n the last," he said. "Come and have a look."

As we entered the bridge, I saw that we were perhaps ten or twelve meters beneath the sea. It had resumed its more comfortable shades of blue-going-to-green-and-back-again. Sunlight penetrated the clean water at this depth, and there were occasional fish nosing past the prow.

"Looks pretty normal to me," I said, leaning against the navigator's table.

"It is," said Bischoff. "The sea takes a long time to change."

"What's our location?" said Ruffin.

"We're approaching the Straights of Magellan."

"Cape Horn?" I said.

Bischoff nodded.

"Supposed to be some bad storms around here, right?"

"That's why we're submerged," said the first mate.

"You have any idea what temporal period we're in?" asked Ruffin.

"What *what?*" Bischoff looked truly perplexed.

"I think he means what age of the earth, what stage of civilization things are in. . . ." I said, smiling.

"Oh," said Bischoff. "Well, don't know for sure. Must be the age of sail though. We saw a frigate on the horizon shortly after passing through." He turned from us to check his headings at the instrument panel, made some corrections, and queried one of the operators. I stood there watching the ever-changing face of the sea, wondering what it was like on the surface, when it could be so utterly tranquil just meters beneath the wind and the air.

Bischoff did not seem like he wanted to continue the conversation and busied himself with the instruments and his charts. He never was much for excess verbiage, and I didn't feel like pushing him. When Nemo arrived there would plenty to talk about it.

Twenty minutes passed before the captain arrived. He appeared somewhat flushed, and his eyes seemed to be darker than I had ever seen them. "All detection equipment on highest gain!" he shouted, storming past us. "Action stations!"

"He talked?" I said, staring at him.

"Lord-all-friday he talked! If he got through, *The Kraken's* in our wake!"

"What're we going to do?"

"First, Mr. Alexander, we shall determine whether or not Robur is indeed accompanying us. If he is, I shall try to lose him in this fluxworld."

"We can't fight him?"

"We could, but I don't want to risk *The Nautilus* in her present condition. If we lose our engines in these waters, we have no way to repair her, or get back to our own world."

"What world is this, anyway? Bischoff didn't know for sure."

"Must you ask such things now?" Nemo glared at me and addressed the operator, Mr. Gray. "Anything yet, Gray?"

"Not certain, sir. I'm getting some confusing signals. Must be a bad storm going on up there."

"Have we rounded the cape yet?" said Nemo.

"No, sir," said Bischoff. "We're just approaching Tierra del Fuego."

Nemo turned from us and consulted some additional charts at the table. Producing his fountain pen, he scribbled some figures on the edge of the charts quickly. "We rendezvous with the 'gate in fifty-six minutes," he muttered mainly to himself. "All right, all ahead full, Mr. Bischoff, and take her up to bridge level."

There was a surge as The Nautilus' engines increased their thrumming and eased gently toward the surface, leveling off as its prow briefly broke the whitecaps then dropped down so that only the eye-ports were exposed to the air. Immediately the deck rocked and yawled under our feet, everyone grabbing for a handhold. The sky above us was almost black and streaked with ugly grays. Lightning flashed and danced across the water like water bugs on very long legs.

"Rig for surface running," said Nemo. "Storm alert at all stations, Mr. Bischoff."

"Why are we surfacing?" I asked, as the high seas continued to pound the crap out of us.

"We'll make better time, once we clear the cape," said Nemo. "And if Robur's behind us, I want to see if he follows us to the surface. Apparently, he's willing to lay back instead of making a fight of it."

"Got a fix," said Gray. "Three thousand meters aft! It might be The Kraken!"

"Is he holding his position?"

"Aye, sir, but he's riding a little deeper in the water."

"Inform me immediately if he changes course or position."

Outside the sea was cruel and capricious, and totally indifferent to our presence. It was difficult to estimate, but many of the swells and waves looked over ten meters high. There were times when The Nautilus would seem to tip over an edge of cascading water and drop as if on a mud slide. My stomach was registering these movements a few seconds after the fact; I felt like I was on an amuse-

189

ment park ride. Sure I did. Several times lightning crackled over the hull and the prow would glow in neon blue light. The gray skies seemed so low and close that you could reach out and touch them.

But Nemo's ship was strong and tough, and it pushed steadfastly through the storm, rounding the cape where the waters were not so terribly rough. At one point we sighted a three-masted ship on our port side. She was leaning into the wind, trying to feather her sails. The wind ripped and tore at her like hawk's talons, and she veered so close to us that I could see the desperate sailors scrambling across her wooden decks, hanging onto lines that whipped across the gunwales like angry snakes. You could almost hear the cracking of her sails as they would catch a full burst of storm wind, and I expected the mainsail to be ripped from her at any second. Men were swarming up ratlines in the gale, trying to gather in the rigging and the remaining pieces of canvas. I felt sorry for the poor bastards.

"What's her colors?" I asked Nemo, as we drew closer to the struggling ship.

"Portuguese. Seventeenth century. Probably full of Jesuits bound for Osaka or Nagasaki. They're the only ones who knew this route back then. A bunch of brave but crazy fools they were!"

I stared at the foundering ship. It had not reached the raging center of the cape's fury. The ship looked so small and fragile. It was a miracle that any of those ancient ships ever made such a dangerous passage. It was at that point that *The Nautilus* made its closest passage to the three-master. In spite of the raging storm and the high seas, many of the sailors took great notice of our ship. No doubt with its sleek lines and its two great glowing eyes, it appeared to be a fierce creature to them. That we could see the men so clearly at the short distance, I was amazed that they could not also see us through the glass of our ports. But if they did, they gave no notice. It would have been interesting to gauge their reactions had we been on calmer seas. A few harpoons and cannonballs might have been clattering off our hull if they had not been otherwise engaged with a storm that was probably going to kill them all.

The Portuguese ship disappeared aft in a cloak of hammering, gray mist, and *The Nautilus* churned forward, while somewhere further back lurked the enemy vessel of Robur.

For the next several minutes, we ploughed through the calming seas, while Bischoff calculated our position. If *The Kraken's* torpedo turret had not been damaged in the last flight, I'm sure we would have bought several charges up our rear sections. But Robur was not totally deranged. His plan obviously was to follow the stricken, wounded *Nautilus* back to its lair, where it would eventually have to return if it would ever be battle-ready and completely seaworthy again. Once learning the location of Nemo's base, Robur could organize a suitable attack and wipe out his nemesis once and for all.

In an incredibly short time, the storm waters were behind us and the sky began to clear. I had no conception of the way the weather worked in such extreme latitudes, but it is no wonder then that the capes of Africa and South America had always been known as mariners' nightmares. Bischoff took some readings in the clearing skies and calculated them on the charts. "We're getting close, sir," he said to Nemo.

"Where's the enemy, Mr. Gray?"

"Holding his position, sir. I've got a good fix on him, now. It's Robur for sure."

Nemo checked his timepiece, did some mental calculating. "Take her down, Mr. Bischoff. We'll try to lose him, come up quickly and slip through the 'gate before he can reach it."

"You're going to leave him here?" I asked.

Nemo stared at me for a moment, no longer flushed and agitated, once again thinking smoothly and clearly. "Why not, Alexander? At last I'd be rid of him."

I did not bother to answer him. *The Nautilus* had already begun its dive and was careening into the sea at an

191

extreme angle. It was back to the handholds for everybody. Gray continued to monitor the movements of *The Kraken*, and Nemo seemed delighted to learn that the enemy submarine was following us down. Nemo's plan, as he outlined it to us, as we neared the nadir of the dive, was to take advantage of *The Kraken's* damaged diving planes. It was hoped that the enemy would have difficulty making a sharp and rapid ascent in following us, and that *The Nautilus* could gain the next fluxgate, pass through it, and be gone before *The Kraken* could even get close to passing through. It was an admirable tactic, which I assumed took a great amount of timing and not a small amount of bravado. There was of course, the chance that *The Nautilus* could also miss the rendezvous, leaving us both stranded in a Secret Sea until the next cycle—whenever that might be.

"Take her up, Mr. Bischoff!" Nemo yelled, and the engines whined, the deck began to level off for a moment, before changing angles again. The only factor Nemo had not provided for was the loss of one of the sub's two gyroscopes, which greatly aided in the stability and change of direction of the vessel. Hence our quick-change maneuver was not as quick nor as smooth as it normally would have been. Gray kept feeding back reports of the position of the enemy. It seemed that, damaged diving plane or no, Robur was managing to keep pace with us, closing, in fact, as if the mad inventor sensed what Nemo had in mind.

We continued knifing upward with all the power the engines would give us. Breaking the surface like a Great Blue whale, pluming into the air for an instant, everyone braced for the impact as the prow smacked down upon the swelling sea. "Hard starboard, ten degrees. It should be appearing any second now," said Nemo, his eyes affixed to the eye-ports anxiously.

The Nautilus stabilized itself and began cutting through the water, while I imagined that close behind was *The Kraken* breaking on top and taking after us as fast as possible. Up ahead a rolling mist seemed to be forming above the water, and I watched it begin to coalesce into what was now a more familiar, though no less awesome sight. I think if I saw one of these dimensional gaps forming every day for the rest of my life, I wouldn't be any less cowed by what it represented, by what it actually was. It was like all the magic mirrors, the lost lands, the fairy-tale contrivances into other worlds all rolled into one massive, roiling, monstrous thing. The torus shape began to take on a grayish metal cast, appearing once again to be a solid object of immense size, hanging in the sea in a place where nothing by all rights should be. How many unsuspecting sailors over the millennia had seen such a sight and been drawn terrified into its timeless, spaceless depths, never to return to their own world?

The green glow had also started forming in its center, and the hull was starting to resonate from the roaring, groaning sound that emanated from the depths of the fluxgate. Our speed seemed to jump a bit as the forces which gave life to the 'gate caught us, sucked us inexorably toward the center. Nemo called out for a reading on *The Kraken,* but the operator shook his head. Apparently the electromagnetic fields set up by the dimensional warp were blanking everything.

"Where does this one let us out?" I asked as the ringed edge of the 'gate passed above the ports.

"Somewhere in the mid-twentieth century . . . quite close to your own time," said Nemo. "But a different world . . . nonetheless."

The fluxgate devoured us, and there was an instant of grayness, of timelessness, and then we were again floating in a rough, choppy sea.

"Where're we geographically?" said Ruffin.

"Somewhere in the mid-Atlantic," said the captain. "I'll know as soon as I can get a fix. It should be close to the coordinates in my charts, however."

Turning from us, Nemo addressed Mr. Gray. *"The Kraken!* Did he make it?"

Gray remained hunched over his console, hands clasped to his earphones. "Think so, sir. I have something

... getting a signal, now. Yes, sir, He's made it. . . ."

"God damn him!"

"Two thousand meters and holding, sir."

"Keep a watch on his position," said Nemo, turning once again to his charts. "Got to rethink this thing, got to figure out a way."

"What about having it out with him, sir?" asked Bischoff. "He's on our tail. We could use the deck gun . . ."

Nemo paused, rubbing his left hand over his thick beard. "Risky. Very risky, Mr. Bischoff. I just don't know."

"How far till the next 'gate?" Bischoff leaned over the charts with his captain.

"Oh, about another two hours. The position is not far from here though. Right here," said Nemo, pointing to a spot on the chart.

"Does Robur have any surface armament?" I asked.

"Nothing like we've got," said Bischoff.

"What about his torpedoes? Could he fire them without using the turret?" This was Ruffin.

"I don't know. It's possible, isn't it, Captain?" Bischoff regarded Nemo who was still lost in thought, apparently trying to discover the correct tactical path out of the maze.

"Yes, it's possible. You've got to go careful with a man like Burton. . . . He might be crazy, but he's still bright, and goddamned dangerous." Nemo looked out the eye-ports at the eastering sky. It was just after dawn in this fluxworld, and the sky and sea were contrasting shades of blue. "Steady as she goes, Mr. Bischoff. Ahead two-thirds."

Nemo drifted off into his own thoughts again, staring out at the barren waterscape. He left us all to our thoughts, and I felt like we were all dangling on the end of a thin line, about to drop in between the most mythical of bad situations: a rock and a hard place.

We passed a little time like that, thinking and staring and not saying a damn thing, and all knowing that *The*

Kraken was hanging tough a couple of thousand meters to the aft.

Things would have stayed like that a little longer I guess . . . if it wasn't for the Zeros.

TWENTY-ONE

APPROPRIATELY, I guess, they came straight out of the sun, smoking down on us like chickenhawks.

Actually we heard them before we saw them, and we heard their machine-gun fire stitching across the water and pinging off the dorsal armor before we even heard their engines. There were four of them flying in a tight formation, and they split into groups of two—not wanting to discriminate against poor Robur bringing up the rear of our little convoy.

"Good Christ!" yelled Ruffin, as he ran to the eye-port and watched the two tan fighter planes with the big, red spots on their wings go ripping past us to bank around for another straffing run. "Zeros, Bryan! Japanese Zeros! In the North Atlantic! I don't believe it."

Nemo joined us at the eye-ports, watching the fighters regrouping and coming back again. He was clearly fascinated by the flying machines, and visibly impressed by the maneuverability and speed as they cut through the air. "They're beautiful," he muttered. "Beautiful!"

"Yeah, and they might be able to blow us right out of the water!" said Ruffin. "We've got to dive!"

The Zeros came in low, their wings flickering from the machine-gun fire, and the bullets traced a trail across *The Nautilus'* hull, pinging and ringing, but causing no appreciable damage. I looked to see if they had anything under the wings as they passed overhead, but they appeared to be clean. Apparently a reconnaissance flight that just happened to spot us rolling along down here on the surface. Exactly what the Japanese were doing in the North Atlantic *was* an interesting question. It was conceivable that the United States had lost control in the Pacific early on in the war, or perhaps they were now allied with the Japanese against Hitler, or . . . well, it could have been any number of variations. It really didn't matter how or why, since the cold facts were that the Japanese considered us an enemy of some sort and they were trying to rub us out.

"We've got to dive," Ruffin said again, this time breaking Nemo out of his adoring trance.

"Their bullets have little effect, Mr. Ruffin," said the captain coolly.

"That doesn't matter, don't you see?" said Ruffin. "They've probably realized that too. They'll be calling in some help!"

"Help?" said Nemo. "What kind of help?"

"Destroyers," I said, wishing that Nemo had seen a few of the old World War II movies so that I would not have to explain everything when time was, as they say, of the essence. "Big armored ships. They have undersea bombs that can blow hell out of us, and they've got detection equipment that makes your stuff look like a crystal set."

"What's a crystal set?" said the captain.

"Hey, look," said Derek. "Never *mind* that, okay? Just listen to us! You've got to take her down! Now!"

Outside, the Zeros had completed their sweeping turns and were now angling in for a third attack-pattern.

"But if I take her down, we will not be able to rendezvous with the final fluxgate, don't you see that, gentlemen?" Nemo looked from one of us to the other with what he assumed to be implacable logic.

"How long before we have to hit the next one?" I asked.

Bullets stung the hull, sounding like hailstones on a tin roof.

"Approximately forty minutes," said Nemo after consulting his timepiece.

"Where?" asked Ruffin.

"Approximately right where we are now," said Nemo.

"Jesus, that's great," said Ruffin, who had begun to pace awkwardly behind the row of operators, who were all watching the fighter planes as they pirouetted through the gray sky, forming up into a four-plane formation once again.

"Excuse me, Captain, but they're leaving," said Bischoff.

We all rushed to watch the Zeros bank off toward the east.

"Probably going back to their carrier," said Ruffin.

"Their what?" Nemo again.

"Their aircraft carrier," I said. "Imagine an enormous floating island constructed on top of a ship's hull. Something big enough to carry and launch fifty or sixty planes. That's a carrier."

"Incredible!" said the captain. "What a marvelous idea!"

"Look, Bischoff," said Ruffin. "Do me a favor, tell your captain that we're in grave danger, will you? Tell him we've *got* to dive!"

The large, bald man stared at Ruffin, obviously upset that he would put the first mate in such an indelicate position. "I cannot tell my captain any such thing. The decision is not mine, Mr. Ruffin."

Just at that point I saw three streamers of black smoke curling off the horizon, and getting thicker, and therefore closer, with every second passing.

"Derek, look," I said, tapping his arm.

"All right, see!" he said to Nemo. "Now do you believe me? They're coming after us. We gotta get outa here!"

"But they seem like they're so far away," said Nemo. "Surely, we have plenty of—"

"Listen, they *are moving!* And they've probably already picked us up on their . . . their instruments. If we wait around, we're cooked."

Nemo stared for a few seconds at the black streamers coming in from the east. They were thicker now, and you could even see the stacks and part of the superstructure of the lead vessel. "Very well, gentlemen, I'll take your word on this account, but we must surface in less than forty minutes to make our fluxgate passage."

I could not imagine us being on the surface with those modern warships and having any kind of a chance. If they

198

didn't get us with their depth charges, their deck guns could schmice us just as easily.

Nemo gave instructions to dive, with Ruffin adding that he should take us as deep as the ocean floor would allow. Bischoff took the helm and nominal control of the vessel, while the captain leaned over the chart table and began calculating times and positions. Every so often he would mutter something to himself, shake his head, nod or emit a soft sigh, then return to his furious scribbling.

As the angle of descent increased, he looked up. "Sorry, but there is no other way to make the passage to our home world but through this 'gate opening soon. If we miss this one, we are trapped in this fluxworld for weeks. And even then, the next 'gate opening won't take us to my home world. We must make this passage, gentlemen."

"Fifteen hundred meters," said Bischoff, recording our descent. "Two thousand . . ."

Nemo called out to Mr. Gray, "Position of *The Kraken*. . . . Is he still with us?"

"He's holding, sir."

"Thirty-five hundred . . . four thousand meters . . ." said Bischoff. "We're approaching bottom terrain. Have to level off with five hundred meters, Captain."

"Steady as she goes. Level as you may, Mr. Bischoff."

Through the eye-ports I could see the rocky bottom of the North Atlantic rising up to greet us. It was a rolling, partially jagged, partially sandy landscape, where untended crops of seaweed and kelplike growth slowly waved at our approach. A school of sea bass rose up past the prow and scattered in the face of our running lamps. Somewhere above us the Japanese destroyers would be circling, probing with their sonar, priming their charges.

"Where's your enemy, Mr. Ruffin?" said Nemo, smiling slyly.

"He's up there," said Derek. "We'll be hearing from him soon enough . . ." He looked through the eye-port cautiously. "His instruments are very sophisticated, and I think we will have more of a chance if we can shut down as many mechanical systems as possible."

"What? Shut *down*! . . ." Nemo was aghast.

"He's right," I said. "They will even be able to hear someone clanging a wrench on a pipe. You've got to do it."

"Incredible!" said Nemo. "Who did you say this enemy is?"

"Japanese," I said. "The United States entered a war with them in my world in 1941."

"Orientals! Incredible that they should have achieved such a technology after so many centuries of feudal ignorance. . . . In so short a time!"

"Listen, this is no time to be discussing world politics and economics," said Ruffin. "You've got to turn everything off and get this ship quiet!"

Nemo turned to protest, but he never got the words out. The entire submarine shuddered under the thunderous explosion of a depth charge which must have detonated right above our heads. The hull of *The Nautilus* rang like a bell being struck with a monstrous hammer. For a moment my ears clogged, and I could hear nothing except the echo of the explosion in my inner ear. Nemo had grabbed a handhold and kept his footing, but Bischoff had been shaken loose from the helm and was on his knees. The operators were scrambling back to their chairs.

"Good Lord!" cried Nemo. "What in God's name—?!"

"I told you they were going to blow hell out of us!" yelled Derek. "We've got to move off this spot and then shut down everything. . . ."

Nemo nodded quickly and issued a series of quick commands. The crew leaned into the task, easing *The Nautilus* across the sandy bottom, down a sloping gradient toward a gently rising formation of igneous rock. He sent Bischoff off on an all-stations alert to shut down all nonessential machinery and command that everyone on board remain perfectly still and by all means quiet. When the engines came to a slow but eventual stop, you could hear everyone breathing on the bridge in quick rapid intakes and exhalations. Nemo's pocket watch sounded like a jackhammer when he pulled it out to check on our timetable.

"Twenty-four minutes," he whispered.

Just then all the lights in the bridge went out, except those on the instruments and several safety lamps built into the walls. Aside from the faint aquamarine glow of the sea, and the scant emergency lighting, we were in darkness.

Bischoff returned, whispering something about being on battery power, and all stations secure.

Another depth charge went off, this time further away, but still rocking the crap out of us. Shock waves and sound waves travel through water with incredible speed and force. Two more charges went off, also some distance away, but each one felt like gigantic hammer blows applied to our collective heads. I was beginning to wonder if the welding and riveting which put *The Nautilus* together were strong enough to withstand a sustained attack such as this. Not even worrying about a direct hit—no sense worrying about that—but rather just the constant vibration and shock to the vessel's superstructure. But I figured there was no sense mentioning that to Nemo. He'd probably already considered it, and even if he had not, there was no sense bothering him with it now. Either we survived or we did not. It was that basic.

"How long will this continue?" whispered Nemo.

"I don't know," I said. "Sometimes they'll just saturate the area and forget about it, hoping that they got lucky. It depends on lots of things. If they're on a particular mission, they might not have much time to fool with us . . . or they might not have anything better to do except wait until they see some of our oil and parts float up to the surface."

"Wonder what old Robur thinks of all this. . . ." said Ruffin. "Probably crapping bricks trying to figure out what we've dragged him into." He laughed a shade on the way to hysteria, and I felt like joining him.

"No doubt he is emulating our own maneuvers if he wishes to survive," said Nemo.

Another salvo of charges blew in our neighborhood.

The fish had all scattered after the first barrage. The sea outside looked as cold and lonely as the moon, but nowhere near as safe.

Nemo checked his timepiece again. "Alexander! We have only minutes left! We cannot stay down like this and miss the cycling of the fluxgate."

"If we go up now, it's suicide," said Ruffin. "I'll take our chances missing it and picking up the next one that comes through . . . whenever it is."

"We cannot take a chance like that. We must pass through."

"There's no way," I said, and another depth charge went off as if to emphasize my words.

"There may be one way," he said, moving to the navigation table and fumbling with his charts and figures. He stood thusly in the dim light, muttering to himself for several minutes. More explosions erupted around us, one so close that I expected the inner hull plates to start buckling inward, the smell of seawater preceded only by a rush of very cold water. But through all this mayhem, Nemo stood his calculating ground, lost completely in his ciphers.

Finally, he was prepared to speak again but first paused to check his timepiece. "Our only chance is to time our ascent perfectly, reaching the surface at the exact moment the fluxgate is opening. We break the water and slip through before the Orientals can open fire on us."

"That sounds insane," said Ruffin.

"No, wait. These depth charges they're sending down here . . . what is their mechanism?" Nemo stared at Ruffin.

"Not sure *exactly* how they work. But I think they're preset to go off at a particular depth."

"Of course!" said Nemo. "As I imagined! Now listen: if we begin with the most rapid ascent possible, we should by all rights be able to clear the depths through which most of their bombs are primed to explode. Then we face no further peril till we reach the surface and the destructive power of their surface cannon, correct?"

"Yeah, but what about then?" said Ruffin. "They'll slaughter us!"

"But no, Mr. Ruffin," said Nemo. "Not if we strike the fluxgate at just the proper moment. There will be no chance for them to fire upon us."

"Sounds crazy to me," said Ruffin, "but you know, it might make some sense, it might just work . . ."

"Of course it shall work," said Nemo, checking his timepiece again. "Lord!, we've just enough time. Rig for running, Mr. Bischoff. I'll take the helm."

Bischoff started bellowing out orders through the phone systems and then down the spiral ladder he ran. The engines started slowly, then rising to a high-pitched insect-like whine. The lights came up and *The Nautilus* was moving slowly across the sea bottom. Another two charges went off, closer than most of the others. Up on the surface, I imagined the sonar operators getting a new fix on our position, passing it along to gunnery crews and the depth bombers.

The gyroscope geared up, the diving planes set at their most extreme angles. The engines were rammed all ahead full, and suddenly *The Nautilus* was climbing through the dead waters. Nemo stood at the helm, checking his instruments, guiding the submarine through an unseen maze in his mind that would bring him to the surface where the only point of escape would lie. Somewhere behind us, Robur and his own vessel, if he did indeed survive the present depth charging, was probably trying to duplicate our maneuvers. But Nemo had seemed to have forgotten all about his original nemesis in light of this greater danger.

Upward we surged, Nemo checking his timepiece occasionally, nodding to himself, watching his guidance instruments and the shimmering reverse mirror of the surface coming closer and closer. Far below us the concussions of more depth charges rattled in the water but had no effect on us. If the Japanese destroyers knew we were surfacing, knew that we were coming fast upon them, they had yet to indicate it.

"Within a minute now!" cried Nemo. "Stand by!"

203

Because of the extreme angle of our ascent, the view from the bubbled eye-ports was limited, but at any moment I expected to see the bottom of a large destroyer crossing our bow, or worse, that we would intersect one of the big mothers and spear him like a swordfish.

What followed next was a succession of strobelike images, only half-perceived and half-imagined because of our vantage point within the bridge. But I'll try to reconstruct what happened so that you can get the whole picture . . . the big picture as they say in the media business.

The Nautilus broke the surface in much the same way as we had earlier done when trying to evade Robur. As the prow slapped down into the choppy waters, I could see that Nemo's aim had been a bit off, but if he had been running things by some instinctive sense of the sea and his position in it, he had not done badly. To our starboard side, we could all see the fluxgate already foaming and curling and resolving itself into a palpable form. We were perhaps one hundred meters from its center when we first surfaced. The engines vibrated through the hull of the ship as Bischoff pushed them to their limits, and we ploughed up rooster tails of water driving for the torus shape of the 'gate. To our port side, a looming gray shape steamed into view. The Japanese destroyer was leaning into us, her bow curving up out of the water like the business end of a very big hatchet. The front turret guns were swiveling around, and the elevation of the barrels was dropping to get us into their sights. Above the ship, a thick, oily column of smoke rolled, being fanned outward by the sea wind and the speed of the gray monster as it bore down on us. I figured we were about fifty meters from the fluxgate—now large and solid and glowing like a big neon sign advertising a doughnut shop—when the destroyer opened with the first salvo. A triad of shells impacted across our bow, literally blowing a hole in the sea for a few milliseconds and The Nautilus seemed to fall for a moment into the empty trough momentarily created. Still we steamed ahead. The destroyer was smoking down on us, less than two hundred meters from our intersection with the 'gate, which had now started pulling us in faster by means of its attractive field. The destroyer fired again, and three more explosions ripped up the water just by the eye-ports. A few more seconds and we were within the outer ring of the torus—we were going to make it, it seemed—and the groaning, thrumming sound of the fluxgate overwhelmed all the sounds of the sub and the raging explosions outside. There was a grayness and blankness for another second and then we were emerging into the bright, cold sunlight of an almost stormy sea in Nemo's world. Behind us, things must have been getting very interesting. Nemo continued away from the egress of the 'gate at full speed, while we watched through the rear port to see *The Kraken* emerging from what appeared to be the nothingness of the air itself. The guy might have been crazy, but he had *chutzpah, cojones,* or whatever you want to call it. He was a hell of a fighter in his own right, and he must have been on our dorsal fin like a pilot fish to make it through.

As we stood watching, at first in amazement at Robur's feat, it quickly turned to horror as we saw the giant gray bow of the Japanese destroyer also emerging from thin air. Those crazy bastards had followed us right through and they were still going to blow us out of the water.

But a curious thing happened.

Before the destroyer could pass all the way through, the 'gate started closing. As we watched, the entire half of the warship that was visible on our side of the 'gate was enveloped in a bright green light. The light became a green, liquid fire that seemed to surge and flow about the superstructure of the bow, the gun turrets, the stacks, and the jutting superstructure. Even at our distance, we could hear the sounds of cracking and breaking, swept up in a moaning roar like the wind out of hell itself. The destroyer seemed to be breaking up into crystalline, snow-flakelike fragments, each one flickering briefly in the eerie green light. The ship was caught between the shifting tangents of two universes, and unable to be pulled through into either one, was being banished into some nether world where nothingness was king. Suddenly there was a brilliant flash, brighter than the sun, but no sound . . .

And then it was gone.

TWENTY-TWO

AFTER SUCH a spectacular display, the sight of *The Kraken* cutting through the sea a few thousand meters aft was not such an awesome thing. Admittedly, the evaporation of the destroyer was a hard act to follow, but one had to keep things in perspective. Robur's ship had somehow followed us through, and he was intent upon sending us to the bottom.

Nemo quickly reminded us of this fact and rechecked his enemy's position. "All ahead full, Mr. Bischoff. Follow standard course coordinates. You know where we are now."

Bischoff nodded and took the helm.

"And now," said Nemo, looking aft to the dark shape of *The Kraken* keeping silent pace, "we must deal with the madman."

"What've you got in mind?" I asked.

"Obviously he plans to follow me to my base. Once discovering its location, he will try to make a run for it, then return with more fire power and a plan to destroy me. Unfortunately for Robur, he will be blundering into a trap from which there will be no escape. He will be forced to fight me in my own territory and he will be at a distinct disadvantage."

"How far are we from your base?" said Ruffin.

"Within the hour we shall be quite close." Nemo turned away and consulted his charts once again.

Outside the submarine was quietly slipping beneath the surface, joining the familiar seas of its own world. The water was clear and brilliant, and the myriad creatures swarmed and schooled past as we cut through them. The sea bottom was not deep here and the light drove far into the clear waters. I could not tell what geographic location this might indicate, other than that we must be in the vicinity of the continental shelf or at least on the downslope of a large island chain or volcanic formation.

While the first mate went below to prepare for return to the base, I stayed on the bridge watching the changing undersea terrain, thinking over the events of the last twenty-four hours—God, was it only that long?—and wondered when it would end. I knew that my appetite for "adventure," and "mystery," and whatever else I thought was lacking in my life had been satisfied for a long time to come. I started thinking about the kind of life Nemo and his crew must have, and there was nothing very romantic about it. In fact, they all must have had at least a slight case of misanthropy, and more than a few of them must have been closet misogynists. And I was discovering, even after just a few days on board the submarine, that I was not cut out to be either of those types. During all the tight spots we'd been in, I had tried not to think about *never* getting back to our own time/world, but in the more quiet moments, it would start to prey on me. I never had gotten a chance to talk to Nemo about taking us back, but I had the feeling that he would not be too averse to the idea. Then there was the problem of a ship. Derek's fine little schooner was scattered all over the Pacific, and we would have to use something once we were dumped off in our own world. It was possible that Nemo could provide us with some kind of dinghy, but floating around the open sea, even *with* land in sight, struck me as just this side of insanity rather than any kind of high adventure. I just wanted to be out of this damned submarine. I wanted to talk on some dry land and kick through some wooden path with lots of crispy orange and brown leaves under my boots and the sunlight coruscating through the trees and a young lady on my arm while we carried a wicker basket with sandwiches and a bottle of cheap burgundy and maybe some cannoli for desert. I always liked cannoli.

But I digress from the tale at hand.

Behind us, *The Kraken* was plumbing the depths and maintaining a safe but pursuing distance. It was very crazy to me that Robur would simply hang on our tail like this without trying to do something nefarious—I've always like that word—or at least offensive. If I had been Nemo's nemesis, trailing him like he was, I would have been working furiously to jury-rig that torpedo system so that at the very least I could squeeze off one shot into our aft section. But so far, all he had done was hang on our wake, waiting, as Nemo had suggested, to finally locate his headquarters. The whole strategy struck me as very odd, much the same way the military tactics of the prerevolutionary British Empire would strike a modern general as foolishness. But as they say, these were strange times I was living in, and things were definitely different here.

Watching the terrain ahead of us, I noticed that it was beginning to slant upward very gradually. The sea bottom was less sandy here, and the vegetation was becoming more sparse as the rocky, jagged bottom assumed a more fierce aspect. We were approaching some kind of geologic formation that was distinctly different from the surrounding sea bottom. I sensed that things were drawing to their eventual climax.

Bischoff returned to the bridge and consulted with Nemo in low whispers that I had difficulty hearing. Outside, their attention was drawn to several large fissures that had appeared beneath us. There was one yawning chasm that split into the sea bottom, as if there had been some sort of awesome upheaval here at one time. An earthquake or perhaps the eruption of some vast undersea volcano.

"All engines one-third," said Nemo, and the submarine began to power down, drifting silently forward toward the center of the chasm that lay beneath us like an open wound. We began settling into its center ever so slowly, and the shadows from the sea-filtered light grew long and dark. Aft, *The Kraken* continued to follow us doggedly, and I was wondering, like Robur himself, I'm sure, whether or not this was some kind of diversionary trick of Nemo's, or if we were drawing temptingly close to the captain's hidden lair. If I had been Robur, I would have been ambivalent about following *The Nautilus* into unfamiliar and possibly dangerous waters. From under the sea, there was no way of positively identifying the area, and there had been no stars out when we entered the fluxworld. It was possible that Robur had not been able to gather a definitive fix on our position.

Whatever his motivations, Robur and his ship mimicked our maneuvers and began drifting slowly into the depths of the great canyon. It grew progressively darker, and Nemo switched on all the outside running lamps, sending out beams of light into the darkness ahead of us.

"Steady as she goes," said the captain. "Should be coming up soon."

Ruffin and I crowded as close to the ports as we could, straining to see whatever it was they were looking for. Still seeing nothing distinctive, I heard Bischoff say, "All right, sir. Coming up now . . ."

"All ahead full! Take the helm, Mr. Bischoff and get us through," Nemo said as he turned to regard *The Kraken* which was still following us down.

Ahead, the running lamps had fallen upon a large cave-like entrance in the side of the canyon. The hemispherical opening was split in several places by large fault lines, and although it was more than large enough to accommodate a ship four times the size of *The Nautilus* it remained a hazardous maneuver to guide the submarine through.

Nemo stood at the aft port studying the enemy vessel, waiting to see if Robur would duplicate our maneuver. The running lights on *The Kraken* were like bright yellow lances, spearing the dark waters to our port side as we pulled out of his pursuing path. Then the beams of light shifted direction, seeking us out once again.

"He's coming through!" cried Nemo. "He's coming on! All ahead full, Mr. Bischoff. Draw him in."

The Nautilus had aligned itself with the cavern entrance now and was burrowing straight down its center into total darkness. We had cleared the entrance and were passing jagged peaks and ridges below and above. *The*

210

Kraken followed, although not at nearly the same speed, since Robur was undoubtedly fearful of the rock formations that could open his ship like a can of soup. Nemo kept watching until certain that *The Kraken* had cleared the cavern entrance, then he turned quickly to the control consoles, muttering to himself.

"I've got him now! I've got him, do you hear!? Close the gates, Mr. Bischoff. The gates! Shut them down!"

The first mate leaned over the board and threw several levers quickly.

"What's going on?" I asked as Nemo practically danced around the bridge, unable to control his obvious elation.

"What gates?" asked Ruffin.

"We have constructed a portcullis to protect the cavern entrance," said Nemo, still beaming, openly smiling for the first time in what seemed like a long time. "My men in the diving suits. Took them almost a year to complete the task, but it proved its worth today! I can control its opening and closing by means of an electronic beam, and now I've got *The Kraken* sealed in. He shall never escape me now!"

"Approaching the entrance, sir," said Bischoff.

"Take her up! Let the fool follow me now!" said the captain, going completely manic as he tasted apparent victory over his lifelong rival.

The Nautilus began a rapid ascent, angling treacherously close to the walls of the undersea passage, but the roof of the chamber was also angling up and away from us and suddenly there was open water above us. I could see the shimmering whiteness of the surface fast descending to greet us, and then we were through into the open air.

"Battle stations!" cried Nemo. "Gun crews and militia teams topside!"

Bischoff scurried down the spiral ladder, and two of the operators rose and quickly followed him.

As I looked out of the eye-ports I could see that we were now sailing in a calm, inland sea. The light was diffused, not as strong as sunlight should be. On the distant

211

shore, I could see the sharply angled walls of sheer cliffs rising up so high as to dwarf a large collection of buildings and docks and other unrecognizable structures.

Ruffin, who was still watching from the aft port, suddenly shouted. I turned to see *The Kraken* also surfacing roughly fifteen hundred meters behind us.

Then Nemo was at our shoulders. "Come on lads, let's get topside and finish him off!"

Following the ecstatic captain, we worked our way through the corridors to the hatch which opened outside the bridge section. The decks were still spilling off foam and seawater as the gun crew cranked the seventy millimeter weapon up onto the deck. There was a man in the cage already, squinting into the gunsight, waiting to swing the entire rig into position. Other men had deployed themselves on the deck, armed with rifles that were similar in design to the Civil War Winchester.

The Kraken, apparently realizing now what had happened, had slackened its pace and was angling sharply away from us. Crewmen had also appeared on her decks and were furiously working at something on her dorsal rear section. Nemo pulled glasses to his face and studied their movements. "Bischoff, get that gun crew cracking! Looks like they've got some kind of new armament. . . . Lord, they've got themselves a cannon, too!"

Just then there was a loud report as the seventy-millimeter got off its first round. The shell dropped a good fifty meters in front of the enemy, sending up a tremendous spray. The spotter for the gun crew shouted out corrections, and the team cranked like little windup men. The cannon was loaded again, and another shot rocked the entire ship with its recoil. Another spray of water, this time closer to *The Kraken*.

"Come on, damn you!" cried Nemo, standing with his glasses and beginning to feel helpless as he watched the enemy gun swing into position. I watched at his side as a bright orange blossom appeared on its barrel, followed quickly by a loud cracking report. *The Kraken's* shell whistled over our heads and entered the water beyond us with a shuddering explosion.

212

"They're getting the elevation," said Ruffin. "Drawing a bead on us . . ."

The Nautilus' cannon opened up again, the deck rocked, and there was a small explosion near the prow of *The Kraken*. The militia team cheered as the gun crew began reloading and fine-tuning their aim for a knockout shot to the enemy gun position. The prow of the enemy submarine was smoldering, and there was a column of oily smoke rising up from the grazing shot.

Suddenly the air was ripped from our mouths as the explosion ripped into *The Nautilus*. Ruffin was thrown off the railing and something hot and sharp sliced through my right leg. There was a white-out as the blast swallowed up the section of the deck that Nemo's seventy millimeter gun had occupied. Smoke swirled up from blackened, twisted wreckage. The crew was gone, blasted into presumably small pieces; half the militia team had also been obliterated and the others were floundering in the water, some screaming for help, others just struggling to stay afloat. What was left of the cannon looked like a few twisted pieces of black metal falling into slag.

Running into the bridge, Nemo was in a panic, calling for all engines full. The gun crew on *The Kraken* didn't waste any time, though, and another shell rocked into our aft section, sending up a fine spray of metal and flame.

I looked down at my leg where a piece of shrapnel had tried to amputate me just above the knee. The blood wasn't running as freely as I would have thought, and I realized that it must have just grazed me as it went by. It didn't look exactly superficial, but I could tell I wasn't mortally stricken. Somebody was hauling Ruffin back on board, and he was yelling something at me. In a kind of half daze, I tried to make out his words.

"Get the gun! Get the gun, Bryan!"

"The gun's gone!" I cried, figuring that he meant the cannon.

He was up on the side, breathing hard, struggling to get out the words. "No! No! The Magnum . . . the Weatherby! Get it up here fast!"

When I knew what he was getting at, I rushed from the

213

bridge and stumbled, hobbled, "ran" down the corridor to my quarters. I could hear the ship's engines groaning all through the ship's interior. That last hit had probably fouled up the rudders and the screws. It didn't seem like we were making much headway.

Reaching my cabin I dove down to the sea chest and fumbled through the piles of books. On deck another shot rang home and the concussion dropped me hard to the floor. I hoped that the armor plate was holding out, or we would soon be deep-sixing it. I pulled out the rifle with the mean-looking scope and the box of cartridges, jamming it into my belt and fumblingly loaded the chamber. I'd never fired the thing in my life and I wasn't even sure I was loading it right.

Then it was back to the bridge and Ruffin, who was coming through to meet me. "Give me that damn thing!" he yelled as he saw me, and yanked it from my obliging hands.

After a quick check of the chamber he snapped it down and dropped into a sharpshooter's crouch. He sighted the Leupold optics on *The Kraken* gun crew.

The gun sounded like a cap gun compared to the cannon they were using, but it was an incredibly accurate weapon. Derek squeezed off two quick shots, and two men slumped over their stations. One guy in the gunnery cage and the spotter. While they were pulling the dead ones out of the way, Derek put two more of them away: the loader and the halyard man. He was so cool and smooth about it. Slowly taking aim, lining up the poor bastards in those precision cross-hairs, then easily squeezing off the hollow head shells. It must have been like a shooting gallery where you're only ten feet away. Each time one of the gunners would catch a shell, the would get knocked back about ten feet and off the deck.

Like a surgeon, Derek continued to fire and had effectively cleaned out the entire gun crew. As more crewmen surged around the gun, Derek would calmly open up and pick them off. Pretty soon they got the message, and nobody was getting near the cannon. It was like a Mexican standoff.

214

"Splendid shooting, Ruffin!" said Nemo's voice as he emerged from the bridge hatch. "Excellent! That's a fine weapon, Alexander. Fine weapon!"

"I can keep them away from the cannon at least," said Ruffin, still sighting through the scope at the huddle of terrified crewman bunched up by the conning tower of *The Kraken.*

Bischoff stepped through the hatch, soaking wet, smeared with oil and grease. "We're dead in the water. One of their shots knocked out the whole rudder and screw assembly. . . ."

Nemo shook his head, and I could see the pain in his eyes as he contemplated such damage to his beloved ship. "We'll have to put ashore," he said finally. "Robur is trapped here. We can deal with him at our leisure."

"Wait a minute," I said. "What about Ruffin? You going to leave him here with the rifle all day?"

Nemo considered this problem for a moment, but before he could answer, Ruffin started shouting. It seemed as if Robur was going to save us the trouble of working things out.

"He's moving off!" cried Ruffin. "Look!"

Everyone stood silently watching the sleek bulk of *The Kraken,* its twisted prow still smoldering, but the fires apparently under control. A shallow wake fanned out from its aft section as it moved slowly from left to right, describing a large, sweeping arc about two thousand meters away from us.

"What's he doing?" I asked.

"Hold on, hold on . . ." said Nemo.

The Kraken continued the arc, gathering speed, its wake growing wider and higher. For a moment I found my attention drifting, as if in a dream, and I scanned the shoreline of the inland sea. The sheer walls I had seen behind the catch of buildings and docks soared high into the air, completely encircling the sea in which we were now lying. High above us was a seemingly small, round aperture at the top of an enormous cone. Nemo's base, his inland sea, everything, was contained within a monstrous, dead volcano. He was correct. There was no escape for

215

Robur—or for any of us—and everyone's fate would be decided here and now.

"He's turning . . ." said Bischoff, breaking me out of my daze, and my attention returned to the enemy submarine, which seemed to have sunk several meters deeper into the water.

"Coming right at us!" cried Ruffin. "He's going to ram us!"

Like a wolf circling his prey, the ship had completed its arcing maneuver and was now homing in on our position. I couldn't be sure of its speed, but it was enough to throw up rooster tails of foam and spray, and he was coming at us like an arrow.

Some of the crew that had scrambled back on the decks were now diving back into the water on *The Nautilus'* opposite flank. For a moment, Nemo stood transfixed, watching the enemy advance in a final suicidal move. You had to hand it to old Robur—he had a lot of class, real panache.

"We've got to abandon ship, sir," said Bischoff, prepared to go belowdecks and sound the final alarm. He waited, hanging on Nemo's response, but the captain stared out at *The Kraken,* saying nothing.

"Captain? . . . Captain Nemo, sir!" Bischoff reached out and grabbed his commander's sleeve, shaking it.

Slowly, Nemo turned, as if surprised to even see Bischoff at his side. "What is it, Bischoff?" he said softly.

"We've got to get off! Abandon ship?"

Nemo smiled. "No, mate, we'll stay on board. It's all right. *The Nautilus* will hold! Damn him and his submarine!" He shouted at the advancing vessel, now less than three hundred meters away and cutting through the water like a knife.

Everything started to slip into a sort of slow-motion, freeze-frame kind of view. I watched everything happen with a delicate precision, as if each image was held in my mind for a second or two longer than it was really happening. I was going to die . . . I could feel it, and I kept thinking slowly and repeatedly, *Is this the way it's going to end? Is this the way I'm going to die?* Over and over again, the thoughts passed through me, and I was curious that I felt no fear, no surge of body juices, no steel-trap muscle tension.

No one moved, except for Ruffin, who bravely pumped high-powered bullets into the glass of the enemy's conning tower. Cracks and fracture lines spider-webbed the glass as each shell pierced the thick glass. The course of the sub veered off slightly to our right but remained on a collision course. There was no sound, except for the surge of the sea as it was cleaved by the advancing submarine, looking like a wounded shark on its final attack.

And then there was a wrenching, groaning sound as metal met metal. The deck surged upward, buckling and splitting under the impact, as the gutted prow of *The Kraken* rammed into our starboard side. Ruffin was thrown into the air, as from a catapult, in a graceful arc to the water. Bischoff also went over the side, but Nemo and I were thrown through the hatch and down the ladder into the bridge, which was caving in, buckling, splitting slowly and inexorably. There was an explosion which rocked both vessels, and I could hear raining fragments of metal pinging down upon the hull. Another explosion and then the cries of men.

Footsteps surrounded us, and I could see the remaining crew streaming up onto the decks armed with pistols, axes, harpoons, their bare hands. Nemo was struggling to his feet, a gash over his forehead, which he ignored. I stumbled up after him and stood in the hatch. Both submarines were locked in a final death grip, *The Kraken's* prow aflame, and the heat actually fusing its metal hull to the armor plate of *The Nautilus*. But Nemo had been right; his ship had held her ground, absorbed the terrible collision, and was still afloat, waiting for more.

On the decks, men swarmed from the hatches of both ships. It was combat reduced to its lowest, most time-hardened denominator. Man against man. Nemo stood by me on the twisted rail of the bridge, watching as the two groups joined in a free-for-all with no rules. Pistols cracked in the air, axes swung wildly, fists flying. It was an insane crush of insane men, driven now past any rationality or even a sense of duty. It was down to kill him or be killed, regardless of *who* he was.

Beyond the small battle on the deck of *The Nautilus,* I saw a solitary figure emerge from the rear deck of *The Kraken.* He was a short man, wearing a gray suit and a black turtleneck. He wore thick glasses that resembled goggles, and he carried a handgun.

"Damn you!" cried Nemo upon seeing him. "Damn you to hell, you monster!" The captain became livid, seething with unstoppered rage and hate. I stood for a moment, paralyzed by the outburst, as he leaped off the rail and fell onto the deck, obviously after his arch rival.

As Nemo scrambled to his feet, Robur raised the handgun and fired off two shots. The first bullets ricocheted off the conning tower and by my ear, and that kind of upset me; the second caught Nemo in the left arm, slapping him down upon the deck again.

Jumping down, I helped him up to a sitting position. He was shocked by the impact of the bullet. He didn't look good, but at least he wasn't dying. "Get him! Get him, Alexander!"

It was all very dramatic, I grant you, but this whole encounter meant a lot to the good captain. I don't know what came over me when I looked down to see this great, but complex and driven, man in my arms. I felt suddenly charged to help him, to serve him.

The battle between the two crews had subsided somewhat after its initial fury, and Nemo's men were cleaning up on the remaining crewmen of *The Kraken.* A few more minutes and they would have things completely in hand. Sensing this, and probably figuring that he had mortally felled his opponent, Robur had scrambled down the aft section of his ship, where he was bent low, working at something I couldn't see. Just then, there was a splashing at the side of the sub, and Ruffin was hauling himself on board.

"You okay?" I yelled. "You all right?"

"Yeah, I'll make it. What happened to the old man?"

I told him about Robur's lucky shot, then looked back
218

to the man in question. He was getting into a small boat that had been attached to the outer hull of *The Kraken,* and he was obviously deciding to leave the party.

"Get him! For God's sake, get him!" said Nemo, after I had directed his attention to our fleeing villain.

"Come on, Derek," I said. "Let's *do* something!" I stood up, watching Robur rowing furiously away from us, looking like a two-legged water bug on the calm, mirror-like surface.

We left Nemo as comfortable as possible and jumped across the intersecting mess of the two vessels. The fighting down on *The Kraken's* decks was over. Ten of Nemo's men were now herding together six surviving enemy crewmen. I saw the cannon further aft and looked at Ruffin. "Think you can figure out how to work that thing?"

"Duck soup," he said.

I laughed, and we ran down the edge of the deck, climbed over some of the crew which Ruffin had earlier disposed of. The fact that they were dead bodies, something I'd had little contact with over the years of my quiet life, did not bother me. Something had changed inside, and I was facing hard realities of conflict, which washed away all my usual ethical feeling and moral pronouncements. I remember thinking that as I helped Ruffin maneuever the deck gun around in Robur's direction.

By this time the madman had put a fair amount of distance between the submarines and himself—maybe a hundred meters. The breech clanged shut as Ruffin loaded a shell into it. Then he paused, studying the firing mechanism. "You want to aim it?" he asked.

"Hell, no. I can't aim this thing!"

"Then get out of the way," and he was pulling me from the cage where the gunsight was located. "You see that cord back there?"

"Yeah," I said, not seeing it yet, but looking furiously for it, glad when at last I spotted it hanging from a lever next to breech. "Yeah!" I yelled again, this time joyed that I was not lying.

There was a lump in my throat, and my hands started

219

shaking as Ruffin cranked on the hand wheels in the cage, bringing the gun into position, drawing a bead on the little dinghy.

"This's going to be a piece of cake," he said.

"You ready?"

"Almost . . . get that cord in your hand! Yank it when I yell. Easy . . . easy . . . FIRE!"

The cannon erupted with an ear-shattering roar, and the recoil knocked me on my back, and as I rolled over to my side, I just caught a glimpse of Robur's little boat swallowed up in an orange white flower of flame.

A chorus of cheers erupted behind us as the crew applauded Ruffin's marksmanship. I never did know where he'd learned to handle weapons like he did, but he was damned good, that was for sure.

"Nice shot," I said, looking out to the spot where Robur had been. There was a wisp of smoke drifting away from the surface, and that was all. He probably never knew what hit him. It was too bad in a way, because although I'd never met him, he sounded like an interesting character. But I'm sure Ghengis Khan was pretty interesting too, right?

Then the crew was surrounding us, slapping backs, shaking hands, escorting us back to the stricken *Nautilus* where Nemo stood wounded but full of pride. Despite his bad arm he hugged both of us and promised anything we could possibly desire.

I looked at Derek, wet and full of grease and bilge, and smiled. "Take us home," I said. "I think we want to go home."

Nemo laughed and nodded his head. "Yes, I suppose you do!" he said, slapping me on the shoulder. "And you shall, gentlemen. And you shall . . . as soon as we get my *Nautilus* seaworthy once again. But we've got a lot of work ahead of us. . . ."

And we did.

TWENTY-THREE

NEMO'S FACILITIES at the volcanic base were a magnificent model of efficiency and design. Within four weeks of towing *The Nautilus* into his docks, his crew had repaired most of the damage and had begun reoutfitting for another cruise. Derek and I helped as much as we could, not knowing a tremendous amount about steelwork or "electrics" as Nemo called it, but we learned and we worked hard.

The battered hulk of *The Kraken* was also towed in and placed up on large stanchions, like a monument, down by the main quay. Nemo displayed it proudly, as would a fisherman who had hooked the largest marlin of the season, and I frankly could not blame him.

My Uncle Valery, poor man, was given a court-martial-style trial by his peers and found to be guilty of espionage. It turned out that he had encountered Robur initially in Iceland, fell under the madman's influence, and the rest, as they say, is psychology . . . or something like that.

Our voyage out from the base to a rendezvous with the proper fluxgate that would return us to our own world was uneventful, but the conversations with Nemo were a joy as usual. At one point he offered to provide us with a "rutter" which could guide us through the Secret Sea, if we ever wished to return to his world of Victorian wonder, but we both flatly turned him down. He did this out of eternal gratitude, I think, for saving his life, and his marvelous submarine. He also prepared for us a small sailing ship, five meters in length, which would get us safely to shore once he passed us through the 'gate.

We landed on the 26th Street beach at Ocean City, Maryland, causing quite a stir among the bathers and the Beach Patrol.

But that's another story.

LOST AMERICAN FICTION

☐	THE CUBICAL CITY Janet Flanner	03096-8	$1.50
☐	DRY MARTINI John Thomas	03093-3	$1.50
☐	THE DEVIL'S HAND Edith Summers Kelly	03101-8	$1.50
☐	FLESH IS HEIR Lincoln Kirstein	08548-7	$1.75
☐	MR. AND MRS. HADDOCK ABROAD Donald Ogden Stewart	08593-2	$1.95
☐	PREDESTINED Stephen French Whitman	08521-5	$1.75
☐	THE PROFESSORS LIKE VODKA Harold Loeb	03087-9	$1.50
☐	QUEER PEOPLE Carroll & Garrett Graham	04188-9	$1.95
☐	THE RED NATION Floyd Phillip Gibbons	04016-5	$1.95
☐	SINGLE LADY John Monk Saunders	04221-4	$1.95
☐	SUSAN LENOX, HER FALL AND RISE David Graham Phillips	04155-2	$2.50
☐	THEY DON'T DANCE MUCH James Ross	03110-7	$1.50
☐	THE WEDDING Grace Lumpkin	04090-4	$1.95
☐	WEEDS E. S. Kelley	03086-0	$1.50
☐	YESTERDAY'S BURDENS Robert M. Coates	03134-4	$1.50

Buy them at your local bookstores or use this handy coupon for ordering:

FAWCETT BOOKS GROUP
P.O. Box C730, 524 Myrtle Ave., Pratt Station, Brooklyn, N.Y. 11205

Please send me the books I have checked above. Orders for less than 5 books must include 75¢ for the first book and 25¢ for each additional book to cover mailing and handling. I enclose $_____ in check or money order.

Name_____

Address_____

City_____State/Zip_____

Please allow 4 to 5 weeks for delivery.

FREE
Fawcett Books Listing

There is Romance, Mystery, Suspense, and Adventure waiting for you inside the Fawcett Books Order Form. And it's yours to browse through and use to get all the books you've been wanting . . . but possibly couldn't find in your bookstore.

This easy-to-use order form is divided into categories and contains over 1500 titles by your favorite authors.

So don't delay—take advantage of this special opportunity to increase your reading pleasure.

Just send us your name and address and 35¢ (to help defray postage and handling costs).

FAWCETT BOOKS GROUP
P.O. Box C730, 524 Myrtle Ave., Pratt Station, Brooklyn, N.Y. 11205

Name_____
(please print)

Address_____
City_____State_____Zip_____

Do you know someone who enjoys books? Just give us their names and addresses and we'll send them an order form too!

Name_____
Address_____
City_____State_____Zip_____

Name_____
Address_____
City_____State_____Zip_____